THOMAS HARDY IN OUR TIME

Thomas Hardy in Our Time

Robert Langbaum

MACMILLAN

First published in Great Britain 1995 by
THE MACMILLAN PRESS LTD
Houndmills, Basingstoke, Hampshire RG21 2XS
and London
Companies and representatives
throughout the world

A catalogue record for this book is available
from the British Library.

10 9   8   7   6   5   4   3
04 03 02 01 00 99 98 97 96

ISBN 0–333–61075–X

Printed and bound in Great Britain by
Biddles Ltd, Guildford and King's Lynn

First published in the United States of America 1995 by
Scholarly and Reference Division,
ST. MARTIN'S PRESS, INC.,
175 Fifth Avenue,
New York, N.Y. 10010

ISBN 0–312–12200–4

Library of Congress Cataloging-in-Publication Data
Langbaum, Robert Woodrow, 1924–
Thomas Hardy in our time / Robert Langbaum.
p.   cm.
Includes bibliographical references and index.
ISBN 0–312–12200–4
1. Hardy, Thomas, 1840–1928—Criticism and interpretation.
I. Title.
PR4754.L36 1995
823' .8—dc20   94–14199
                                                  CIP

Contents

Preface

There is a boom just now in the production of interesting new books on Hardy. Since Hardy wrote so much and with great understanding about women, he is making a special appeal to feminist critics. And since he criticised his own society and was especially revolutionary in his criticism of marriage and the conventional ethics of sexuality, he is appealing to politically radical critics. Far from apologising for adding still another book to the stream, I am delighted to contribute to so lively a discourse a book which I hope will prove relevant and will succeed in projecting Hardy as a still commanding figure for our time. Every genuine critical act, I believe, is a new start, a fresh encounter between critic and author distinguished from all previous encounters, just as every genuine poem and novel is a fresh encounter between author and life – life as mediated by the literary tradition.

For this reason *Hardy in Our Time* is organised, not as a chronological survey of all Hardy's work (such surveys have been well done), but according to my perception of the different current issues relating to Hardy that need arguing. The major works are treated in varying degrees of detail; the rest are at least alluded to – the proportions are determined by the requirements of the argument. My method is to describe the works discussed at sufficient length so that people who have not read them or not read them recently can follow my argument. I have also tried in my critical commentary to convey the sense of what it is like to read the work, both for the first time and after many informed readings.

Chapter 1, 'Hardy and Lawrence', reflects the evolution of my interest in Hardy from my work on Lawrence about whom I have written extensively in *The Mysteries of Identity*. When I came to realise that Hardy was the principal influence on Lawrence, that in commenting on Hardy's novels in his *Study of Thomas Hardy* Lawrence was rewriting Hardy as a way of arriving at his own novels, I felt the urge to write about Hardy. Although Hardy's novels may seem Victorian largely because of their well-made plots, the plots contain exaggerations verging on fantasy that suggest twentieth-century symbolisations of the unconscious. Hardy's psychological insights into the unconscious and sexuality seem contemporary with Lawrence's. There are, as we shall see, passages in both novelists that might have been written by either. The comparison of Hardy and Lawrence involves a discussion of several Hardy novels, especially *Tess of the d'Urbervilles* and *Jude the Obscure*.

In Chapter 2, 'The Issue of Hardy's Poetry', the first issue is the question whether the recently increased estimation of Hardy's poetry expresses a reaction, mainly in Britain, against the classic modernist poets – Yeats, Pound and Eliot. The next issue is the question whether in comparison to these modernists Hardy emerges as a first-rate minor poet whose influence gave rise in Britain to a generation of poets who in reaction against Yeats, Pound and Eliot aimed at the small, precise perfections of minor poetry – a generation best represented by Hardy's self-declared disciple Philip Larkin. My attempt to formulate a theory of the differences between major and minor poetry leads me through a discussion of Hardy's poems to argue that Hardy wrote so many major poems as to be considered a major poet who, after his successful career as a novelist, gave himself the luxury of writing mostly minor poems in order to enjoy the *craft* of poetry in all its variety. Since Hardy modernised and transmitted to the twentieth century what was usable in nineteenth-century poetry, I discuss at length the influence on him of nineteenth-century poets to show him as thoroughly absorbed in the nineteenth-century tradition though critical of it.

There follows still another issue (a favourite argument among Hardy's admirers): which is greater – Hardy's poems or his novels? My major–minor distinction helps to answer this question, for it helps to develop a standard for evaluating Hardy against the classic modernists by showing that he is mainly successful on another scale. The distinction helps to develop a criterion for distinguishing between Hardy's major and minor poems and for distinguishing between his poems and major novels. Thus, I argue here and in the succeeding chapters that Hardy's poetry on the largest scale, requiring the largest extension of imagination, is to be found, albeit in prose, in the major novels.

To pursue this argument, I devote the next two chapters to the pastoral novels – *Under the Greenwood Tree, Far from the Madding Crowd, The Return of the Native* and *The Woodlanders*. Chapter 3 begins, '*The Return of the Native* is Hardy's greatest nature poem.' I also trace the development away from the pure pastoral of *Under the Greenwood Tree* through the nearly tragic *Far from the Madding Crowd* to the tragic *The Return of the Native* to the dark comedy and antipastoralism of *The Woodlanders*. In defining the genre of *The Woodlanders*, I try to indicate how that neglected novel should be read, its sustained ironies appreciated, if it is to rank among the major novels, if we are to understand why Hardy 'in after years. . . . often said that in some respects *The Woodlanders* was his best novel'.[1]

I trace a continuing critique of idealism which is first manifested in the social idealism of Clym Yeobright in *The Return of the Native*. The critique continues with the epistemological idealism of Fitzpiers and the pastoral idealism of Giles Winterborne in *The Woodlanders*, the Shelleyan idealism of Angel Clare in *Tess of the d'Urbervilles*, the Utopianism of Sue Bridehead and Jude Fawley in *Jude the Obscure* and the Platonic idealism of Jocelyn Pierston in Hardy's last novel *The Well-Beloved*.

Finally in Chapter 5 I discern a change of direction in Hardy. Up to this point I have discussed, with an approach owing a good deal to Freud, Hardy's interest in sexuality and also the rich eroticism of his novels. But Chapter 5 is called 'The Minimisation of Sexuality' and deals with *The Mayor of Casterbridge* and *The Well-Beloved*. Why this minimisation? In *Mayor* sexuality is minimised most notably in Henchard, but in most of the other characters as well, perhaps because Hardy wanted to throw the emphasis on moral choice and the novel's tragic structure. In *The Well-Beloved* Jocelyn cares more for his feminine ideal, his Well-Beloved, than for the numerous real women who temporarily embody her, because this ideal is the subject of his sculpture. Hardy may be demonstrating in this novel the price paid in sexual over-idealisation or sublimation for the artistic temperament, hence the novel's subtitle *A Sketch of a Temperament*. Hardy also rounds out his study of sexuality by reversing his usual emphasis on it.

A theme throughout is Hardy's connection with George Eliot. The anonymous serialisation of *Far from the Madding Crowd* was attributed by one reviewer to George Eliot, and Hardy's novels were often compared by reviewers to George Eliot's. A generation ago F. R. Leavis conceived the fruitful idea of a Great Tradition running through the English novel from Jane Austen to George Eliot, through Conrad and James, to D. H. Lawrence.[2] Since Leavis had little respect for Hardy's novels, he omits him from the Great

Tradition. I hope to show that Hardy is the missing link in Leavis's scheme between George Eliot and Lawrence.

All three begin with the provincial scene (Hardy uses rustics for comic relief in George Eliot's manner), yet achieve a widely applicable exploration of human nature and society through a medium of sophisticated ideas. Taking issue with Matthew Arnold who as a critic attacked English provincialism, Hardy writes in the *Life*:

> Arnold is wrong about provincialism, if he means anything more than a provincialism of style and manner in exposition. A certain provincialism of feeling is invaluable. It is of the essence of individuality, and is largely made up of that crude enthusiasm without which no great thoughts are thought, no great deeds done. (146–7)

Hardy seems to have taken from George Eliot the valorisation in art of a realistic objectivity and an often expressed preference for fictional characters who see the world objectively and exhibit competence at work. He seems to have taken from George Eliot and passed on to Lawrence the morally serious exploration of society, the interest in women, especially intelligent women with their problems in choosing husbands, and above all the psychological approach to characterisation. 'It was really George Eliot who started it all', the young Lawrence told Jessie Chambers. 'It was she who started putting all the action inside.'[3] But George Eliot mainly concentrates on the psychology of the conscious mind; she seldom carries psychology beyond the depth where it would obliterate moral choice (Maggie Tulliver in *The Mill on the Floss* can only yield to her unconscious desire for her brother by drowning with him in his arms). Hardy goes farther than George Eliot, and Lawrence goes farther than both in letting the unconscious have its way against social and moral restrictions. This change in subject matter is determined by historical change and does not suggest artistic improvement, that the later novelist is artistically superior to the earlier.

Hardy's middle position between George Eliot and Lawrence makes him, by comparison to George Eliot, modern, but not like Lawrence modern*ist*. Although George Eliot and Hardy are sceptical of religion and critical of society and marriage, Hardy explores the unconscious and sexuality more explicitly than she does. As projections of the unconscious, Hardy's powerful use of folklore adds a mythical dimension to his realistic stories; also his use of coincidences, suggesting that there are no accidents, that we all share one mind, indicates a mythical view. In comparison to Lawrence, Hardy is not modern*ist*, because his plots for all their strange moments remain well made and still describe a society that sends forth signals strong enough, even if of doubtful validity, to torment his characters. In Lawrence's middle and later novels, such signals have ceased: social conventions are no longer an obstacle to anyone's desires. Therefore, Lawrence substitutes for social notation the externalising of subjectivity, creating in *Women in Love* (1920) and the ritualised scenes of *The Rainbow* (1915), a new genre that exists on the borderline between myth and the novel. Thus, Lawrence's revision of the novel's form and language is more thorough than Hardy's, hence he is modern*ist*. But Hardy's historical situation (and George Eliot's too) is better for the novel than Lawrence's because it yields an objective social reality complex enough to be worth exploring and powerful enough to be a worthy antagonist to his characters and his social criticism.

In conclusion, I want to thank the generous scholars who took time to read this book and offer valuable comments. Samuel Hynes, Dennis Taylor and Herbert Tucker read Chapter 2, Alison Booth and Karen Chase read the section on George Eliot, Dale Kramer read an early draft of the book, J. Hillis Miller and Norman Page read the book in its penultimate draft. Thanks are due to the University of Virginia for annual research funds and to my very efficient and devoted research assistants. Thanks are also due to the following libraries: Alderman Library of the University of Virginia, the New York City Public Library, the British Library and the Thomas Hardy Memorial Collection in the Dorchester County Museum. Thanks to the Rockefeller Foundation Study and Conference Center, Bellagio, Italy, which enabled me to work on this book amid the princely surroundings of Villa Serbelloni during June 1987.

Chapter 1 appeared in the *Thomas Hardy Annual No. 3*, edited by Norman Page (Basingstoke and London: Macmillan, 1985) and in *D. H. Lawrence and Tradition*, edited by Jeffrey Meyers (Amherst: University of Massachusetts Press, 1985). Part of Chapter 5 appeared in *The Thomas Hardy Journal*, VIII (February 1992) and part of Chapter 2 appeared in *Victorian Poetry*, 30 (Summer 1992). Chapter 3 appeared in *Victorian Literature and Culture*, 20 (1993). Thanks to the editors and publishers for permission to reprint these selections. Thanks also to Oxford University Press for permission to quote from *The Complete Poetical Works of Thomas Hardy*, 3 vols, edited by Samuel Hynes, copyright Samuel Hynes 1982, 1984, 1985.

Thanks to Morgan Daven for help with proof-reading and preparing the index. Thanks finally to my dear wife Francesca who made sacrifices to enable me to write this book and, as for all my books, gave me encouragement and valuable advice.

R. L.

Charlottesville, Virginia

1
Hardy and Lawrence

The best source of comparison between Thomas Hardy and D. H.
Lawrence is Lawrence's curious little book *Study of Thomas Hardy*
(the *Study* is curious in its mixture of literary criticism with metaphysics, authobiography, cultural history and other things). In the
Study, Lawrence implicitly acknowledges Hardy as his master.
Hardy takes on new relevance and stature when we realise that
he is the principal influence on one of the two most innovative,
twentieth-century English-speaking novelists (the other is Joyce),
while we understand Lawrence better when we realise that he differs
only in degree from Hardy and when we can trace the roots of
Lawrence's art back through Hardy to George Eliot and Wordsworth.

To some extent Lawrence's relation to Hardy illustrates Harold
Bloom's theory of influence, in that Lawrence in the *Study* partly
misreads and rewrites Hardy's novels as a way of arriving at his
own art. But the *Study* shows no sign of what Bloom calls 'the anxiety
of influence', in that Lawrence is not out to defeat Hardy. He wants
to complete him, to continue his direction, to fulfil the implications
of Hardy's art that Hardy as a Victorian could not fulfil. It is true
that Lawrence has so assimilated Hardy that 'one can', to borrow
Blooms's words, 'believe, for startled moments' that Lawrence is
'being *imitated*'[1] by Hardy. Such absorption is not, however, necessarily aggressive; it can be a way of learning all one can from the
precursor before going on to take the inevitable next step of finding
one's identity as a writer.

Although Lawrence criticises Hardy for allowing his metaphysic
or moral judgement to outweigh his sympathy for his convention-
breaking characters, he writes about Hardy's novels with such
affectionate understanding that his admiration is what we remember. 'Nothing in [Hardy's] work', says Lawrence,

> is so pitiable as his clumsy efforts to push events into line with
> his theory of being, and to make calamity fall on those who
> represent the principle of Love. . . . His feeling, his instinct, his
> sensuous understanding is, however, apart from his metaphysic,

1

very great and deep, deeper than that, perhaps, of any other English novelist.[2]

Lawrence also expresses his admiration for Hardy in places other than the *Study*, for example: 'They are all – Turgenev, Tolstoi, Dostoevsky, Maupassant, Flaubert – so very *obvious* and coarse, beside the lovely mature and sensitive art of . . . Hardy' (letter of 27 November 1916).[3] The same criticism – that strong sensibility compensates for a too obtrusive metaphysic – is often made about Lawrence.

If we recall at what point in his career Lawrence wrote the *Study of Hardy*, we realise that Lawrence places himself in Hardy's line in order to understand himself as a novelist, to understand where he comes from and where he is going. It was on 15 July 1914, a moment of triumph, when he had married Frieda and confidently sent off *The Rainbow* to Methuen, that Lawrence asked a friend to lend him Hardy's novels and Lascelles Abercrombie's book on Hardy, because he planned 'to write a little book on Hardy's people'. August was a month of reverses. Methuen returned the manuscript and the war broke out. On 5 September Lawrence wrote to his agent: 'What a miserable world. What colossal idiocy, this war. Out of sheer rage I've begun my book about Thomas Hardy' (*Letters*, II: 198, 212). The book on Hardy was conceived, however, in a moment of happiness and there is no rage in it. *Study of Hardy* is, like the final version of *The Rainbow* to which it provides the skeletal structure, optimistic about the possibility for the evolution of human consciousness through the right kind of marriage.

The apparent digressiveness of the *Study* has led most readers (and Lawrence himself at times) to conclude that Hardy is a mere pretext for Lawrence's expression of his own philosophy[4] and that the three chapters dealing directly with Hardy's novels – Chapters III, V, IX – have little to do with the other ten chapters. I want to argue, instead, that the *Study* does hang together, that the metaphysic no less than the criticism derives from Lawrence's understanding of Hardy's novels. 'Normally, the centre, the turning pivot, of a man's life', writes Lawrence in Chapter VII of the *Study*, 'is his sex-life, the centre and swivel of his being is the sexual act' (444). Hardy thought so too; he is the first Victorian novelist, perhaps the first English novelist to have thought so. That is why he was always in trouble with the bowdlerizers and censors. Lawrence says that in the division of human life between the purpose of self-preservation and the sexual-creative purpose (the distinction corresponds to Freud's between the reality and pleasure principles), Hardy's people are mainly committed to the sexual-creative purpose. Thus, Lawrence's metaphysic – which sees all life as sexual and equates sexuality with spirit – can be said to derive from his understanding of Hardy, but is also used as a means for understanding Hardy. Writers of course have always dealt with sex. The difference in Hardy and especially in Lawrence is the centrality of sex – the fact that sex is self-justifying, that it is not subject to judgement by other values but is indeed the source of other values. The ironic subtitle, *A Pure Woman*, to *Tess of the d'Urbervilles* challenges the quite opposite conventional judgement of Tess.[5]

Far from being a digression, then, the chapters on the metaphysic – especially those that account for our cultural and psychic history by the necessary opposition of male and female principles – are necessary for an understanding of Lawrence's readings of Hardy's novels. To cite another example, the flaming of the evanescent poppy, in Chapter I, leads to the legend of the phoenix and to the conclusion that 'The final aim of every living thing, creature, or being is the full achievement of itself' – a crucial principle in Lawrence's understanding of Hardy's people (403). Lawrence begins his discussion of Hardy's novels in Chapter III by accounting for the *Study*'s apparent digressions: 'This is supposed to be a book about the people in Thomas Hardy's novels. But if one wrote everything they give rise to, it would fill the Judgment Book' (410).

Lawrence's valid insights outweigh his misreadings, making him Hardy's best critic, the first to understand Hardy's innovativeness and relevance to the twentieth century. We can never read Hardy in the same way once we have encountered Lawrence in the *Study* and in his novels, and have come to realise that Lawrence took from Hardy the great new subjects of sex and the unconscious.

Lawrence's *Study of Thomas Hardy* influenced the final version of *The Rainbow*, as is amply demonstrated by Mark Kinkead-Weekes who shows that Lawrence needed to write the *Study* in order to find out what he had been up to in the vast draft, called *The Sisters*, which by the time of the *Study* was separated into *The Rainbow* and what would be called *Women in Love*. Lawrence, according to Kinkead-Weekes, learned two main things from Hardy's example: he learned the necessity for and the danger of a metaphysic. 'Every novel,' Lawrence writes in the *Study*, 'must have the background or the

structural skeleton of some theory of being, some metaphysic.' Hardy
anticipated the modernists in being the first Victorian novelist and
poet who felt the need of a system – a system he finally worked out
in his mammoth epic poem *The Dynasts* (1903–8). It is because of
Hardy's metaphysic that Lawrence places him on a level with Tolstoi,
but their metaphysics, says Lawrence, damaged the art of both
novelists when it overcame 'their living sense of being. . . . The
metaphysic must always subserve the artistic purpose beyond the
artist's conscious aim. Otherwise the novel becomes a treatise.'
Lawrence seems to be thinking of the defeat by society of Hardy's
Tess and Tolstoi's Anna Karenina when he goes on to say that
'Hardy's metaphysic is something like Tolstoi's. "There is no reconciliation between Love and the Law", says Hardy. "The spirit of
Love must always succumb before the blind, stupid, but over-
whelming power of the Law"'(479–80).

   In determining that 'the metaphysic must always subserve
the artistic purpose beyond the artist's conscious aim', Lawrence
arrives at a theory of the proper subordination of conscious to unconscious intention. This connects with the other main thing that
Lawrence probably learned from Hardy – a new sense of unconscious or impersonal identity. Lawrence found in Hardy, says
Kinkead-Weekes, 'a language in which to conceive the impersonal
forces he saw operating within and between human beings', which
helped him discover 'a "structural skeleton" on which to re-found
[his novel] in a new dimension', involving 'a new clarification of
what the novel he had been trying to write was really *about*'.[6] It was
about the new sense of identity, which is why Lawrence felt im-
pelled, as a way of retracing his steps for the sake of understanding,
to write about Hardy's *people*.

   Hardy's new sense of identity is clearest, Lawrence implies, in
the way he relates characters to landscape. In *The Return of the Native*,
the people

> are one's year's accidental crop. . . . The Heath persists. Its body
> is strong and fecund, it will bear many more crops beside this. . . .
> And the contents of the small lives are spilled and wasted. There
> is savage satisfaction in it: for so much more remains to come,
> such a black, powerful fecundity is working there that what does
> it matter?   (415)

Out of this passage and the *Study's* metaphysic of female and male
principles emerge the great opening passages of *The Rainbow* (written

after the *Study*),[7] where the Brangwens are portrayed as passing manifestations of the fecund landscape. The men are absorbed by organic connection with the female earth, by 'blood-intimacy': 'the pulse of the blood of the teats of the cows beat into the pulse of the hands of the men'; whereas the women look upward to the male church tower and aspire to a life of spirit.[8] The sexualization of landscape derives from Hardy – from the voluptuous landscapes in *Far from the Madding Crowd* and from passages in *Tess* such as this one:

> Amid the oozing fatness and warm ferments of the Froom Vale, at a season when the rush of juices could almost be heard below the hiss of fertilization, it was impossible that the most fanciful love should not grow passionate. The ready bosoms existing there were impregnated by their surroundings.[9]

Hardy and Lawrence sexualise Wordsworth's living landscapes.

That is because Hardy and Lawrence are post-Darwinians. 'Man has a purpose,' says Lawrence in a statement in the *Study* describing his own novels while describing Hardy's, 'which he has divorced from the passionate purpose that issued him out of the earth into being' (415). Human identity, in other words, is split between our conscious, individual purpose and the unconscious, biological purpose we also carry within us. Hence, the importance of marriage in *The Rainbow* and in the *Study's* theology of marriage as a way of reconciling our two purposes. Lawrence is more optimistic about marriage than Hardy, who mainly attacks the institution. The difference partly derives from their different experiences of marriage (Hardy's first marriage became unhappy). But it may also derive from the fact that Hardy is still a social reformer, still out to free us from the bonds of established institutions, while Lawrence wants to restore values to a society disastrously free of them. The difference may be one reason why Hardy is ironic, while Lawrence is mainly without irony.

Lawrence's optimism also derives from Hardy's post-Darwinian metaphysic about the inevitable evolution of human consciousness, even consciousness of an Innate Will in nature. 'The sexual act,' says Lawrence in the *Study*, 'is not for the depositing of the seed. It is for leaping off into the unknown', for serving evolution (441). The sense of beyondness is the criterion of good sexual relations in *The Rainbow* and the novels that follow.

There emerges from Lawrence's analysis of Hardy's people a new

diagram of identity as a small, well-lit area surrounded by an
increasingly dark penumbra of unconsciousness opening out to
external, impersonal forces. This leads to a system of judgement
which condemns the attempt to shut out the darkness and live im-
prisoned in the well-lit ego. Thus, Lawrence's analysis in the *Study*
of the idealistic Clym in *Return of the Native*:

> Impotent to *be*, he must transform himself, and live in an ab-
> straction, in a generalization, he must identify himself with the
> system. He must live as Man or Humanity, or as the Community,
> or as Society, or as Civilization. . . . He already showed that
> thought is a disease of the flesh, and indirectly bore evidence that
> ideal physical beauty is incompatible with emotional develop-
> ment and a full recognition of the coil of things.

Clym – who 'was emotionally undeveloped. . . . Only his mental
faculties were developed' – shut out the penumbra of unconsciousness connecting him with the heath. The fenced-out darkness can seem as demonic as the fenced-in ego: 'Was it his blood,
which rose dark and potent out of Egdon [Heath], which ham-
pered and confined the deity [within him], or was it his mind, that
house built of extraneous knowledge and guarded by his will, which
formed the prison?' (416–17).

Ursula in *The Rainbow* arrives at a similar diagram of her identity:

> This lighted area, lit up by man's completest consciousness, she
> thought was all the world: that here all was disclosed for ever.
> Yet all the time, within the dark, she had been aware of points of
> light, like the eyes of wild beasts, gleaming, penetrating, vanish-
> ing. And her soul had acknowledged in a great heave of terror
> only the outer darkness.   (xv: 437)

She succumbs to the darkness because she has had only momentary, ego-centred intuitions of it as fenced out, hence the wild beasts,
who are menacing when repressed. But Ursula advances beyond
Clym because she learns to reconcile consciousness with unconsciousness.

In assimilating Clym to his novel in progress, *The Rainbow*,
Lawrence is not misreading. His analysis of Clym is brilliantly valid.
The sign of this is that Clym, with his lofty intellectual ambitions,
studies so hard that he becomes blind and his blindness leads him
back to the heath – he finds contentment in the lowly occupation of
furze cutter. Clym's salutary blindness, though Hardy does not

describe it as such, may have given Lawrence the idea for his short story 'The Blind Man', in which Maurice Pervin's blindness restores 'the almost incomprehensible peace of immediate contact in darkness'.[10] Pervin's blindness or immersion in the unconscious improves his marriage; whereas Clym's blindness destroys his marriage because Clym alternates between consciousness and unconsciousness while his wife Eustacia insists on his having both – his consciousness for worldly prestige, his unconsciousness presumably for sex. Clym's blindness seems to symbolise a decline in sexuality – a point Hardy leaves surprisingly obscure.

According to Lawrence's analysis in the *Study*, the two human purposes – individual and biological – determine the structure and imagery of Hardy's novels as well as his characterisations. There exists in Hardy's novels, writes Lawrence,

> a great background, vital and vivid, which matters more than the people who move upon it. . . . The vast unexplored morality of life itself, what we call the immorality of nature, surrounds us in its eternal incomprehensibility, and in its midst goes on the little human morality play, with its queer frame of morality and its mechanized movement; seriously, portentously, till some one of the protagonists chances to look out of the charmed circle, weary of the stage, to look into the wilderness raging round. Then he is lost, his little drama falls to pieces, or becomes mere repetition, but the stupendous theatre outside goes on enacting its own incomprehensible drama, untouched. (419)

The characters' two purposes parallel the two areas where the action takes place – the small, well-lit circle of human morality (and ego) versus the constantly encroaching amoral wilderness around it. (In traditional literature, instead, the human moral scheme envelops the universe.) Hardy's men – like Clym and Angel Clare on the side of 'goodness' and Alec d'Urberville on the side of 'badness' – alternate between the two areas. Hardy's tragic figures – usually women, like Eustacia and Tess; Jude is the exceptional male – inhabit both areas and are torn apart by the conflict. A sign of the tragic conflict is *Tess's* earliest manuscript title: *The Body and Soul of Sue* (Tess's original name).[11]

Lawrence, I think, derives his metaphysic in the *Study* from the conflict he discerned in Hardy between conscious and unconscious principles. Since Hardy's heroes are mainly weighted on the side of consciousness and his heroines on the side of unconsciousness, it follows that Lawrence in his metaphysic (confirming cultural prejudice) calls the conscious principle *male* and the unconscious principle *female*, while acknowledging that each person and historical epoch combines a different mixture of the two.[12]

The men in Hardy who are in touch with unconscious forces of sexuality are mainly villains – like Alec in *Tess* and Troy in *Madding Crowd* (Arabella in *Jude* is the exceptional woman in this group) – because they are seducers: they exploit sexuality. Lawrence, as we might expect, is more favourable to these sexually charged characters than most readers up to his time have been. But when Hardy ventures to say of Angel in *Tess*, who displays the Victorian virtues of chastity and strict moral judgement, that 'with more animalism he would have been the nobler man' (v, xxvi: 205), when Hardy says this, he is on the way to becoming Lawrence.

The great achievement of Lawrence's dialectical system in the *Study* is the recognition of the female principle as a positive force, equal if not superior in vitality to the male principle. When women in traditional literature are strong, they tend to be dangerous – like Clytemnestra or Medea or Lady Macbeth or Thackeray's Becky Sharp. The intelligence and strength of will of Lawrence's mother, as portrayed in *Sons and Lovers*, is on the whole damaging. Lawrence's recognition of a healthy female vitality must have come from his long tussle with his wife Frieda, a female power-house whom he called 'the devouring mother' while recognising that he by his own weakness had given her that forcefulness. As a way of resisting he sought a domination that she refused to let him have. 'Hence our fight'.[13]

Lawrence's respect for a healthy female vitality also derived from Hardy's women who, beginning with the managerial Bathsheba in *Far from the Madding Crowd*, are usually more intelligent and stronger-willed than the men. The same can be said of the Brangwen women in *The Rainbow* and *Women in Love* (only Birkin is a match for them). The theme of many Hardy novels is the superior woman's problem in finding a suitable mate – a theme Hardy took from George Eliot, from Dorothea's problem in *Middlemarch*. When Lawrence writes that the germ of his early draft *The Sisters* was 'woman becoming individual, self-responsible, taking her own initiative' (*Letters*, II: 165), he is continuing the theme of George Eliot and Hardy with additions to Hardy's increase of the theme's sexual ramifications.

The month before Lawrence announced his projected book on

Hardy's people, he wrote in the well-known 'carbon' identity letter of 5 June 1914 a description of the impersonal identity to be found in *The Rainbow*. Although the 'carbon' identity letter precedes the letter proposing the *Study*, we have to remember that Lawrence when he wrote the 'carbon' identity letter was about to *re*read Hardy and that what he had fundamentally learned had been learned from earlier readings and was already mainly incorporated in the novel he had just sent to Methuen. ('Have you ever read *Jude the Obscure*?' he asked Louie Burrows as early as 17 December 1910; *Letters*, I: 205). The near coincidence of the 'carbon' identity letter with the 15 July letter announcing his plan to write on Hardy's people suggests Lawrence's feeling that the new sense of identity in *The Rainbow* derived from Hardy and his consequent need to retrace his steps as a way of understanding what he had accomplished. *Study of Hardy* confirms and systematises the 'carbon' identity letter.

'You mustn't look in my novel', Lawrence writes in this letter, 'for the old stable ego of the character. There is another ego, according to whose action the individual is unrecognisable'. This other ego is the unconscious, impersonal element, the 'carbon' identity. 'That which is physic – non-human, in humanity,' Lawrence writes, 'is more interesting to me than the old-fashioned human element – which causes one to conceive a character in a certain moral scheme and make him consistent. . . . The ordinary novel would trace the history of the diamond – but I say "diamond, what! This is carbon." . . . and my theme is carbon' (*Letters*, II: 183, 182).

In the *Study*, Lawrence says much the same thing when he points out the inconsistency of Hardy's characters:

> Nowhere, except perhaps in Jude, is there the slightest development of personal action in the characters: it is all explosive. . . . The rest explode out of the convention. They are people each with a real, vital, potential self . . . and this self suddenly bursts the shell of manner and convention and commonplace opinion, and acts independently, absurdly, without mental knowledge or acquiescence. And from such an outburst the tragedy usually develops. For there does exist, after all, the great self-preservation scheme [society], and in it we must all live.   (410–11)[14]

In the 'carbon' identity letter and the *Study*, Lawrence is saying that he and Hardy treat their characters' social selves – the whole concern of the novel of manners – as the mere tip of the iceberg. The real action goes on underneath, rising to the surface sporadically in explosive or symbolic manifestations the logic and motives of which remain as mysterious to the characters as to the reader. In carrying the regression as far back as inanimate carbon, Lawrence goes a step beyond Hardy, who roots his characters in vegetated landscape. Behind them both stands Wordsworth, who was the first to root his characters in landscape and to intensify their being through regression as far back as inanimate objects: the quality of the old leech-gatherer's existence, in 'Resolution and Independence', is that of a huge stone which seems slightly, mysteriously animate. The innovation in Wordsworth, Hardy and Lawrence is the partial portrayal of characters as states of being rather than as totally defined by social class and moral choice. There remains, however, more social determination in Hardy than in Lawrence.

I have already quoted Lawrence's remark that 'it was George Eliot who started it all. . . . It was she who started putting all the action inside' (E. T., *Lawrence*, 105). But George Eliot seldom carries psychology to the depth where it obliterates moral choice. Hardy goes farther than George Eliot and Lawrence goes farther than both in letting the characters' unconscious desires have their way against social and moral restrictions.

The paradigms of 'carbon' identity and explosive characterisations are especially apparent in *Women in Love*, which proceeds through a series of discontinuous stills or set scenes each designed to manifest the characters' unconscious or 'carbon' identity. Gerald and Gudrun seal their sado-masochistic union in the scene on the island, where Gudrun defies the male principle by chasing away bullocks and finally by slapping Gerald across the face – a totally unexpected manifestation of desire. Their relationship proceeds through arbitrary, unprepared for scenes in which Gudrun swoons with masochistic excitement while Gerald torments his mare and subdues a huge hare whose savage energy, as first Gudrun and then Gerald hold him by the ears, suggests phallic power. Lawrence's use of animals to reveal to his characters their unconscious desires may derive from Hardy – from a scene like the sheep-shearing in *Far from the Madding Crowd*, in which Gabriel and Bathsheba discover their desire for each other through Gabriel's sexually suggestive way of handling a ewe while Bathsheba watches. Gabriel, we are told, dragged

> a frightened ewe to his shear-station, flinging it over upon its back with a dexterous twist of the arm. He lopped off the tresses

about its head, and opened up the neck and collar, his mistress quietly looking on. 'She blushes at the insult,' murmured Bathsheba, watching the pink flush which arose and overspread the neck and shoulders of the ewe where they were left bare by the clicking shears. . . . Poor Gabriel's soul was fed with a luxury of content by having her over him.[15]

Similarly, in *Sons and Lovers*, Paul's sexually suggestive cherry-pelting of Miriam before their first intercourse may derive from Alex d'Urberville's sexually suggestive way of feeding Tess strawberries on their first meeting: 'Tess eating in a half-pleased, half-reluctant state whatever d'Urberville offered her. . . . She obeyed like one in a dream' (I, v: 34). This is the pattern of her later rape-seduction by Alec. *The Rainbow*'s spectacular dance under the moonlight, which releases the erotic unconscious of Ursula and Skrebensky, echoes the scene in *Return of the Native* where Eustacia, temporarily fleeing her unhappy marriage to attend a village picnic, meets there by Hardyan coincidence (as the fulfillment of her unconscious desire) her former lover Wildeve, who is also unhappily married. Their dance under the moonlight provides erotic release: 'a riding upon the whirlwind. The dance had come like an irresistible attack upon whatever sense of social order there was in their minds.'[16]

The analysis of Hardy's explosive characterisations is Lawrence's most illuminating insight into Hardy's novels. It accounts in *Madding Crowd* for Bathsheba's sudden entanglement with Sergeant Troy, which runs counter to the sequence of events so far and to her conscious intentions. Troy is a stranger when one night in her garden his spur becomes entangled in her dress. The invisible body contact excites Bathsheba because of its outrageousness. When he sees her face, 'She coloured with embarrassment' (xxiv: 128): 'She blushes at the insult', she had said of the *undressed* ewe. This scene leads to the sealing of their union in the wildly explosive sword-exercise, which with its phallic and sado-masochistic symbolism reveals to Bathsheba a stratum of sexual desire she knows nothing about. As Troy makes his sword cuts within a hair's breadth of her body, she feels penetrated: 'Have you run me through?' The experience becomes psychologically an intercourse: 'She felt powerless to withstand or deny him. . . . She felt like one who has sinned a great sin' – this last in response to what turns out to have been a mere kiss. The phallic performance takes place in a vaginal or

womblike 'hollow amid the ferns' (xxxviii: 142–6) to make the most
Lawrencean scene in Hardy, though we probably have to know
Lawrence or Freud to appreciate the blatancy of its symbolism.

Bathsheba, the masterful woman who expresses her sexual interest in Gabriel Oak by tormenting him, gets a sexual thrill out of
being brutally subdued by Sergeant Troy. Hardy's understanding
of sado-masochism, which to some extent came from Swinburne,
points towards Lawrence whom Yeats wrongly credited with having
discovered the cruelty in love. Edmund Gosse, Hardy's friend and
Swinburne's biographer, wrote that Swinburne had 'prepared the
way for an ultimate appreciation of Mr Hardy'.[17] Tess's relation with
Alec d'Urberville is also sado-masochistic. Alec subdues her at the
outset by driving her at terrifying speed to the d'Urberville man-
sion where she will be a servant. Then he 'gave her the kiss of
mastery' (I, viii: 45). The master–servant relation intensifies sado-
masochism: Gabriel is Bathsheba's servant, Troy her servant's lover.
When Alec in the end insists that Tess return to him, she (pointing
toward the scene in which Gudrun strikes Gerald) slaps him across
the mouth with her heavy glove, drawing blood.

> 'Now punish me!' she said turning up her eyes to him with the
> hopeless defiance of the sparrow's gaze before its captor twists
> its neck. 'Whip me, crush me . . . I shall not cry out. Once victim,
> always victim – that's the law!'

Alec in replying fills the role required of him: '"I was your master
once! I will be your master again"' (VI, xlvii: 275). Tess returns to
him. This interchange can also be read as signifying class oppres-
sion; Tess exemplifies the way in which Hardy, in John Lucas's
words, 'uses his fictional women to focus on precisely those issues
of class and separation which his novels explore'.[18] Nevertheless, an
accompanying psychological interpretation is made inevitable by
such *extreme* remarks.[19]

Lawrence's analysis of Hardy's explosive characterisations accounts for the ambiguities of Tess's behaviour at crucial moments
of her life. Why does Tess take the job at the d'Urbervilles when it
is clear from the start that Alec will be a danger to her? Why, after
all her determined resistance to him, does Tess, on that most crucial
night of her life, suddenly leap behind him on his horse and allow
herself to be carried into the dark wood where she falls asleep so
willingly that it remains impossible to determine whether she is

then raped or seduced? (Did Lawrence learn from this scene how to portray Gerald's rape-like way of taking Gudrun the first time when, with the mud from his father's grave on his boots, he steals at night like a criminal into her family's house and breaks into her bedroom determined to have her?) Why cannot Tess, despite her good intentions, bring herself to tell Angel before their marriage about her relations with Alec? Angel might not then have felt betrayed by the confession which came too late. When Tess learns that Angel never saw the confessional letter she slipped under his door because the letter slid under a rug, she lets this accident make the decision for her not to confess. According to the Victorian reading, the accident is a typically contrived Hardy coincidence. If we take a deep psychological view of the accident, however, it exemplifies an advanced technique for making an external event confirm an unconscious desire – Tess's desire to let nothing impede her marriage to Angel.

Why does Tess go back to Alec? And why, after Angel's reappearance, does Tess murder Alec when all she has to do is leave him? And why, finally, does Tess show so little interest in escaping with Angel after the murder? Why in the end does she lay herself down, almost willingly, as a human sacrifice on the altar at Stonehenge to be captured and executed?

Hardy's explanations are in the deep psychological manner overdetermined – which is to say that they are all partly valid, yet no one of them is the complete explanation. The reason Tess takes the job at the d'Urbervilles is to help her family financially and that is one reason she goes back to Alec, though the reason seems even less satisfactory than before as a complete explanation. The night of the rape–seduction, she leaps onto Alex's horse in order to avoid a fight with his former mistress, but also to triumph over the other woman by leaping onto the horse in front of her. Hardy suggests a deeper reason by saying that Tess 'abandoned herself to her impulse . . . and scrambled into the saddle behind him' (I, x: 58). Her unconscious acquiescence is confirmed by her falling asleep and by Hardy's further explanation that Tess was still a child with a woman's body. Another recurrent explanation makes Tess the victim of a malignant fate.

Tess's problem throughout is her combination of strong conscience with strong sexual desire. She has one foot in what Lawrence calls Hardy's 'human morality play' and the other in the swirl of amoral biological forces that join our life to the cosmos. It is partly ly's meagre fortune, that impels her toward Alec. Instead of hating Angel for his abandonment of her, she takes the blame upon herself and goes to work on the brutal Flintcomb-Ash farm, with its infernal landscape, as a kind of penance. Most of Tess's misery is created by her conscience, for she condemns herself more strongly than does anyone else.

Equally strong is Tess's unconscious desire for a biological fulfilment leading through sexuality to death. Like Gabriel Oak in *Far from the Madding Crowd*, Tess falls asleep at crucial moments that advance her destiny. Here is Hardy's description of the conflict in Tess between conscience and biological destiny. She has just left Angel after promising to answer in a few days his proposal of marriage and tell him about her past.

> Tess flung herself down upon the rustling undergrowth of speargrass, as upon a bed, and remained crouching in palpitating misery broken by momentary shoots of joy, which her fears about the ending could not altogether suppress. In reality, she was drifting into acquiescence. Every see-saw of her breath, every wave of her blood, every pulse singing in her ears, was a voice that joined with nature in revolt against her scrupulousness. . . . In almost a terror of ecstasy Tess divined that, despite her many months of lonely self-chastisement, wrestlings, communings, schemes to lead a future of austere isolation, love's counsel would prevail. (IV, xxviii: 150)

Similarly Clym, while waiting for Eustacia, often flings himself down amid vegetation as if to draw erotic strength from nature. Birkin in *Women in Love* flings himself down so, after Hermione tried to kill him, as if to draw restorative strength from nature.

Hardy's deep explanation as to why Tess finally consents to marry Angel without having confessed looks back to Wordsworth and forward to Lawrence by way of Darwin: 'The "appetite for joy" [a Wordsworthian phrase] which pervades all creation, that tremendous force which sways humanity to its purpose, as the tide sways the helpless weed, was not to be controlled by vague lucubrations over the social rubric' (IV, xxx: 161). A strongly crossed-out passage in the manuscript shows how far Hardy, had he not feared censorship, would have made Tess go in letting passion overrule the social rubric. In wondering whether to tell Angel about Alec, Tess reflects:

As a path out of her trying strait she would possibly have accepted another kind of union with him [above line: purely] for his own [above line: beloved] sake, had he urged it upon her; that he might have retreated if discontented with her on learning her story.[20]

The same biological drive leads Tess to seek death as well as love. She expresses throughout her longing for death. Her murder of Alec is a way of bringing on her own death, but it is also a fulfilment of their own murderous sexual relation, a relation like that of Gerald and Gudrun. Gudrun's words to Gerald after she has slapped him across the face would apply to Tess after she strikes Alec. '"You have struck the first blow"', says Gerald. '"And I shall strike the last"', Gudrun replies.[21] After the murder Tess tells Angel: '"I have killed him! . . . I feared long ago, when I struck him on the mouth with my glove, that I might do it some day"' (VII, lvii: 318).

There has emerged since Lawrence's time two ways of reading *Tess* and Hardy's other major novels – the Victorian moralistic way and the Lawrencean deep-psychological way. According to the moralistic reading, Tess is entirely Alec's victim – she entertains no sexual feeling for him.[22] She goes to him only to help her family; their first intercourse is a rape, and she murders him to avenge the harm he has done her. The novel is largely a reformist attack on the double standard of sexual morality. According to the moralistic reading a malignant fate is the prime mover of events, while fate is hardly mentioned in the *Study*. We need to combine both interpretations, but it is the deep psychological interpretation that reveals the full measure of Hardy's greatness and accounts for what have seemed flaws in his characterisations and plots. Through our reading of Lawrence, both in the *Study* and the novels, we have come to understand that Hardy is important in the history of the English novel because he is the first to elaborate the sphere of unconscious motivation. The Brontes show intuitive flashes into it; Dickens, we now realise as the Victorians did not, symbolises the unconscious through projections of it on the world of objects. But Hardy is the first English novelist to treat the unconscious analytically and to organise characterisation and plot for the purpose of revealing it. Hence, the mysteriously explosive characterisations which force us to look for motives deeper than the obvious ones. Hence, the much criticised Hardyan coincidences which, when they work well, are,

as I have already suggested, fulfilments of the characters' unconscious desires or make such fulfilments possible.

In *Jude the Obscure*, Sue Bridehead is the best example of explosive characterisation. Sue's crucial decisions are never prepared for;
it requires the deepest psychology to understand them and many
remain unfathomable. Why does she marry Phillotson and even
more puzzling why does she entirely on her own initiative return
to him (repeating the pattern of Tess's return to Alec) when she is
still in love with Jude, to whom she has borne children? The usual
answer is that she wants to do penance for having lived in sin with
Jude, but the return of her repressed Christian conscience seems to
mask deeper motives.

Why, in the chain of events leading to the children's deaths, does
Sue tell the landlady that she and Jude are not married? Sue's
unnecessary confession leads to the family's eviction from the only
lodging they could find. The eviction and refusal of other lodgings
make a terrible impression on the oldest boy, who concludes: '"It
would be better to be out o' the world than in it, wouldn't it?"'
Instead of comforting him, Sue agrees:

> 'It would almost, dear.'
> ''Tis because of us children, too, isn't it, that you can't get a
> good lodging?'
> 'Well – people do object to children sometimes.'
> 'Then if children make so much trouble, why do people have
> 'em?'
> 'O – because it is a law of nature.' ...
> 'I wish I hadn't been born!'
> 'You couldn't help it, my dear.'
> 'I think that whenever children be born that are not wanted
> they should be killed directly, before their souls come to 'em.'

Instead of assuring the boy of her love, 'Sue did not reply'.[23] And
she unnecessarily volunteers the information that there will be another baby. The boy responds with such horror as to indicate that
this last news makes him hang the other children and himself.

Hardy, in his usual way of offering an inadequate explanation in
order to suggest others, begins this episode by saying that 'Sue had
not the art of prevarication' (vi, 1: 261). Would it have been a lie to
tell the boy she loved him and to have withheld the information
about the new baby? For all her beauty, intelligence and idealism,
Sue emerges as defective because she lacks instincts.

After the children's deaths, Sue comes to the 'awful conviction that her discourse with the boy had been the main cause of the tragedy'. She explains to Jude:

> I talked to the child as one should only talk to people of mature age. . . . I wanted to be truthful. I couldn't bear deceiving him as to the facts of life. And yet I wasn't truthful, for with a false delicacy I told him too obscurely. . . . I could neither conceal things nor reveal them! (VI, 2: 266–8)

The things she concealed were the facts of sex, thus making her explanation even more terrifying to the boy. Sue's fear of sex is always the deeper motive beneath her apparent ones. Yet she subscribes – showing Hardy's analysis here and elsewhere of self-deceiving idealism – to an abstract ideal of free sex.

In his 1912 Postscript to *Jude*, Hardy refers to a German reviewer's description of Sue as 'the woman of the feminist movement – the slight, pale "bachelor" girl – the intellectualized, emancipated bundle of nerves that modern conditions were producing' (8). This accords, as Elaine Showalter demonstrates, with attacks of the time against the New Woman.[24] But the deep psychological treatment of Sue individualises her.

Lawrence in the *Study* brilliantly tells us how Jude and Sue do not feel that, in living together without marriage, they have sinned against the community but that they have lied to themselves. 'They knew it was no marriage; they knew it was wrong, all along; they knew they were sinning against life, in forcing a physical marriage between themselves.' Their uneasiness makes their union seem illicit to others. Theirs was no marriage because Sue 'was no woman'. It was wrong of Jude to have forced sex upon her and wrong of her to have borne children in order to make a false show of being a woman. Because their marriage had no consummation in the interchange of male and female principles, 'they were' – says Lawrence in a poetic passage that shows his deep response to the novel – 'too unsubstantial, too thin and evanescent in substance, as if the other solid people might jostle right through them, two wandering shades as they were': Dantesque shades (506–7).

Lawrence again reveals motives deeper than the ostensible Christian one in explaining Sue's return to Phillotson after the children's deaths:

Then Sue ceases to be. . . . The last act of her intellect was the utter renunciation of her mind and the embracing of utter ortho- doxy, where every belief, every thought, every decision was made ready for her, so that she did not exist self-responsible. And then her loathed body . . . that too should be scourged out of existence. She chose the bitterest penalty in going back to Phillotson. . . . All that remained of her was the will by which she annihilated herself. That remained fixed, a locked centre of self-hatred, life- hatred so utter that it had no hope of death. (508–9)

This sounds like a Lawrence novel. The last three sentences could be describing Gudrun, who chose the bitterest penalty in giving herself up to Loerke. The analysis also applies to Jude and Gerald who, having emotions, are granted the relief of death; Sue and Gudrun, who live entirely in the head, cannot achieve oblivion.

Lawrence's fundamental statement about *Jude the Obscure* is that 'Jude is only Tess turned round about. . . . Arabella is Alec d'Urberville, Sue is Angel Clare' (488). Since Lawrence says that both Tess and Jude contain within themselves the conflict between female sensuality and male intellect, one wonders why he goes on to speak of Jude as though he lived entirely in the head like Sue. Jude like Tess is strong in sexuality and conscience; that is why Jude succumbs to Arabella as Tess succumbs to Alec. The differ- ence is that Jude is not on such friendly terms with his unconscious as Tess is with hers; he does not like Tess fall asleep at crucial moments.

Jude and Sue – Sue even more than Jude – are alienated from their unconscious. That is what makes them Hardy's first distinc- tively twentieth-century characters. Angel's repression of his un- conscious is still Victorian in that it can be explained by attachment to traditional morality, as Jude's and Sue's cannot. Hardy's remark that Tess expresses 'the ache of modernism' (III, xix: 105) does not gibe with her whole character, but the phrase suits Jude and Sue who appeared only four years later (in 1895). It requires Lawrence's metaphysic – in which he traces the cultural evolution of the West from 'female' communal Judaism to 'male' individualistic Protes- tantism – to account for the astounding fact, finally stated in the *Study*'s penultimate chapter, that the male principle should have come to reside in a certain kind of modern woman. 'Sue', says Lawrence, 'is scarcely a woman at all, though she is feminine enough. . . . One of the supremest products of our civilization is

Sue, and a product that well frightens us' (496–7). The point is that Sue is an 'advanced' woman whose case in not uniquely pathological but symptomatic of a coming desexualisation of our culture.

Recent feminist critics defend Sue against the Lawrencean criticism of her as sexless or frigid. Penny Boumelha, while noting that Hardy's revisions increase Sue's sexual reserve, argues against equating 'such changes with a total absence of sexual feeling, or with frigidity'. The reserve is connected with the intellectual 'woman's sense of selfhood', it is a necessary stand against being reduced to the 'womanly'. Boumelha quotes Hardy in a letter to Gosse to show 'that it is irrevocable sexual commitment which she fears and abhors, and that she has attempted to retain control of her sexuality by a straightforward restriction of her sexual availability'.[25]

I shall quote Hardy's letter to Gosse more amply than does Boumelha:

> There is nothing perverted or depraved in Sue's nature. The abnormalism consists in disproportion, not in inversion, her sexual instinct being healthy as far as it goes, but unusually weak and fastidious. . . . Though she has children, her intimacies with Jude have never been more than occasional, even when they were living together (I mention that they occupy separate rooms, except towards the end), and one of her reasons for fearing the marriage ceremony is that she fears it would be breaking faith with Jude to withhold herself at pleasure, or altogether, after it; though while uncontracted she feels at liberty to yield herself as seldom as she chooses. This has tended to keep his passion as hot at the end as at the beginning, and helps to break his heart. He has never really possessed her as freely as he desired.[26]

These last two sentences, not quoted by Boumelha, suggest that from Jude's point of view a word like 'frigid' would apply to Sue.

'*Jude the Obscure* offers a challenge,' writes Boumelha, 'to contemporary reformist feminism', to the notion that 'the home or the love-relationship . . . could be reformed by individual acts of will and intention.' *Jude* shows 'rather the unimaginable nature of female–male relations as they would exist outside the economic and ideological pressures which [in this novel] wrench the relationship back into pre-determined forms of marriage'. Jude is quoted: 'Perhaps the world is not illuminated enough for such experiments as ours!' (150). The world of this novel is certainly not ready, perhaps we are only now getting ready, for the kind of emancipation Sue requires, though the emancipation may bring its own kind of trouble to love relationships. Boumelha finally admits that *Jude* is 'in conscious dialogue with both feminist and anti-feminist fiction of its time' (153).

Rosemarie Morgan goes farther than Boumelha in that she enlists Hardy in the ranks of the feminists, seeing Sue as 'the objective voice for Hardy's own . . . political views'. Admitting Sue's sexual coolness, she argues that 'a sexually passionate nature in Sue would . . . threaten to diminish her political voice', as it diminishes the political voices of the voluptuous Bathsheba, Eustacia and Tess. Were Sue endowed, Morgan says felicitously, with the 'sensuality, sexual luxuriance and physical self-delight that Hardy sees as the birthright of his strong women', the novel 'would lose its hard edge of bitter repression, its sharp focus upon the harsh codes that govern the lives of women struggling for independence, for autonomy'.[27]

Although Morgan's feminist commitment leads to misinterpretation of certain male characters whom most readers find attractive but whom she condemns as 'the spying Oak, the policing Venn' (162), she is persuasive in arguing that Sue is sexually disarmed by Jude's idealisation of her: '"All that's best and noblest in me loves you, and your freedom from everything that's gross has elevated me."' 'How can Sue', Morgan comments, 'yield now out of any other feelings than guilt and responsibility, and a frightening sense that at all costs she must not appear "gross" (sexually passionate)?' (140). Hardy, says Morgan, uses Arabella's sharply intuitive, woman-to-woman assessment of Sue in the end 'to ensure that readers do not fall into the trap of reading Sue as Jude reads her' (144). Arabella's

> insight into the unguarded, passionate, sensual Sue struggling to break from the curbing 'ennobled' mould which imprisons her, presents the reader with a deeper understanding of the strong, vital woman conceived by Hardy and tragically misconceived by Jude. (153–4)

This notion of the heroine as creation of what Kaja Silverman, in her article on figuration in *Tess*, calls the 'colonizing male gaze' is recurrent in feminist criticism. 'What is at stake', Silverman argues, 'in the representation of Tess as a surface upon which certain things are figured is precisely *her accessibility as image.*' Whereas her father has 'a stable and knowable appearance, co-extensive with his social, economic and physical circumstances, his daughter has *no* integral visual consistency, but must be painted, imprinted and patterned in order to be seen'. Thus, after her rape–seduction the narrator asks: '"Why was it that upon this beautiful feminine tissue, sensitive as gossamer, and practically blank as snow as yet, there should have been traced such a coarse pattern?"'[28]

So far Jude's manhood has been taken for granted while Sue's womanhood has been treated as problematic. But a recent gender study – Elizabeth Langland's 'Becoming a Man in *Jude the Obscure*' – traces Sue's place in the construction of Jude's masculinity. Jude sees his cousin Sue as a version of himself, but middle class and feminine where he is working class and masculine. It is after he has been denied access to the middle-class scholarly life that Jude turns with increased passsion to Sue as 'pivotal to the construction of [his] identity'.[29] It is such multiple interpretations of a novel in which the characters find life problematic that, according to Irving Howe, make *Jude the Obscure* 'Hardy's most distinctly "modern" work'.[30]

Tess and *Jude* are the two Hardy novels Lawrence discusses in detail. We can see why since they are the two that treat sex explicitly. The chapter on *Jude* is the *Study's* climax and in this chapter the discussion of Sue makes the most important bridge to Lawrence's work. For it is in the character of Sue, as Lawrence and others analyse her, that Hardy makes the definitive break with the Victorian novel, in which the problem is to arrive at the point of sexuality by finding the right mate while staying within the laws of God and society. With Sue sexuality itself becomes the problem, whether a problem in pathology or in the relations between the sexes. From Sue on, we encounter characters (especially in Lawrence) who do not want sex or want it perversely. The connection in Sue of idealism with sexual deficiency points toward Miriam in Lawrence's *Sons and Lovers*. Sue admires roses in what will be Miriam's manner: '"I should like to push my face quite into them – the dears!"' (*Jude*, v, 5: 235). Paul Morel's choice between Miriam and Clara resembles Jude's choice between Sue and Arabella, with the difference that Paul has his own problem in an Oedipal attachment to his mother. Lawrence reads more sexual problems into Jude (perhaps because he identifies himself with him) than most readers would find.

With Sue, as Lawrence points out, Hardy makes a first attack on the cult of virginity, on all those virgins who have in novels been held up as eminently desirable for marriage. With Sue, Hardy shows how virginity can become a pathological state of mind. Sue remains psychologically a virgin (her name Bridehead suggests maidenhead, a sign of virginity) even after she has slept with Jude and Phillotson and given birth to Jude's children. We can read back from Hardy's explicit treatment of sexual deficiency in Sue to find hints that the idealism of earlier characters like Angel and Clym may be linked with sexual deficiency; so that the characterisation of Sue brings to a climax (a climax maintained in the next and last novel *The Well-Beloved*) Hardy's continuing critique of idealism.

Thus far Lawrence goes along with Hardy, explaining what he considers to be Hardy's conscious intentions. Lawrence breaks with Hardy over the issue of the sexually potent characters whom Lawrence calls 'aristocrats' and over the issue of society's role in the novels. On these issues Lawrence apparently feels he is fulfilling Hardy's *un*conscious intentions. Hardy, we are told, has the predilection of all artists for the aristocrat, because 'the aristocrat alone has occupied a position where he could afford to *be*, to be himself'. Lawrence's phrase in the *Study*, '*prédilection d'artiste*' (436), comes from Hardy's *A Laodicean*, where the rich bourgeois Paula Power expresses her aesthetic preference for aristocratic ancestors.[31] But Hardy also shares the bourgeois moral antagonism to the aristocrat, making his aristocrats die or making 'every exceptional person a villain' (436). Lawrence seems to have derived from Hardy a romantic notion of aristocracy as signifying existential potency rather than social class. Hardy likes to give his existentially potent characters vaguely aristocratic or pseudo-aristocratic connections – Tess, Alec, Eustacia, Troy and Fitzpiers are examples. Through the three versions of *Lady Chatterley's Lover*, Lawrence keeps refining the gamekeeper in order to show that he rather than Sir Clifford Chatterley is the true aristocrat.

Hardy's fault, says Lawrence, is that he always stands 'with the community in condemnation of the aristocrat' when 'his private sympathy is always with the individual against the community'. Unfortunately Hardy gives some of his distinct individualities – Troy, Clym, Tess, Jude (Lawrence should have added Sue) – 'a weak life-flow, so that they cannot break away from the old adhesion' to communal morality. Tess, for example, 'sided with the community's condemnation of her' (439–40) – internalising, as I have suggested, a social condemnation harsher than anything objectively apparent until her execution, which is itself curiously muted.

'Hardy is a bad artist', says Lawrence, 'because he must condemn Alec d'Urberville, according to his own personal creed.' But Alec, 'by the artist's account, . . . is a rare man who seeks and seeks among women for one of such character and intrinsic female being as Tess'. Similarly it is Arabella's distinction that she chooses 'a sensitive, deep-feeling man' like Jude, which no 'coarse, shallow woman' would do. 'Arabella was, under all her disguise of pig-fat and false hair, and vulgar speech, in character somewhat an aristocrat. She was, like Eustacia, amazingly lawless, even splendidly so. She believed in herself and she was not altered by any outside opinion of herself' (488–90). This last sentence would not apply to Jude or Sue or Tess.

Alec and Troy, we are told, 'could reach some of the real sources of the female in a woman, and draw from them. . . . And, as a woman instinctively knows, such men are rare. Therefore they have a power over a woman. They draw from the depth of her being.' But 'what they draw they betray. . . . What they received they knew only as gratification in the senses; some perverse will prevented them from submitting to it, from becoming instruumental to it' (484). The same applies to Arabella. These sensualists betray the depths they draw on because they are exploitative in love – they gratify themselves without giving back the male or female principles that would create an interchange. They are unwilling to submit to the development in themselves required for the male–female interchange that yields full consummation. 'Jude, like Tess, wanted full consummation. Arabella, like Alec . . . resisted full consummation' (490). It is a sign of their inability to develop that both Arabella and Alec go through a period of evangelical conversion which leaves no permanent effect upon them.

In *Women in Love*, Lawrence uses as a criterion of approval the capacity for development. Ursula and Birkin are the only characters with this capacity. Lawrence – whose aim is to reconcile the conflicts that Hardy leaves unreconciled – works out a way of achieving full consummation through what he calls a 'star-equilibrium' between the sexes – a metaphor probably suggested by Hardy's description, in *Return of the Native*, of Clym's and Eustacia's harmonious first months of marriage: 'They were like those double stars which revolve round and round each other, and from a distance appear to be one' (IV, i: 187).

Lawrence in the *Study* criticises Hardy for coming down, in the conflict between the individual and society, on the side of society when social judgements no longer express God's judgement but are merely relative. 'Eustacia, Tess or Sue', says Lawrence, 'were not at war with God, only with Society.' Yet they

> were all cowed by the mere judgment of man upon them, and all the while by their own souls they were right. . . . Which is the weakness of modern tragedy, where transgression against the social code is made to bring destruction, as though the social code worked our irrevocable fate. (420)

Actually Hardy is no less critical of society than Lawrence and agrees, more than Lawrence realises, about the relativity of social judgement. I have already quoted the passage in which he says that Tess's desire for Angel 'was not to be controlled by vague lucubrations over the social rubric' (IV, xxx: 161). Tess feels ashamed of having suffered over mere conscience, when she beholds nature's cruelty in the pain of pheasants left wounded by hunters. Wringing the pheasants' necks to end their torture, 'she was ashamed of herself for her gloom of the night, based on nothing more tangible than a sense of condemnation under an arbitrary law of society which had no foundation in Nature' (V, xli: 233). The injustice of society is attacked throughout *Jude*.

What surprises Lawrence is that Hardy portrays a world where society, as I suggested in the Preface, still sends out signals strong enough, even if of doubtful validity, to torment his characters. In Lawrence's middle and later novels, such signals have ceased: social conventions are no longer an obstacle to any one's desires. Lawrence portrays a world that has become increasingly apparent since World War I. In their treatment of society, the difference between Hardy and Lawrence is one of historical situation. Hardy's historical situation is better for the novel than Lawrence's, since the novel's original subject is the protagonist's exploration of and conflict with social reality. For such a subject the novelist requires a social reality complex enough to be worth exploring and powerful enough to be a worthy antagonist to his characters. Because such a society has largely disappeared by the time of *Women in Love* (1920), Lawrence evolves there and later a genre – the first signs of which

are the ritualised scenes in *The Rainbow* (1915) – that substitutes for
social notation the externalising of subjectivity: this genre exists on
the borderline between myth and novel.

Already in Hardy's novels, where society still pretends to an
authority it has lost, we find the beginnings of a transition to the
mythical mode. The transition can be detected in Hardy's technique
of presenting characters first as distantly perceived figures barely
separable from the landscape before they approach and take on the
lineaments of individuals. The transition can also be detected in
Hardy's much criticised use of coincidences and other 'clumsy' narrative devices, all of which sacrifice verisimilitude to set up highly
concentrated scenes that permit the explosive revelation of internal
states of being. Hardy's coincidences point toward Lawrence's
Freudian dictum that there are no accidents; for Hardy's coincidences, when they are successful, allow his characters to fulfil their
desires and destinies. Hardy's irony derives from the fact that there
is a society out there worth attacking ironically and from the fact
that what appears to be chance turns out to be design – that of fate
and/or the characters' unconscious.

In the 'Moony' chapter of *Women in Love*, Lawrence uses a
Hardyan coincidence and accounts for it psychologically. Ursula is
walking by a lake in the moonlight at a time when Birkin is abroad.
'She wished for something else out of the night'. Soon 'she saw a
shadow moving by the water. It would be Birkin', she thinks before recognising him. 'He had come back then, unawares'. That last
word is ambiguous; it is the adverb Wordsworth uses with equal
ambiguity when the narrator of 'Resolution and Independence' suddenly beholds the old leech-gatherer standing by a pool: 'I saw a
Man before me unawares'. In Lawrence 'unawares' seems to mean
that Birkin has returned without telling her, also in response to
her desire, also that he is unaware of being observed. Ursula justi-
fies spying on him by thinking: 'How can there be any secrets, we
are all the same organisms? How can there be any secrecy, when
everything is known to all of us?' (xix: 322). Hardy's coincidences
– I have already cited some and will cite others – can be justified by
the possibility that all the characters share one mind. The possibility dissolves the distinction between the event and the character's
individual unconscious – a dissolution which Hardy often, too often,
represents as fate.

In *Study of Hardy*, Lawrence rewrites Hardy's novels and criticises
Hardy's deficiencies in such a way as to arrive at his own novels

by an unbroken continuum. The *Study* is important as criticism just because it tells us as much about Lawrence as about Hardy, to the enlargement of both writers' stature. When we think of all Hardy managed to say under the restrictions laid down by readers and editors even more prudish than the ones who harrassed Lawrence, we can only conclude from what Lawrence shows us in the *Study* that Hardy, with his sensitivity to historical change, would, had he been born a generation later, have become a novelist very much like D. H. Lawrence.

2

The Issue of Hardy's Poetry

When I told the American poet Theodore Weiss that I was writing on Hardy's poetry, he snorted contemptuously saying Hardy was being used nowadays as a stick with which to beat the modernists, such as Yeats, Eliot and Pound. Weiss argues this view powerfully in the *Times Literary Supplement* of 1 February 1980. Irving Howe, instead, in the *New York Times Book Review* of 7 May 1978 defends the taste for Hardy's poetry in just the terms feared by Weiss.

> As we slowly emerge from the shadowing power of the age of modernism, Hardy's poems can be felt as more durable . . . than those of, say, T. S. Eliot. . . . Reading Eliot (or even Yeats) one may say, 'ah, here in fulfillment is the sensibility that formed us.' Reading Hardy one may say, but 'this is how life is, has always been, and probably will remain.' (11)

In his book *Thomas Hardy* Howe says that Hardy 'through the integrity of his negations' helps make possible the twentieth-century 'sensibility of problem and doubt', but 'he is finally not of [this century]. That his poems span two cultural eras while refusing to be locked into either is a source of his peculiar attractiveness' (161).

It is Donald Davie who, in his *Thomas Hardy and British Poetry* (1972), defines most acutely the crisis for modernism represented in Britain by the 'conversion' to Hardy. Davie begins by declaring that 'in British poetry of the last fifty years (as not in American) the most far-reaching influence, for good and ill, has been not Yeats, still less Eliot or Pound, not Lawrence, but *Hardy*'. Davie cites as the model for post-World War II British poetry Philip Larkin's significant 'conversion . . . from Yeats to Hardy in 1946, after his very Yeatsian first collection'.[1] The post-World War II British poets renounced the grand resonances emerging from the modernists' allegiances to the tradition and to various myths – the 'common myth-kitty', as Larkin put it (Davie, 42) – settling for the smaller, drier tones of a precisely noted quotidian reality. In learning to read the great modernists we had to assent to mysticisms, religious orthodoxies and reactionary politics most of us would not dream of living by. But we thought only such views could in our time supply the symbols necessary for great poetry. Here, says Davie, lies Hardy's importance as 'the one poetic imagination of the first magnitude in the present century who writes out of . . . political and social attitudes which a social democrat recognizes as "liberal" '. Hardy shows that poetry can be made out of the common sense working ethic of most English-speaking readers – an ethic Davie aptly describes as 'scientific humanism' (6, 5), a scientific world-view tempered by humanitarianism, by what Hardy in the Apology to *Late Lyrics* (1922) calls 'loving-kindness'. In the Apology Hardy decries the 'present, when belief in witches of Endor is displacing the Darwinian theory'.[2] Hardy is probably responding to Yeats's occultism.

Most contemporary American poets seem able to reconcile admiration for the modernists with a taste for Hardy. Even in Britain, pre-World War II poets like W. H. Auden and Cecil Day Lewis could admire Eliot without repudiating their earlier passions for Hardy (Day Lewis's passion remained so strong that he had himself buried near Hardy in Stinsford churchyard). Auden tells how Hardy first gave him the sense of modernity: 'Besides serving as the archetype of the Poetic, Hardy was also an expression of the Contemporary Scene.' Hardy 'was my poetical father'.[3] A generation earlier Ezra Pound declared the same filial relation to Browning ('Ich stamm aus Browning. Pourquoi nier son pere?'[4]), who educated him in the rough diction, broken syntax and *difficult* music of modern lyricism. In a generation still earlier Hardy, as we shall see, learned the same things from Browning, while from Swinburne he learned modern ideas delivered in classic metres ('New words, in classic guise'[5]).

Davie, however, insists that for post-World War II poets 'the choice cannot be fudged' between mythical and realistic poetry. The contemporary poet must decide whether like Yeats to try 'to transcend historical time by seeing it as cyclical, so as to leap above it into a realm that is visionary, mythological' or like Hardy to confine himself to 'the world of historical contingency [linear time], a world of specific places at specific times' (4, 3). While mainly agreeing with Davie, I find difficulties in his position which I will try to puzzle out.

Having begun by saying that Hardy is the one twentieth-century poet 'of the first magnitude' to express the liberal ethos, Davie subsequently casts doubt on whether Hardy's poetry is indeed 'of the first magnitude'. He goes on to criticise Hardy's too obvious symmetries, attributing them to the hand of an engineer influenced by Victorian technology or to a poet educated in the regularities of architecture (though Hardy spoke of having learned from his experience with Gothic the art of irregularity). Davie uses the question of symmetry as a criterion of evaluation, showing that the best poems display asymmetries that have slipped past the surveillance of the poet's 'imperious' will (25). Despite his high evaluation at the beginning, Davie seems subsequently to approve of Blackmur's argument that Hardy's successes are 'isolated' cases, that he had expertise but lacked 'technique in the wide sense' because he lacked 'the structural support of a received imagination'.[6] 'Hardy is not a great poet,' writes Davie, 'because, except in *The Dynasts*, he does not choose to be' (39). Davie proposes Hardy as a precursor of Larkin and the other contemporary British poets who in reaction against modernism deliberately set out to be precise and minor. Is the implication then that liberal, realistic poets are not first-rate?

While admitting that Hardy is a much larger figure than Larkin, Davie still considers him minor because his poems deliver an untransformed reality. This, however, is the characteristic of Hardy's poetry which, after the transcendentalising nineteenth century, later poets took over as particularly modern. Thus, Yeats, in the one sentence he devotes to Hardy in the Introduction to his *Oxford Book of Modern Verse*, belittles Hardy's 'technical accomplishment' but praises 'his mastery of the impersonal objective scene'.[7] Italy's leading modernist poet, Eugenio Montale, finds Hardy's relation to objects congenial to his own art, as we see by his translation into Italian of Hardy's 'The Garden Seat', but Montale wonders at Hardy's 'rigidly closed' forms and 'impeccably traditional' stanzas.[8] Davie concludes his discussion of Hardy's poems as follows:

> And so his poems, instead of transforming and displacing quantifiable reality or the reality of common sense, are on the contrary just so many glosses on that reality, which is conceived of as unchallengeably 'given' and final. . . . he sold the vocation short, tacitly surrendering the proudest claims traditionally made for the act of poetic imagination. (62)

Yet for an atheistic realist Hardy populates his poems with a
surprising number of ghosts. And if he does not draw on the 'myth-
kitty', he does in his poems and fiction draw on observed folklore
which, as the mythology of the illiterate, is older and more fundamental than the myths available through the literary tradition.
Hardy's ghosts are not only the folklore ghosts of his ballads, but
in his lyrics they are also psychological ghosts of Wordsworthian
involuntary memory, wrapping the poems in mystery, dissolving
fixities of place and time. Even 'The Garden Seat', a realistic portrayal of an abandoned garden seat, evokes the ghosts of those who
used to sit upon it (II: 331). The ghost of Hardy's dead wife Emma
flits through these pages, as in 'After a Journey' (which Davie calls
a 'phantasmagoria'), where the ghost is placeless: 'Hereto I come
to view a voiceless ghost; / Whither, O whither will its whim
now draw me?' (II: 59), or in 'The Voice' where Emma's ghost is a
timeless, placeless auditory experience:

> Woman much missed, how you call to me, call to me,
> . . .
>
> Or is it only the breeze, in its listlessness
> Travelling across the wet mead to me here,
> You being ever dissolved to wan wistlessness,
> Heard no more again far or near?
>
>   Thus I; faltering forward,
>   Leaves around me falling,
> Wind oozing thin through the thorn from norward
>   And the woman calling.
>
>   (II: 56–7)

'Or is it only the breeze' continues the romantic tradition of natural–
supernaturalism, while the shortened lines and changed metres of
the last stanza produce the break in symmetry which by Davie's
criteria (and mine) mark this poem as major.

The ghost of involuntary memory is best exemplified in 'During
Wind and Rain', where scenes from the past rush back with un-
bearable poignancy to overwhelm a present represented only by
wind and rain: 'Ah, no; the years O! / How the sick leaves reel

down in throngs!' (II: 239). In 'Wessex Heights', a ghost poem of eschatological magnitude, the heights, realistically evoked by place-names, seem to represent a detached state of existence comparable to the afterlife:

> and at crises when I stand,
> Say, on Ingpen Beacon eastward, or on Wylls-Neck westwardly,
> I seem where I was before my birth, and after death may be.

'In the lowlands', instead, 'I have no comrade'. 'Down there I seem to be false to myself, my simple self that was.' It seems misleading to try to identify, as does J. O. Bailey in his *Commentary*,[9] the people being accused of betraying the speaker since he accuses himself as well. 'Too weak to mend' and 'mind-chains do not clank where one's next neighbour is the sky' suggest self-accusation, so does 'I am tracked by phantoms' and 'I cannot go to the great grey Plain; there's a figure against the moon, / Nobody sees it but I, and it makes my breast beat out of tune.' The ghosts who enter the next stanza seem to represent a purgatorial experience:

> There's a ghost at Yell'ham Bottom chiding loud at the fall of
>   the night,
> There's a ghost in Froom-side Vale, thin-lipped and vague, in
>   a shroud of white,
> There is one in the railway-train whenever I do not want it
>   near,
> I see its profile against the pane, saying what I would not
>   hear.

The speaker finally saves himself through the liberating perspective achieved through loneliness on the heights: 'And ghosts then keep their distance; and I know some liberty' (II: 25–7).

There are also poems in which Hardy portrays himself through the analogy to ghostliness. 'He Revisits His First School' begins:

> I should not have shown in the flesh,
> I ought to have gone as a ghost;
> It was awkward, unseemly almost,
> Standing solidly there,
>   (II: 258–9)

as though, Hardy says, I still belonged to the same vigorously living species that inhabits this classroom. I should have waited and returned from the tomb. In the similar 'Among School Children', Yeats's strong presence takes over the scene, whereas Hardy projects his relative absence: his ghost would have made a stronger presence. Absence is again projected in 'The Strange House (Max Gate, A.D. 2000)', in which future inhabitants sense only faint ghostly stirrings of the Hardys' life there (II: 346–7). The most uncanny of the ghostly self-portrayals is the early poem, 'I Look into My Glass', in which the aged speaker, seeing himself wasted in body and wishing his 'heart had shrunk as thin' so he could wait his 'endless rest / With equanimity', is horrified by the youthful passions that still shake his 'fragile frame' (I: 106) – as though he were a ghost who could not find rest. (This poem, though symmetrical, seems major because it springs a surprise, whereas Hardy's minor poems are as predictable in content as in form.) One wonders how much Hardy's sense of himself as ghostly emerged from his knowledge that he was at birth taken for dead.

'For my part', he wrote in his diary,

> if there is any way of getting a melancholy satisfaction out of life it lies in dying, so to speak, before one is out of the flesh; by which I mean putting on the manners of ghosts, wandering in their haunts, and taking their views of surrounding things. . . . Hence even when I enter into a room to pay a simple morning call I have unconsciously the habit of regarding the scene as if I were a spectre not solid enough to influence my environment.
> (*Life*, 209–10)

I have cited all these examples to show, in answer to Davie, that many of Hardy's poems do transform reality, even if the poems of common sense reality, poems such as 'A Commonplace Day', are admittedly most characteristic. Yet even that poem, which contains such finely realistic lines as 'Wanly upon the panes / The rain slides', begins with the line, 'The day is turning ghost' and opens out in the end to a cosmic speculation that accounts for the speaker's regret over the dying of so commonplace a day (I: 148–9). In the Apology to *Late Lyrics*, Hardy tries to reconcile the two sides of his work by dreaming of 'an alliance between religion . . . and complete rationality . . . by means of the interfusing effect of poetry' (II: 325).

And in the *Life* he speaks of his 'infinite trying to reconcile a scientific view of life with the emotional and spiritual, so that they may not be interdestructive' (148).

We cannot classify Hardy the poet simply as an antimythic, commonsense realist when his great novels are wrapped in the mystery noted by Virginia Woolf who, in her essay on him in *The Common Reader*, describes him as a novelist of unconscious intention and when so many of his plots are modelled on the mythic patterns of Greek and Shakespearean drama. We cannot finally assess Hardy's poems without remembering that he began publishing his poems when already an elderly successful novelist and that readers were first drawn to the poems because of the novels. Too many critics of the poems (Davie included) write as though the novels did not exist.[10]

Davie describes the difficulty of assessing Hardy's poetry. 'Affection for Hardy the poet is general', he writes, '. . . but it is ruinously shot through with protectiveness, even condescension. Hardy is not thought of as an intellectual force.' 'None of Hardy's admirers have yet found how to make Hardy the poet *weigh* equally with Eliot and Pound and Yeats' (5, 4). Davie does not try to accomplish this end. He and other critics have in effect withdrawn Hardy from the competition by judging him according to another scale – as, though most critics avoid the term, a first-rate *minor* poet. John Crowe Ransom, in the *Southern Review* Hardy issue, calls him 'a great minor poet' (14).

Most critics note in Hardy's prodigious output an inevitable number of bad poems, a majority of interesting, well-made poems comprising a refreshing variety of subjects, verse forms and tones, and a dozen or two major poems. But there is no agreed upon Hardy canon for the poems as there is for the novels. Everyone of course agrees upon a few poems as major, otherwise each critic chooses different poems for discussion. Most critics (Yeats is an exception) praise Hardy's craftsmanship, and the question arises whether the major poems are to be viewed as happy accidents or as a main criterion for evaluating his poetry. In speaking of Hardy as ambitious technically but, except in *The Dynasts*, unambitious in every other way, Davie is suggesting that Hardy *chose* to work on a minor scale and that the major poems are happy accidents, moments when the creative impulse escaped from the watchful eye of the technician and the wilful self: hence the chapter titles, 'Hardy as Technician' and 'Hardy Self-Excelling'.

Before proposing my own different evaluation, I want to see how far Hardy can be considered minor in a non-pejorative sense, since many minor poets have become classics. It is the minor scale of Hardy's poetry that makes him useful as an influence. His admirers display an intimate affection for him differing from the awe inspired by the great modernists. More recent poets have found Hardy supportive because he points a direction without pre-empting their own ideas and feelings. He is, in other words, a precursor from whom much can be learned, but not a competitor.

Auden speaks of his debt to Hardy for 'technical instruction'. Hardy's faults 'were obvious even to a schoolboy, and the young can learn best from those of whom, because they can criticise them, they are not afraid'. Hardy was useful as a teacher because no other English poet 'employed so many and so complicated stanza forms' and because his rhymed verse kept Auden from too early an excursion into free verse which to a beginner looks easy but is really the most difficult of verse forms. Hardy 'taught me much about direct colloquial diction, all the more because his directness was in phrasing and syntax, not in imagery' – for example, 'I see what you are doing: you are leading me on' ('After a Journey') and 'Upon that shore we are clean forgot' ('An Ancient to Ancients'). 'Here was a "modern" rhetoric which was more fertile and adaptable to different themes than any of Eliot's gas-works and rats' feet [imagery] which one could steal but never make one's own' (Guerard, ed., *Hardy: Critical Essays*, 141–2). Acually 'An Ancient to Ancients', which was first published in 1922, the year of *The Waste Land*, contains modern *imagery* comparable to Eliot's:

> Where once we danced, where once we sang,
>   Gentlemen,
> The floors are sunken, cobwebs hang,
> And cracks creep; worms have fed upon
> The doors. . . .
>
> The bower we shrined to Tennyson,
>   Gentlemen,
> Is roof-wrecked; damps there drip upon
> Sagged seats, the creeper-nails are rust,
> The spider is sole denizen.
>
>   (II: 481–3)

But Auden's point is that the apprentice can take what he wants from a minor poet while still calling his style his own.

What then is the difference between major and first-rate minor poetry? The difference does not lie in Hardy's unevenness; Wordsworth is more uneven, yet most of us would agree that he is major. Auden, in introducing his anthology of nineteenth-century British minor poets, says that the major poet is likely to 'write more bad poems than the minor'. As for enjoyment, he says, 'I cannot enjoy one poem by Shelley and am delighted by every line of William Barnes, but I know perfectly well that Shelley is a major poet, and Barnes a minor one.'[11]

What then is the difference? A major poet seems to me to be one whose world-view and personal character determine each other and determine the diction, imagery and central myth running through all his poetry. His poetry is thus *characteristic* down to its unconscious elements; its originality of content and form emerges from its characteristicness or inner compulsion. That is why major poetry gives the impression of unfathomed depths, leaving us with the desire to *re*read as soon as we have read. Not so minor poetry which, deriving from the poet's will, can usually be understood and enjoyed with one or two readings, though we may return to it many times to admire its skillful clarity of meaning and form. The symmetries of minor poems are obvious, sometimes too obvious, whereas major poems favour asymmetries and leave a final impression of openness even though the older poems employ formal closures.[12]

T. S. Eliot tries to define minor poetry in writing about another poet–novelist, Rudyard Kipling, whom Eliot calls a writer of '*great verse*'. Kipling exhibits

that skill of craftsmanship which seems to enable him to pass from form to form, though always in an identifiable idiom, and from subject to subject, so that we are aware of no inner compulsion to write about this rather than that – a versatility which may make us suspect him of being no more than a performer. . . . I mention Yeats at this point because of the contrast between his development, which is very apparent in the way he writes, and Kipling's development, which is only apparent in what he writes about. We expect to feel, with a great writer, that he *had* to write about the subject he took, and in that way. With no writer of equal eminence to Kipling is this inner compulsion . . . more difficult to discern.[13]

Auden, too, employs the criterion of development. 'In the case of the major poet,' he says in his Introduction to *Minor Poets*,

> if confronted by two poems of his of equal merit but written at different times, the reader can immediately say which was written first. In the case of a minor poet, on the other hand, however excellent the two poems may be, the reader cannot settle their chronology on the basis of the poems themselves. (16)

If we judge by these criteria, most of Hardy's poems would count as minor, but a significant number would count as major. The New Critics – if we take as an example the contributors to the *Southern Review*'s Hardy Centennial issue (Summer 1940) – divide evenly between on the one side Ransom and Tate, who praise Hardy's poetry with qualifications, and on the other Blackmur and Leavis who have hardly a good word to say about the poetry. Critics of note nowadays, instead, are unqualified in their praise, beginning with Pound who in *Guide to Kulchur* asks: 'When we, if we live long enough, come to estimate the "poetry of the period," against Hardy's 600 pages we will put what?' (285). Philip Larkin 'would not wish Hardy's *Collected Poems* a single page shorter, and regards it as many times over the best body of poetic work this century so far has to show'.[14] 'It is generally agreed today', writes J. Hillis Miller, 'that Thomas Hardy is one of the greatest of modern poets writing in English.'[15] Harold Bloom calls Hardy a *strong* (that is, a major) poet, 'Shelley's ephebe'.[16] Christopher Ricks describes 'the recovery of the conviction of Hardy's greatness as a poet', but speaks of him as 'the poet who owed so much to Browning'.[17]

We might reconcile these varying judgements by saying that Hardy is a major poet who *chose* for long stretches to work in the minor mode, probably because (now that he had given himself the luxury of writing poetry after all the years of writing fiction for money) he wanted to test his skill at as many poetic forms as possible, wanted to indulge in the *craft* of poetry. Most Hardy poems are successes in the minor mode, in that they make their points completely with symmetries that are obvious, sometimes too obvious. The symmetries of thought and form in 'The Convergence of the Twain' are in my opinion too obvious. Yet 'His Immortality' is successful though it establishes in an unvarying stanza of obvious symmetry a quickly predictable pattern of thought. The poem begins:

I saw a dead man's finer part
Shining within each faithful heart
Of those bereft. Then said I: 'This must be
His immortality.'

It is clear that the dead man's immortality must diminish as the
friends who remember him die. Each stanza describes another step
in this diminution until in the final stanza the dead man finds 'in
me alone, a feeble spark, / Dying amid the dark' (I: 180). The imagery, however, suggests ironically that the speaker's immortality
is equally vulnerable. The ironical twist to the fulfilment of our
expectations of thought and form make this poem successful in a
minor mode.

As for the question of development, it is a commonplace that
Hardy the poet – in contrast to Hardy the novelist – shows no
development, that his volumes of verse mix earlier and later poems
with no discernible differences of period, unless dated or distinguished by subject such as the Boer War. Hardy dated his early
poems, suggesting that in his view they differed from the later
poems. Yet if an early success like 'Neutral Tones' (1867) were not
dated, could we discern its period? Looking back over Hardy's
poems in the *Sunday Times* of 28 May 1922, Edmund Gosse con-
cluded that the poetry had 'suffered very little modification in the
course of sixty years'.

Dennis Taylor, however, in his *Hardy's Poetry, 1860–1928*, argues
for development, finding it in Hardy's development of the meditative lyric and in the flowering of pastoral poems in his last volumes. While conceding that Hardy's 'poetry does not display the
obvious and clearly defined stages' of 'other poets', Taylor shows
that Hardy himself thought his volumes of verse displayed development, writing in his preface to *Times Laughingstocks* (1909) of the
first-person lyrics in that volume: 'As a whole they will, I hope, take
the reader forward, even if not far, rather than backward.'[18] By the
criterion of development Hardy's poetry falls on the border between
major and minor poetry.

Having myself discerned little development in Hardy's poetry, I
did note in my latest reading a steady increase in plain colloquial
diction and syntax. Hardy developed, as Samuel Hynes puts it,
'toward a more consistent and more effective control of that tone
which we recognize as uniquely his'.[19] Most importantly I noted,
beginning so late as *Human Shows* (1925), the last volume published

during Hardy's lifetime, a new imagist style which projects emotion entirely through closely observed objective correlatives. 'Snow
in the Suburbs' is the best known example: 'Every branch big with
it, / Bent every twig with it'. Objective correlatives to emotion appear
later: 'Some flakes have lost their way, and grope back upward,
when / Meeting those meandering down they turn and descend
again' (III: 42–3). Although written in couplets throughout, the stanzas vary in line lengths and in the last stanza in number of lines,
suggesting a freeing-up of the verse.

Other examples are 'Green Slates', 'An East-End Curate' and
'Coming up Oxford Street: Evening' (1925) which could be early
Eliot:

A city-clerk, with eyesight not of the best,
Who sees no escape to the very verge of his days
From the rut of Oxford Street into open ways:
And he goes along with head and eyes flagging forlorn,
Empty of interest in things, and wondering why he was born.

(III: 25)[20]

These couplets vary in the number of syllables and are much longer
than the lines in the previous longer stanza, which vary in the
number of syllables and rhyme scheme – suggesting again a freeing
up of the verse, already seen in such early poems as 'My Cicely'
and 'The Mother Mourns' with their many unrhymed lines.

Still other examples are 'The Flower's Tragedy', also 'At the
Aquatic Sports' which sounds like Frost ('So wholly is their being
here / A business they pursue', III: 104) and in the posthumous *Winter
Words* (1928) the admirably restrained 'The New Boots'. In the
moving poem 'Bereft' (1901), a working-man's widow laments his
death with the ballad-like refrain:

Leave the door unbarred,
The clock unwound,
Make my lone bed hard –
Would 'twere underground!

(I: 263)

In 'The New Boots', instead, the widow's grief is projected through
a neighbour's description of the boots which the husband bought
joyfully but never lived to wear. The widow's grief is all the more
apparent because of her muteness: 'And she's not touched them or
tried / To remove them. . . .' (III: 244).

It is not clear whether Hardy's imagism developed from his own objective realism (already evident in 'On the Departure Platform', 1909), or whether he was influenced by the Imagist poets. He appears to have read volumes sent him by Ezra Pound in 1920–1 and by Amy Lowell in 1922, but his responses to these young Imagists do not suggest influence (*Letters*, VI: 49, 77–8, 186). The phrase in his last volume, 'Just neutral-tinted haps' ('He Never Expected Much', III: 225), explains what he always aimed to convey, so that the neutrality characteristic of imagism was incipient in his earliest poems 'Neutral Tones' and 'Hap'. Hardy's objective realism or metonymy is more characteristic of his poetry than are metaphor and symbol.[21]

If we apply to Hardy Eliot's remark about Kipling's variety, we find that as poet Hardy exhibits even more variety than Kipling, in that he passes not only from form to form and subject to subject but also from level to level. For he mixes with humorous verse and melodramatic balladry poems that are serious philosophically and others that are in the full sense 'poetry'.

Yet we do not feel in reading through a Hardy volume the assured pitch of intensity that we feel with indubitably major poets or the equally assured lightness of versifiers. Hardy's variousness can be entertaining if we are alive to his shifts of tone, otherwise we may become impatient with his skilful ballads and narratives because our standards have been determined by the greater depths of emotion and psychological insights offered in the major poems. When an indubitably major poet relaxes into light verse – as does Eliot in his charming little book on cats – we feel that the playful excursion need not be taken into account for understanding him. But Hardy establishes no such criterion for exclusion. He himself recognised this problem when complaining in the Apology prefacing *Late Lyrics*,

> that dramatic anecdotes of a satirical and humorous intention following verse in graver voice, have been read as misfires because they raise the smile that they were intended to raise, the journalist, deaf to the sudden change of key, being unconscious that he is laughing with the author and not at him. I admit that I did not foresee such contingencies as I ought to have done, and that people might not perceive when the tone altered.   (II: 321–2)

Eliot's remark that Kipling's poetry 'does not revolutionise' (*Poetry and Poets*, 293) is inapplicable to Hardy as evidenced by his influence on succeeding poets. Although Hardy did not innovate in verse forms, he did innovate in diction, tone and above all in subject matter. As a novelist Hardy was a major innovator, having developed sex and the unconscious as subjects and mythical rendition as technique. These innovations appear also in the poetry, sex most conspicuously. To the extent that Hardy innovated, he might be considered a major poet; to the extent that he modernised and transmitted what was usable in nineteenth-century poetry, Hardy might be considered a first-class minor poet.

What is the use, one might well ask, of the distinction I am trying to draw between major and minor poetry? I am, first of all, trying to develop a standard for evaluating Hardy against the classic modernist poets by showing that he is in most cases successful on another scale. I am also trying to develop criteria for dealing with the great variety of levels and tones in Hardy's poems. To use the word 'major' for the best of them is to clarify the extent and mode of their success. To use the words 'first-class minor' for many of the others is to recognise their success on another scale. Finally, I want to distinguish between Hardy's poems and novels, to argue, as I shall do in the succeeding chapters, for the great novels as his most consistently major work, containing, albeit in prose, his most massively major poetry.

I have already discussed the aura of unconsciousness in many of the major poems. Hardy's advanced ideas about sex and marriage appear mainly through satire (the poems tend to be more explicitly didactic than the novels). In the bitterly ironic 'The Conformers', the speaker warns his mistress of what will happen to their passion should he surrender to her insistence that they marry (the tone of voice is what counts):

> Yes; we'll wed, my little fay,
>   And you shall write you mine,
> And in a villa chastely gray
>   We'll house, and sleep, and dine.
>   But those night-screened, divine,
>   Stolen trysts of heretofore,
> We of choice ecstasies and fine
>   Shall know no more.

The short concluding line dramatises in each stanza the finality of loss.

> . . .
>
> When we abide alone,
> No leapings each to each,
> But syllables in frigid tone
> Of household speech.

And when we die they will not speak of our 'mad romance', but will see in us 'A worthy pair, who helped advance / Sound parish views' (I: 279–80).

Traditional ideals of marital fidelity are satirised in 'A Wife Comes Back' and 'The Inscription'. In the first a man dreams that his long-estranged wife returns to him in all her youthful beauty. He reaches out to embrace her, 'But his arms closed in on his hard bare breast'. He goes in search of her and eventually finds an old woman who says:

> 'I'd almost forgotten your name! –
> A call just now – is troublesome;
> Why did you come?'
>
> (II: 369–70)

'The Inscription' takes off from a typical medieval tale of fidelity to tell the story of a widow who at her knightly husband's death had vowed eternal fidelity, then falls in love and undergoes great suffering even madness to keep her vow (II: 460–4). Rendered ironical by the medieval language, the poem is a modern study in sexual repression.

Most daring of all is 'Cross-Currents', which satirises romantic scenes of lovers' partings: 'They parted – a pallid, trembling pair'. Surprisingly the lady turns out to be glad that their plan to wed has fallen through, for '"never could I have given him love, / Even had I been his bride"'. While sorry for him, she is pleased to '"have escaped the sacrifice / I was distressed to make!"' (II: 457–8). We have here a case of perversity in that the lady could not have performed sexually (one wonders whether the title derives from Swinburne's novel *Love's Cross-Currents*). In 'The Mound', another advanced poem, a lady tells her current lover about her previous sexual adventures without the least remorse:

> And she crazed my mind by what she coolly told –
>   The history of her undoing,
> (As I saw it), but she called 'comradeship,'
>   That bred in her no rueing.

(III: 176)

The lady in this poem takes quite another direction from that of the relatively conservative Tess and Sue Bridehead who do repent. In 'A Practical Woman', the woman finds herself a man to father a healthy son and then unsentimentally leaves him when 'he'd done his job' (III: 220). Hardy, as he admitted, felt free to say in the poems things he could not have said so openly in the more popular and therefore more censored form of the novel. But in fiction and poetry Hardy led the way in the changing sexual morality of the late nineteenth century. He kept in touch with the advanced novelists, many of them women, who were dealing with the New Woman and the marriage question, and he was discussed favourably by the sexologist Havelock Ellis.

In the pseudo-Greek tragedy *Aristodemus the Messenian*, the modern reader must see a violent attack on the cult of virginity as victimising women (III: 181–6). 'I Said to Love' instead deals with the decline of sexuality in modern times. To Love's threat that with neglect of him '"Man's race shall perish"', the speaker replies: '"We are too old in apathy! / *Mankind shall cease*. – So let it be"' (I: 148).

These are not major poems despite their significant ideas. 'The Trampwoman's Tragedy', with its positive rather than satirical treatment of sexuality, is major; Hardy considered it 'upon the whole, his most successful poem' (*Life*, 312). Based on a local story of some such event, this powerful ballad is Lawrencean in its treatment of pre-industrial, itinerant people for whom sex is a central preoccupation, strong enough to stir up both self-destructive and murderous passions. The abundant use of place-names gives the story its air of reality and its poetry, reproducing minds which operate concretely through locations rather than ideas:

> For months we had padded side by side,
>   Ay, side by side
> Through the Great Forest, Blackmoor wide,
>   And where the Parret ran.

These roaming people live outside society's conventions of marriage, but have their own conventions.

The central event springs from the unconscious, since the speaker has no motive, but out of 'wanton idleness' she 'teased my fancy-man in play' by pretending to prefer another. When her lover asks whether the baby in her belly is the other man's, her wantonness turns destructive: 'But, O despair! / I nodded – still to tease'. Is despair what she feels as she answers, or later, or at both times? Her lover swiftly kills his rival with a knife and is hanged: 'On his death-day I gave my groan / And dropt his dead-born child'. Such desolation requires the breakthrough to the supernatural found in so many of Hardy's best poems. Ballad conventions and the characters' pre-industrial minds make plausible the appearance of the lover's ghost asking her the question that still torments him: '"Was the child mine, or was it his?"' Her answer is deeply moving:

> O doubt not but I told him then,
>   I told him then,
> That I had kept me from all men
>   Since we joined lips and swore.
> Whereat he smiled, and thinned away,

leaving her, like a ghost, to haunt 'the Western Moor' in remorse (I: 244–7) – which turns the story into a local myth. In such powerful imaginativeness we find a criterion for distinguishing Hardy's major from his minor poems.

While most of Hardy's poems are minor (many are triumphs in the minor mode), he has as we will see written enough major poems to count as a major poet – especially since the effect of reading through the bulky *Complete Poetical Works* is to be impressed by the power of prolific creativity and sustained technical virtuosity, so that even when the poems are minor we never cease to feel ourselves in the presence of a major *writer*, the author also of the novels. If we regard the oeuvre as one, we can understand that Hardy wrote his long poems as prose fictions and his short poems as verse, that he was trying in the verse for smaller effects, and we can judge accordingly. He had already used the big sublime voice in the major novels; for the poems he often sought a more astringent voice with less resonance and more wit, which is why some poems may seem more modern than the novels. Imagination, even in the imaginative poems, is limited in scope compared to the novels.

As a measure of imaginative scope in the novels, let us compare with *Tess* the poem 'We Field-Women', written many years after publication of the novel. A choral voice, consisting probably of Tess and her friends Marian and Izz contrast 'How it rained' and 'How it snowed' on Flintcomb-Ash farm to 'How it shone' when they return to the dairy (III: 218–19): in the novel they do not return to the dairy. The parallel passage in the novel to the poem's 'How it snowed' shows the working of the synthesising imagination which brings to bear upon the present scene of oncoming snow images drawn from the most distant reaches of the globe:

> strange birds from behind the North Pole began to arrive silently ... with ... eyes which had witnessed scenes of cataclysmal horror in inaccessible polar regions of a magnitude such as no human being had ever conceived ... and retained the expression of feature that such scenes had engendered.... The snow had followed the birds from the polar basin as a white pillar of a cloud, and individual flakes could not be seen. The blast smelt of icebergs, arctic seas, whales, and white bears, carrying the snow so that it licked the land but did not deepen on it. (V, XLIII: 240–1)

I spoke earlier of Hardy's importance as an influence on later poets, and this ability to influence comes from his powerful connection with the whole nineteenth-century tradition of British poetry. C. M. Bowra rightly called him 'the most representative British poet between Tennyson and Yeats'.[22] The great modernist poets *thought* they were repudiating their nineteenth-century predecessors (Pound's homage to Browning and Yeats's to Blake and Shelley are exceptions), whereas Hardy revised the nineteenth-century poets while still admiring them, even perhaps considering them greater poets than he. Hardy's poetry exhibits many voices, but the voice we discern as modern often derives from realistic revisions of romantic rhetoric and themes – especially revisions of the romanticists he admired most, Wordsworth and Shelley. His most important Victorian influences – Browning and Swinburne – are assimilated without much critical comment. Hardy may be said to have passed on the nineteenth-century tradition in a form usable by twentieth-century poets.

A good example of Hardy's new voice is 'Neutral Tones', a poem written as early as 1867. The first stanza like the title establishes the theme of neutrality, a reaction against romantic colourfulness and significance:

> We stood by a pond that winter day,
> And the sun was white, as though chidden of God,
> And a few leaves lay on the starving sod;
> – They had fallen from an ash, and were gray.

The stanza addresses the central issue of romantic nature poetry – the pathetic fallacy, the projection into nature of human qualities. The neutrality of Hardy's landscape suggests, instead, that nature is indifferent and alien.

Hardy's lovers exhibit a love as depleted of value as the landscape: 'And some words played between us to and fro / On which [of us] lost the more by our love'. Their love was valueless, not only now when it is over, but even while it was operative. Yet the landscape oscillates between objective neutrality and deliberately invoked pathetic fallacy. The movement is from 'And the sun was white, as though chidden of God' to the final lines in which the speaker drops 'as though' and speaks simply, in association with the lover's hated face, of 'the God-curst sun' (I: 13). Here and elsewhere Hardy achieves powerful ironies by invoking the pathetic fallacy in order to suggest its inapplicability but also its psychological inevitability – in order to suggest that under the pressure of emotion we conceive nature's neutrality as malevolent. Such oscillation between nature's neutrality and malevolence runs through the poems and novels.

Instead of romantic projection, Hardy often uses the traditional devices of allegory and personification to make nature yield meaning. In 'The Darkling Thrush', the landscape becomes 'The [Nineteenth] Century's corpse outleant' (I: 187). In 'Hap' (1866), Hardy realises that 'Crass Casualty' would strew 'blisses' in my path as readily as the 'pain' I encounter (I: 10) so that design of any kind, even malevolent design, would be a consolation. Although a later poem 'The Subalterns' (1901) makes the opposite point – that life seems less grim when the speaker realises that Cold, Sickness and Death are like himself helpless agents of natural laws (I: 155) – both poems insist on nature's indifference. Here and elsewhere Hardy's blatant anthropomorphism, as compared to Wordsworth's gentle animation of nature, indicates how utterly *non*-anthropomorphic nature really is. Only the self-referentiality of Hardy's artifical rhetoric can convey the meaning of meaninglessness.

'Hap' and 'The Subalterns' belong to a class of poems cast as dialogues among personified natural forces. The theological purport of such dialogues on nature's indifference ('God-Forgotten' is another example) precludes Wordsworthian feelings of nature's meaning that might emerge from realistic renditions of nature and that do emerge from the few poems where Hardy does treat nature realistically. These theological dialogues do not in my opinion rank among Hardy's best poems, because divorced from sensation, but we could not do without them because they are so Hardyan. What does poignantly shine through these poems, amid the cosmic indifference and blundering, is man's *humanity*, for they show man as more rational and moral than the force that created him. Hardy never reduces man to an automaton, not even in *The Dynast*, which announces its determinism.

Hardy never went further in rendering nature's indifference than in the poems of the 1860s, which were written under the first impact of Darwin's *The Origin of Species by Means of Natural Selection or the Preservation of Favored Races in the Struggle for Life* (1859). Other nature poems of these years are '"In Vision I Roamed"' (I: 10–11), which contrasts the intimacy of love with the endless reaches of space, and 'At a Bridal', subtitled 'Nature's Indifference', which concludes that nature does not *intend* to evolve in an upward direction.

Darwin's influence led to a decline in the importance of Wordsworthian nature poetry, the kind that sought a substitute for orthodox Christianity in the elevated emotions aroused by nature, and there followed a significant change in the nature poetry that went on being written. Hardy was the main executor of this change to a *diminished* nature poetry. Hence the flat, toneless style, the difficult music (learned from Browning) in contrast to Wordsworth's Miltonic resonance. Hardy almost never employs blank verse, probably to avoid the Miltonic sound – he saw the danger before Pound and Eliot did. On the whole Hardy gives less emphasis in his poems than in his novels to nature's beauty; although he does, when turning in later poems to realistic rendition, show in nature a hard-won beauty that looks forward to Frost, Lawrence, Dylan Thomas, Theodore Roethke and Ted Hughes.

A good example is 'A Backward Spring' (1917), which shows the beauty of nature under adverse conditions, defining its difficult music against Wordsworth's notions of nature's benevolence:

The trees are afraid to put forth buds,
And there is timidity in the grass;
. . .

Yet the snowdrop's face betrays no gloom,
And the primrose pants in its heedless push,
Though the myrtle asks if it's worth the fight
  This year with frost and rime
  To venture one more time
On delicate leaves and buttons of white
From the selfsame bough as at last year's prime,
And never to ruminate on or remember
What happened to it in mid-December.

(II: 243)

This strikes me as major work because of the unusual way in which
nature's beauty is evoked. Note the lack of perfect symmetry. The
two stanzas are of different lengths; the two short lines are in the
first stanza interrupted by a long line while the first stanza does
not, like the second, end with a couplet but with a word 'bloom'
that finds its rhyme in the first line of the next stanza, a rhyme
never again appearing. The poem seems a model for Frost's nature
poetry.

Hardy's 'The Fallow Deer at the Lonely House' (II: 366) seems a
model for Lawrence's animal poems, especially 'A Doe at Evening',
in its rendition of the awesome otherness of animal life. The poems
which express Hardy's extraordinary compassion for animals are,
instead, deliberately anthropomorphic – as for example 'Horses
Aboard', about war horses who are sent unwittingly to be slaugh-
tered on foreign battlefields (III: 105), like common soldiers.

In the way Lawrence defined himself as novelist against Hardy
whom he admired, so Hardy defined himself as nature poet against
Wordsworth whom he admired; this we know from Hardy's many
allusions to Wordsworth's poems and prefaces in his published
verse and prose and also in his literary notebooks and marginalia.[23]
Several of Hardy's poems can be read as direct answers to Wordsworth. 'In a Wood', for example, gives us a speaker who, 'City-
opprest', enters a wood, seeking in 'Nature a soft release / From
men's unrest'. He finds, instead, a relentless struggle for existence
– 'Combatants all!' – and returns to human society where 'now and
then', at least, 'are found / Life-loyalties' (I: 83–4). (The subtitle,

'From *The Woodlanders*', confirms that novel's antipastoralism, to be discussed in Chapter 4.) In another Darwinian poem, 'The Ivy-Wife', the ivy, having been repulsed by the trees that survive in the struggle for existence, digs her 'soft green claw' into an ash, destroying them both when the ash collapses (I: 75).

Hardy looks back to Wordsworth and forward to Lawrence in the magnificent poem 'Transformations', which I shall quote in full:

> Portion of this yew
> Is a man my grandsire knew,
> Bosomed here at its foot:
> This branch may be his wife,
> A ruddy human life
> Now turned to a green shoot.
>
> These grasses must be made
> Of her who often prayed,
> Last century, for repose;
> And the fair girl long ago
> Whom I vainly tried to know
> May be entering this rose.
>
> So, they are not underground,
> But as nerves and veins abound
> In the growths of upper air,
> And they feel the sun and rain,
> And the energy again
> That made them what they were!
>   (II: 211–12)

This is Wordsworthian pantheism without the theism. It is unlike Hardy to make such pseudo-statements as the poem depends on (the last stanza rings like a religious credo). But Hardy makes the immortality strictly biological – one organism passes into another by feeding it. Wordsworth's vision of the dead Lucy's pantheistic immortality, 'Rolled round in earth's diurnal course, / With rocks, and stones, and trees'[24] is more mystical. But Hardy's vision, like Lawrence's later, has more biological vitality – a vitality so intensified by the sense of upward growth in the last stanza as to pose a mystery of its own. The simplicity of the last line together with its tantalising suggestiveness as to all that 'they were' and will be exemplifies the open-endedness of major poetry.

The Wordsworth poem most often alluded to is 'Ode: Intimations of Immortality'. In 'The Youth Who Carried a Light', the question, 'What became of that light?' in the young boy's eyes (II: 222), recalls Wordsworth's 'Where is it now, the glory and the dream?' (187). In 'Midnight on the Great Western', a young boy travelling alone on a train is 'Bewrapt past knowing to what he was going, / Or whence he came'. Hardy's question, 'What past can be yours, O journeying boy / . . . / Knows your soul a sphere . . . / Our rude realms far above?' (II: 262) corresponds to Wordsworth's Neoplatonic speculations in the Ode. That final inversion signals Hardy's switch, after his plain diction in the first two stanzas, to the Ode's exalted diction. The fact that Hardy's questions arise from a modern realistic setting defines a difference between the two poets.

Other poems comment ironically on the Ode, disagreeing with Wordsworth. The opening stanza of 'Nature's Questioning' recalls the Ode in content and form:

> When I look forth at dawning, pool,
>   Field, flock, and lonely tree,
>   All seem to gaze at me
> Like chastened children sitting silent in a school.
>
> (I: 86)

'When I look' recalls Wordsworth's complaint that when he looks upon nature he no longer sees what he saw in childhood. But an ironic reversal has taken place; the children are now the natural objects who wait for Hardy to explain their meaning. In *Wessex Poems* (1898) this poem was illustrated by a broken key, the key to nature's meaning. The first two lines echo rhythmically Wordsworth's opening line, 'There was a time when meadow, grove, and stream'; the objects named in the second line appear in Wordsworth's stanza IV, where the single Field and Tree give instruction (186–7). The form of Hardy's stanza, with its reduction from a four-stress to two three-stress lines and final expansion to a six-stress line, is an abbreviated version of Wordsworth's. What begins, however, as a major nature poem is lost in a routine theological fable in which the 'children' give back all too explicitly Hardy's philosophy about the 'Vast Imbecility' or 'Automaton' that created nature. The poem is retrieved

in the end when Hardy returns to a realistic rendition opposite to
Wordsworth's view of nature:

> Meanwhile the winds, and rains,
> And Earth's old glooms and pains
> Are still the same, and Life and Death are neighbours nigh.
>
> (I: 86–7)

Hardy's loveliest treatment of the Wordsworthian themes of
childhood, memory and the evolution of consciousness is the magical 'The Self-Unseeing', which, after Hardy's recollection of a
happy childhood scene by the fire with his parents, ends like this:

> Childlike, I danced in a dream;
> Blessings emblazoned that day;
> Everything glowed with a gleam;
> Yet we were looking away!
>
> (I: 206)

Hardy's answer to Wordsworth is that childhood unconsciousness
was not an advantage, for it made him unaware of his happiness.
This stanza, like the last stanza of 'Transformations', takes an unexpected direction, ending with the suggestive openness of major
poetry.

The most powerfully ironic take-off from Wordsworth is 'An
Upbraiding', which with a small rhyme change employs the three
quatrains of the Lucy poem in which Wordsworth, after praising
Lucy, grieves over her death in the memorable last lines: 'But she
is in her grave, and, oh, / The difference to me!' In Hardy's poem
the dead woman talks back; she is his first wife Emma, who up-
braids the poet for praising her now that she is safely unattainable
but not caring for her while she lived. Here is Wordsworth's first
stanza:

> She dwelt among the untrodden ways
> Beside the springs of Dove,
> A Maid whom there were none to praise
> And very few to love:
>
> (113–14)

Here is Hardy's first stanza:

> Now I am dead you sing to me
> The songs we used to know,
> But while I lived you had no wish
> Or care for doing so.

The dead woman concludes bitterly: 'When you are dead, and stand to me / Not differenced, as now, / ['differenced' points powerfully to Wordsworth's last line] But like again, will you be cold / As when we lived, or how?' (II: 282). The allusive style shows that Hardy relates to the nineteenth-century tradition as Eliot said poetry should relate to the tradition and indeed that Hardy anticipated Pound and Eliot in bringing back the poetry of wit.

   I have already shown how Hardy sums up and writes finis to the Victorian period in 'An Ancient to Ancients'. He does an equally powerful summing up of romanticism in his most anthologised poem 'The Darkling Thrush', dated 31 December 1900. The title recalls Keats's 'Ode to a Nightingale', in which the poet listens 'darkling' to the bird singing in the dark wood. 'When Frost was spectre-gray' recalls Keats's 'spectre-thin' youth, and the thrush who has chosen 'to fling his soul' forth 'In a full-hearted evensong / Of joy illimited' recalls both Keats's nightingale 'pouring forth thy soul abroad / In such an ecstasy!' and Shelley's skylark who 'Pourest thy full heart / . . . Like an unbodied joy'. The earlier birds, however, did not like Hardy's fling their songs upon a *resistant* 'growing gloom' (Keats's dark wood is penetrable, it intensifies the sensuous imagination). The most poignant contrast is in Hardy's lines, 'The tangled bine-stems scored the sky / Like strings of broken lyres' (I: 187–8) which, as John Bayley points out, recall Shelley's 'Ode to the West Wind': 'Make me thy lyre, even as the forest is' (*Essay on Hardy*, 37). By 1900 the sky shows through the tangled bine-stems and the poet's lyre is broken. The climactic irony occurs in the third stanza where we learn to our surprise that the song comes from 'An aged thrush, frail, gaunt, and small', who is unbodied, not because like Shelley's skylark and Keats's nightingale it is too ethereal or poetic to be visible, but because its body has been wasted by age and struggle against a hostile environment. Here is Hardy's realistic comment on romantic poetry.

   Behind the whole poem stands Wordsworth, who is recalled by the Lucy poems' quatrains and by a waste land imagery – 'The

ancient pulse of germ and birth / Was shrunken hard and dry' –
that reverses the vitality of Wordsworth's landscapes. Wordsworth's
poetic method is reversed by the split between the description of
the landscape and the meaning imposed upon it through allegory
not projection. The lines, 'The land's sharp features seemed to be /
The Century's corpse outleant', recall the original allegorical title,
'By the Century's Deathbed', when the poem first appeared in the
Graphic on December 29. It is a sign of the poet's non-projectiveness
that the thrush's joyful song makes no headway against 'the growing gloom', or as Bayley says, 'It is because the pathetic fallacy is so
absolute that the thrush and his song remain wholly outside it' (39).

The first three stanzas move like major poetry through a steady
intensification of the imagery and irony. But in the fourth and last
stanza Hardy retreats to minor poetry by shrugging off the impasse
he posed, with in the last two lines a pat remark the very rhythm
of which is trivial as compared to the rhythm of the previous stanzas' concluding lines. 'So little cause for carolings', he reflects,

> That I could think there trembled through
> His happy good-night air
> Some blessed Hope, whereof he knew
> And I was unaware.
>
> (I: 188)

The thrush's song is so distinctly unrelated to the landscape and
the poet's feelings that the capitalised Hope emerges as the poet's
wishful fancy, a sentimentally optimistic interpretation incongru-
ent with the preceding ideas but which probably accounts for the
poem's popularity.

We find another realistic comment on romanticism in 'Shelley's
Skylark' which reminds us that the bird Shelley hails as 'blithe
Spirit! / Bird thou never wert' was now 'A pinch of unseen, un-
guarded dust' that 'only lived like another bird, / And knew not its
immortality'. He thinks of the bird's death, when it fell one day, 'A
little ball of feather and bone' and of its biological continuance
through the food chain. Only faeries, he concludes – changing direction by praising Shelley's transforming imagination – could find
'That tiny pinch of priceless dust' and lay it in 'a casket silver-
lined'; for the poem not the bird is immortal (I: 133). Given his
uncomfortable unawareness of the disjunction between the real bird
and what Shelley made of it, Hardy would not and could not write

such an immortal poem, but this inability, we are to understand, is a disadvantage. It's just that Hardy as poet must take into account commonplace facts. 'The point is (in imaginative literature)', Hardy wrote in his notebook, 'to adopt that form of romanticism which is the mood of the age' (*Life*, 147).

Hardy wrote 'Shelley's Skylark' at Leghorn (where Shelley wrote his poem) on an Italian pilgrimage during which, we are told in the *Life*, 'two such differing poets as Browning and Shelley ... mingled in Hardy's thoughts ... almost to the exclusion of other English poets ... associated with Italy' (192). In 'The Lyrical Poetry of Thomas Hardy', Cecil Day Lewis finds that 'Browning is the only poet whose idiom is strongly echoed from Hardy's own verse'.[25] If we consider that Browning changed the sound of English poetry by replacing Miltonic resonance and mellifluousness with the rough colloquial diction and rhythms and the fragmented *difficult* music of modern lyricism, then Hardy emerges as the first perpetuator of Browning's style into the twentieth century. A line then emerges from Browning to Hardy to Pound on into our own time.

Hardy is less critical of Browning than of the romantic poets. He mainly follows Browning's direction in diction, verse form and thought, though he does criticise the facile optimism of the Epilogue to *Asolando* (*Life*, 383) and is puzzled by the 'smug Christian optimism ... inside a man who was so vast a seer & feeler when on neutral ground' (*Letters*, II: 216). Nevertheless he had 'Rabbi Ben Ezra', Browning's profession of faith in this life and the next, read to him the night before his death (*Life*, 445–6). Hardy's first volume, *Wessex Poems*, opens with a poem, 'The Temporary the All', which, though employing Swinburnian Sapphic stanzas, is Browningesque in rhythm, diction and thought. Hardy takes issue with Shelleyan idealism in Browning's way, a way including admiration of Shelley. In Shelley's *Alastor* the poet dies because he cannot arrive at the ideal. Hardy's speaker instead settles for the friend, the woman and the lodging chance sends him, while awaiting their ideal conterparts. In the end he realises that the temporary *is* the all, that neither fate nor his own efforts have produced anything better.

This is a Browning theme – successful failure – and it is articulated with the word coinages ('a breath-while') and the elliptical syntax ('Thus I ... But lo, me!') reminiscent of Browning (of, for

example, Browning's 'Drew one angel – borne, see, on my bosom!'[26]).
The two-stress, five-syllable fourth line of each Hardy stanza echoes the alternating two-stress, five-syllable lines in 'A Grammarian's Funeral'. Browning's 'Singing Together' (I: 730) is echoed by
Hardy's 'Fused us in friendship'. Hardy's line 'Life is roomy yet,
and the odds unbounded' (I: 7–8) sounds like Browning and could
have come from 'Grammarian's Funeral', for both poems celebrate
unceasing effort in an imperfect world. The difference is that the
grammarian expected God to 'Perfect the earthen', to complete in
the next life what was not achieved in this one. His disciples at least
envision the absolute that the grammarian by his accomplishments
failed to achieve:

> Here – here's his place, where meteors shoot, clouds form,
>   Lightnings are loosened,
> Stars come and go!
>
> (I: 732–3)

Hardy's poem instead ends with the line, 'Never transcended!' (I: 8).
Browning saw the imperfect as an index to the absolute, whereas
for Hardy imperfection is all we have – it must be justified for its
own sake.

Although Hardy in his prefaces insists, as did Browning and
later Pound, that his first-person poems are 'dramatic' (I: 5, 113), even
using the term 'dramatic monologues' (I: 235), he wrote very few
dramatic monologues and these do not rank among his best poems.
He preferred narratives, often first-person narratives, and dialogues,
where his novelistic talent shows up (the best parts of *The Dynasts*,
in my opinion, are the prose narratives). The lyrics in which the
speaker is some one other than the poet (often a woman) remain
lyrics rather than dramatic monologues.

Hardy's 'The Chapel-Organist' (1922) comes closest to being a
Browningesque dramatic monologue because of the speaker's unusual perspective and fierce fidelity to her character. The poem
employs the hexameter line of varying syllables used in Browning's
'Abt Vogler', the utterance of a male organist whose mind runs
entirely on heavenly things as he extemporises. Hardy's speaker
instead is a beautiful, full-bosomed young woman who shares Abt
Vogler's passion for music, but also likes sex to a degree inappropriate to her job as organist in a Dissenting chapel, especially in 'A.
D. 185–', the mid-Victorian period of strict sexual morality when

the poem takes place. She is eventually fired and, in a kind of love-death, drinks poison after playing the last note of her last performance in the chapel. Her utterance is what passes through her mind just before drinking the poison. Although occasion and auditors are vague, the poem can be called a dramatic monologue because the organist does not in the end regret her sexual freedom – she is more intensely herself than ever: the turn away from conversion toward self-intensification distinguishes the dramatic monologue from other first-person utterances.[27]

> I have never once minced it. Lived chaste I have not.
> Heaven knows it above! . . .
> But past all the heavings of passion – it's music has been
> my life-love! . . .
>
> (II: 411–12)

Like Kierkegaard and Nietzsche, Hardy understood that music and sexuality work together.

Hardy's 'In Tenebris II' contains the line often cited to exemplify his philosophy: 'Who holds that if way to the Better there be, it exacts a full look at the Worst' (I: 208). The line applies in matter and manner to Browning; it serves together with Hardy's phrase 'evolutionary meliorism' (II: 319) to correct oversimple ideas about Hardy's pessimism and Browning's optimism. Line and phrase describe Browning's defence of *The Ring and the Book* against charges of sordid realism.

Browning's influence is strongest in the love poems where Hardy took over the sophisticated modern wit of Browning's 'Respectability', on the advantages of illicit over respectable love (the point of 'The Conformers'), and the wit of Browning's 'A Woman's Last Word', about a marital quarrel in bed between two intellectuals who nevertheless love each other. In Hardy's 'The End of the Episode', one lover coolly calls the whole thing off in accents taking off from Browning's opening lines: 'Let's contend no more, Love, / Strive nor weep' (I: 539). Here is Hardy's first stanza:

> Indulge no more may we
> In this sweet-bitter pastime:
> The love-light shines the last time
> Between you, Dear, and me.
>
> (I: 277)

Browning's 'Love Among the Ruins' is echoed in content and rhythm by Hardy's 'In Time of "The Breaking of Nations"'. Hardy's three-stress line, 'Half asleep as they stalk' (II: 295), combines Browning's two two-stress lines, 'Half-asleep / ... / As they crop' (I: 527). Both poems contrast the meeting of lovers on a pastoral landscape with historical events such as wars, in order to find love more permanently important than history. Browning's poem is more historical in that the contrast is with a pagan, power-worshipping civilisation, which inhabited this very place, whereas Hardy's poem only alludes to war and the passing of 'Dynasties' as remote from landscape and lovers. The difference confirms James Richardson's observation that 'Hardy is deliberately small and localized', substituting unlike Browning 'the homely for the exotic'.[28] The difference, however, applies only to Hardy's settings, for his concerns were as large as Browning's.

Browning figures in the great elegiac love poems of 1912–13 that Hardy wrote for his dead wife Emma. 'The Going' employs Browning's sophisticated colloquial style, drawing out its questions through the stanzas in the manner of 'Two in the Campagna'. The line, 'While Life unrolled us its very best', might have been written by Browning and so might the abrupt colloquial turn into fragmented syntax which in the last stanza breaks the poem's symmetry, marking it as major. The poem moves from the smooth lyricism of

> 'In this bright spring weather
> We'll visit together
> Those places that once we visited.'

to: 'Well, well! All's past amend, / Unchangeable', and

> O you could not know
> That such swift fleeing
> No soul foreseeing –
> Not even I – would undo me so!
>
> (II: 48)

The last line, with its second pause before 'so', recalls the bumpy rhythm of Andrea del Sarto's, 'Nay, Love, you did give all I asked, I think – ' (I: 646). Hardy's great elegy, 'After a Journey', in which he pursues Emma's elusive ghost ('Whither, O whither will its whim now draw me?' [II: 59]), recalls Browning's lesser 'Love in a Life', in which the speaker pursues his mistress's elusive real self through all the rooms of the house (I: 603–4).

Actually Browning's influence is most important just where it can least be picked out, having been assimilated into a style that is Hardy's at his most modern. For example, the striking realism of Hardy's 'while I / Saw morning harden upon the wall', in 'The Going' (II: 47), corresponds to Browning's 'the quick sharp scratch / And blue spurt of a lighted match' in 'Meeting at Night' (I: 451). In the lovely late lyric 'Afterwards', Hardy characterises himself by what the neighbours will say after his death about his powers of observation: '"He was a man who used to notice such things"' (II: 308). In Browning's 'How It Strikes a Contemporary', the poet is portrayed as a steady observer of commonplace things ('He stood and watched the cobbler at his trade') and, therefore, according to the speaker, 'The town's true master if the town but knew!' (I: 605–6). Browning is revising Shelley's declaration, in 'A Defence of Poetry', that 'Poets are the unacknowledged legislators of the world' because 'A poet participates in the eternal, the infinite, and the one'. Hardy agreed with Browning that if poets have that high mission, it is because they *see* more concretely than other men do.

Hardy's favourite Browning poem was 'The Statue and the Bust', in which Browning reprimands two courtly lovers in sixteenth-century Florence who out of timidity and sloth never consummate the adultery they planned, remaining content to look at each other from a distance. When they find their youth fading, they decide to preserve it in statues of themselves, a sign that they are now little more alive than statues. She becomes a bust forever looking into the piazza where he passes; he becomes an equestrian statue looking toward her window.

The surprise lies in Browning's wryly ironic final comments where he answers those who argue that '"delay was best, / For their end was a crime"'. 'Oh, a crime will do / As well,' he replies, 'to serve for a test, / As a virtue'. Whatever game 'you choose to play', play it 'to the uttermost' or you lose your life. 'And the sin I impute to each frustrate ghost', he says with distinct sexual innuendo, 'Is – the unlit lamp and the ungirt loin.' He ends atonally: 'You of the virtue (we issue join) / How strive you? *De te, fabula*' (I: 603). This story is about *you*, virtuous reader – which reminds us, in the doubt cast on the distinction between virtue and vice, of Baudelaire's '*Hypocrite lecteur*' taken over by Eliot in *The Waste Land*.

We can see why Hardy admired 'The Statue and the Bust' which

contains Browning's most revolutionary reflections on sexual morality. The irony here and in Browning's cynical 'A Light Woman'
anticipates Hardy's mordant satires on fidelity in love and those
Hardy poems in which women remain unrepentant of their free
sexuality. 'The Statue and the Bust' is quoted in *Desperate Remedies*,
'An Indiscretion in the Life of an Heiress', *Far from the Madding
Crowd*, *Jude the Obscure* and most interestingly in *The Woodlanders*
where, as we shall see, a reference to the dead Giles's 'frustrate
ghost' helps us judge Grace's decision to abandon her fidelity to
Giles's grave to return to her living, potent, even if imperfect
husband.

Hardy assimilated Browning along with Wordsworth, Shelley,
Swinburne and the whole nineteenth-century poetic tradition to
forge a style which was distinctly his own and transmitable to
twentieth-century poets. In *Map of Misreading*, Harold Bloom points
out the pervading influence of Shelley's *Triumph of Life* over Hardy's 'central meter-making argument . . . a skeptical lament for the
hopeless incongruity of ends and means in all human acts'. Bloom
also perceives the influence of 'Ode to the West Wind' on Hardy's
'During Wind and Rain' ('How the sick leaves reel down in
throngs!'), 'as good a poem', he says of it, 'as this century has given
us' (20–1).

Swinburne's influence began in the sixties, with the publications
of *Atalanta in Calydon* (1865) and *Poems and Ballads* (1866). This was
the decade of Darwin's overpowering influence, and these two
revolutionary figures no doubt merged in the young Hardy's mind.
For he learned not only Swinburne's precisely melliflous metres,
but also his atheism, his novel ideas about sexuality and his imagery
of oblivion. In a wonderful stanza of 'A Singer Asleep', his elegy
for Swinburne, Hardy tells how as a young architect in London he
first discovered the elder poet:

> O that far morning of a summer day
> When, down a terraced street whose pavements lay
> Glassing the sunshine into my bent eyes,
> I walked and read with a quick glad surprise
> New words, in classic guise.
>
> (II: 31)

For 'new words', read 'new ideas'.

Ross Murfin finds the poems composed from 1865 on that form
Wessex Poems (1898)

clearly Swinburnian in their tendency toward deifying abstraction ('Fate,' 'Love,' 'Crass Casualty' . . .), in their obsessively precise metrical . . . sound patterns . . . , in their 'Sapphic' stanza forms, in their plaintive protest against time's ruination of the life-tree at root, and in their implicit denial of transcendental possibilities.[29]

He gives as a prime example 'Amabel' (1865), which employs a 'Sapphic' stanza (four lines with a fourth short line) and speaks of time's ruination. The poem is, I would add, puzzling since its musicality and the lady's name lead us to expect a content opposite to the one we find. The speaker recalls the beautiful young girl he once loved in the aged woman of 'ruined hues' he now beholds. What is surprising and Swinburnian is the speaker's final indifference to Amabel's fate:

> I said (the while I sighed
> That love like ours had died),
> 'Fond things I'll no more tell
> To Amabel,
>
> 'But leave her to her fate,
> And fling across the gate,
> "Till the Last Trump, farewell,
> O Amabel!" '
>
> (I: 9)

The puzzle may be solved if we hear in the refrain's variation within sameness an echo of Swinburne's 'Faustine' which uses a similar stanza to trace the deterioration of a sadistic, promiscuous type of femme fatale from Roman times to our own. Unlike Hardy's, Swinburne's speaker has reason enough to be hostile:

> If one should love you with real love
> (Such things have been,
> Things your fair face knows nothing of,
> It seems, Faustine;
>
> . . .
>
> Curled lips, long since half kissed away,
> Still sweet and keen;
> You'd give him – poison shall we say?
> Or what, Faustine?

Although 'Faustine' appeared in *Poems and Ballads* (1866), a year after the composition of 'Amabel', Hardy probably read 'Faustine' in the *Spectator* of 31 May 1862 (he refers to the *Spectator* publication in a letter of 15 June 1911, *Letters*, IV: 159) and in 'Amabel' he may have taken over Swinburnian cruelty without supplying sufficient reason for it.

'A Singer Asleep' is a skilful work which, as Peter Sacks makes clear in *The English Elegy*, touches all the bases in the tradition of elegies written by one poet for another. Thus, Swinburne, a passionate poet of the sea, buried by the sea, is characterised as a disciple of Sappho who drowned herself for love. Hardy fancies that the two phantoms meet at the water's brim 'as a dim / Lone shine upon the heaving hydrosphere' (II: 32), upon the luminous combination of water and aqueous vapour with which Hardy can identify to join the poetic tradition. Thus, writes Sacks, 'the elegist has performed that absorption of the dead man's power . . . so crucial to the work of mourning and inheritance'.[30]

The poem that follows, 'A Plaint to Man', is the clearest statement of Hardy's atheism and reminiscent of one theme in Swinburne's 'Hertha'. Hardy's God asks human beings why they found it necessary in primitive times to invent him, and as in 'Hertha' goes on to describe the death of God in modern times:

> And now that I dwindle day by day
> Beneath the deicide eyes of seers
> In a light that will not let me stay,

men and women must learn to live 'On the human heart's resource alone', with 'loving-kindness fully blown, / And visioned help unsought, unknown' (II: 34).

Even more like 'Hertha' is 'The Mother Mourns', where the speaker is Mother Nature. But Hardy ironically rewrites Swinburne's poem by criticising Nature as though she were God, whereas Swinburne praises her as the only God. Swinburne's Earth-Mother wants people to develop all their capacities ('I bid you but be'), whereas Hardy's Mother Nature complains that humanity has developed so much intellectual capacity as to turn a critical eye upon her: 'As to read my defects with a god-glance'. The subject here is the death of Nature: 'My species are dwindling, / My forests grow barren' and 'My children have aped mine own slaughters / To quicken my wane' (I: 145–6).

In 'God's Funeral', Hardy complicates Swinburne's atheism by
mourning for the dead God: 'I did not forget / That what was
mourned for, I, too, long had prized'. The death of God raises new
problems: 'Still, how to bear such loss I deemed / The insistent
question for each animate mind'. The best among us recognise the
need of some substitute for God, some 'pale yet positive gleam'.
We can hear Swinburne along with Wordsworth, Shelley and
Browning in the unusually mellifluous 'During Wind and Rain',
perhaps Hardy's most successful poem:

> They sing their dearest songs –
> He, she, all of them – yea,
> Treble and tenor and bass,
>   And one to play;
> With the candles mooning each face. . . .
>   Ah, no; the years O!
> How the sick leaves reel down in throngs!
>
> (II: 239)

In this series of vignettes from the past (drawn from Emma's 'Some
recollections', which Hardy with much emotion found after her
death),[31] the use of memory recalls Wordsworth and the Browning
of 'By the Fire-side'; the word coinage, 'mooning', recalls Browning; the 'sick leaves' come from Shelley; but the *pain* of recollection
is Hardy's. For the idyllic scenes in Emma's recollections of her
early years make Hardy recall with remorse her disastrous later
years, so that he writes a great poem about loss, the loss we all
endure.
    In a poet whose fault has been oversymmetry, we find continual
variation in the number of stresses and syllables and in metres. The
manuscript shows the penultimate line of each stanza as 'Ah, no;
the years O!', but Hardy's revision alternates this refrain with 'Ah
no; the years, the years'.[32] The anapestic last line of each stanza recalls Swinburne. But the syncopation of the second line – 'He, she,
all of them – yea' – and the refrain – 'Ah, no; the years o!' – points
toward Hopkins's metrical innovations. The poem's powerful last
line – 'Down their carved names the rain-drop ploughs' (II: 240) –
renders Hopkins's 'inscape', a surprisingly tangible 'thisness'
achieved by revision from 'On their chiselled names the lichen grows'
(Hynes, ed., *Poetical Works*, II: 240, n28). Hardy and Hopkins began
as Victorian poets, but made their impact in the twentieth century.

Hardy could have seen some of Hopkins's poems since Hopkins's younger brother Arthur illustrated the serialisation of *The Return of the Native* (*Letters*, I: 53n).

I would like finally to discuss the posthumously published 'Proud Songsters', because it shows the complete technical mastery of old artists and because it reminds me, in its prosaic understatement, its subtle music and its serene contemplation of the natural cycle, of Browning's late lyric in 'Parleying with Gerard de Lairesse'. Browning offers his little poem to show how through a precise rendition of spring flowers in a cemetery the modern poet can suggest all that the myths tell us about death and rebirth. Here is Browning's poem.

> Dance, yellows and whites and reds, –
> Lead your gay orgy, leaves, stalks, heads
> Astir with the wind in the tulip-beds!
>
> There's sunshine; scarcely a wind at all
> Disturbs starved grass and daisies small
> On a certain mound by a churchyard wall.
>
> Daisies and grass be my heart's bedfellows
> On the mound wind spares and sunshine mellows:
> Dance you, reds and whites and yellows! (II: 838)

Here is Hardy's poem.

> The thrushes sing as the sun is going,
> And the finches whistle in ones and pairs,
> And as it gets dark loud nightingales
>   In bushes
> Pipe, as they can when April wears,
>   As if all Time were theirs.
>
> These are brand new birds of twelvemonths' growing,
> Which a year ago, or less than twain,
> No finches were, nor nightingales,
>   Nor thrushes,
> But only particles of grain,
>   And earth, and air, and rain.
>
>   (III: 167–8)

This poem is subtly rhymed – one rhyme governs three lines of each stanza, the other three lines remain unrhymed within the stanza but rhyme with three corresponding lines across stanzas. The one-stress, three-syllable fourth line gives an air of irregularity to the four-stress pattern. The poem's final line has three stresses, but with lengthened pauses, echoing Wordsworth's 'With rocks, and stones, and trees' (115). Indeed Hardy repeats his biological version of Wordsworthian pantheism, completing his earlier poem 'Transformations' in which the dead live on through their return to earth. Here the newly born emerge from earth and inanimate matter, completing the natural cycle.

I have tried to show the interesting variety and general importance of Hardy's poems and to point out some of those that strike me as major. Yet I must conclude by suggesting that Hardy's greatest poetry, his poetry of scope, is to be found in his major novels, and this I hope to demonstrate in the next two chapters on the pastoral novels.

3

Versions of Pastoral

The Return of the Native is Hardy's greatest nature poem. Hardy achieves the imaginative freedom and intensity of great poetry by daring to make the heath the novel's central character, the all-encompassing identity from which the human characters derive the individualities that emerge from the pass back into the heath. Hardy ties his characters to the heath by means of a device which is most conspicuous in *Far from the Madding Crowd* and *The Return of the Native*: characters appear for the first time as distant shapes on the heath, mysterious archetypes, taking on individualising lineaments as they approach the observer. Hardy sometimes renews a character's identity by *re*introducing him or her in this manner, making the observer (the technique requires an observer) *re*recognise the character as if for the first time.

Thus, Eustacia, after the opening chapter's powerful description of the heath at nightfall, appears to the observer as a landscape object. The reddleman watches the 'form' of an old man (Eustacia's grandfather) 'as it diminished to a speck on the road and became absorbed in the thickening films of night'. He then looks upward toward a distant hill with a barrow (a prehistoric burial mound) upon it and becomes aware that the barrow's summit

> was surmounted by something higher. It rose from the semi-globular mound like a spike from a helmet. . . . There the form stood, motionless as the hill beneath. . . . The form was so much like an organic part of the entire motionless structure that to see it move would have impressed the mind as a strange phenomenon.[1]

'Strange' in the manner of Wordsworth's old leech-gatherer (probably in Hardy's mind) who, in his stillness breaks upon the observer as a huge stone that can only have moved there supernaturally. Only when Hardy's 'form' moves can it be distinguished from the heath as a woman's figure, which turns out many pages later to be Eustacia. Instead of just evolving from the landscape, as in Wordsworth, Eustacia evolves from the heath through association with a primitive artifact and Guy Fawkes bonfires both of which descend from ancient Celtic culture. Hardy adds to Wordsworth an anthropological view of man's relation to landscape through organically evolved culture.

In *The Return of the Native* Hardy goes beyond Wordsworth in attempting to portray the heath as totally objective, beyond human categories of understanding. In so far as the heath is comprehensible at all, it is comprehensible through contradictory aspects both deriving from and not deriving from human observation. This despite Hardy's usual practice as described in his journal entry of 23 August 1865: 'The poetry of a scene varies with the minds of the perceivers. Indeed, it does not lie in the scene at all' (*Life*, 50). Hardy's art is not so far as is generally thought from that of his contemporary, Henry James; the difference is that Hardy employs many points of view instead of one – almost all his important actions are carefully framed by observers, sometimes animal observers. The heath is unusual because not presented through points of view. Yet in this exceptional instance and others there remains the sense that the landscape or animals (the animals in the dicing scene, for example) are objectively there whether observed or not and that the full intensity of their being exceeds human observation.

For Hardy the objective is that which remains inscrutable. He admired Swinburne's ability to project the inscrutability of things, an inscrutability merging with oblivion of consciousness.[2] Hardy's contribution to nature poetry, as I have suggested, is his portrayal of nature in its inscrutably non-anthropomorphic otherness, whereas in Wordsworth nature's mysteries are the mysteries of imaginative projection.

Because his presentation is exceptional, Hardy's opening description of the heath at twilight exemplifies the aesthetic of the sublime, given the heath's affinity to night and its slightly threatening aspect:

> The heath wore the appearance of an instalment of night which had taken up its place before its astronomical hour was come.... At this transitional point of its nightly roll into darkness the great and particular glory of the Egdon waste began.... It could best be felt when it could not clearly be seen.

Hardy goes on to distinguish between the sublime and the beautiful in the manner of Burke's *The Sublime and the Beautiful* (1756). Its nocturnal and threatening qualities, says Hardy, 'lent to this heath a sublimity in which spots renowned for beauty of the accepted kind are utterly wanting' (I, i: 2–3). The difference is that Burke treats the sublime as an alternative aesthetic, whereas Hardy treats it as anti-aesthetic, as emphatically the taste for the non-beautiful of modern reflective men who through science know the bleak truth about nature. These modern men, we learn when Clym is described, cannot themselves be beautiful because their faces are ravaged by thought and unpalatable knowledge. The modern taste for the anti-aesthetic sublime becomes the post-Darwinian way of relating to nature. 'I feel that Nature is played out as a Beauty, but not as a Mystery', Hardy wrote in his journal for January 1887 (*Life*, 185). With the current revival of interest in the sublime, Hardy's revision of Burke should be especially relevant.

The heath is presented as a particular place but also as the whole earth in 'its nightly roll into darkness'. In *The Return of the Native*, Hardy goes beyond Wordsworth in portraying the landscape as a total environment. The characters move on the heath as fish swim through the sea; the characters are brushed by the grasses they push through, they are observed uncomprehendingly by animals. 'Tall ferns buried [Eustacia] in their leafage whenever her path lay through them, which now formed miniature forests, though not one stem of them would remain to bud the next year' – the last clause will apply also to Eustacia (IV, iii: 202). And of Clym we are told:

> The ferns, among which he had lain in comfort yesterday, were dripping moisture from every frond, wetting his legs through as he brushed past; and the fur of the rabbits leaping before him was clotted into dark locks by the same watery surrounding. (III, vi: 165–6)

As other examples of animal observation we read: 'Clym as he walked forward, eyed by every rabbit and fieldfare [thrush] around' (III, iii: 143), and 'at each brushing of Clym's feet white miller-moths flew into the air just high enough to catch upon their dusty wings the mellowed light from the west' (IV, vii: 228). Such passages (the verse contains nothing more poetic) belie Hardy's stated aim to present the heath as non-beautiful, but there are other passages in which nature is presented as locked in the Darwinian struggle for existence.

The characters' total immersion in nature suggests pastoralism, and indeed *The Return of the Native* brings to a climax the series of pastoral novels beginning with *Under the Greenwood Tree* (1872). But *Return of the Native* is also the first of the great tragic novels constituting Hardy's major period. In making the transition to tragedy, *Return of the Native* seriously modifies pastoral which does not traditionally mix with tragedy. Hardy makes them mix by deepening the psychology to a point usually inappropriate to pastoral, and by taking a Darwinian view so that the nature which totally embraces the characters does not know them. The lovely sentence about miller-moths just precedes Clym's discovery of his mother dying on the heath of a snake bite.

If we begin with the obvious definition of 'pastoral' as an idealising picture of country life implying its superiority to city life,[3] we must ask whether the word aptly describes Hardy's novels after *Greenwood Tree*. In *The Country and the City*, Raymond Williams argues that we misread if we impose on Hardy's novels 'a neo-pastoral convention of the countryman as an age-old figure, or a vision of a prospering countryside being disintegrated by Corn Law repeal or the railways or agricultural machinery'. Corn Law repeal made little difference in Dorset, Williams explains, and 'the coming of the railway gave a direct commercial advantage in the supply of milk to London' as we see in Tess's reflection on the Talbothays milk that will appear on London breakfast tables the next morning. Douglas Brown, instead, powerfully describes the argicultural depression that hit Britain after 1870, causing catastrophic depopulation of the countryside.[4] There is certainly evidence in the novels that this catastrophe was very much on Hardy's mind. To approximate the truth we probably have to combine the views of Williams and Brown.

Certainly Williams's argument that Hardy's sympathy does not rest entirely with the country is supported by Hardy's almost Marxist essay, 'The Dorsetshire Labourer', in which he shows how farm labourers have become as itinerant, free-market oriented and alienated as industrial workers, while arguing that this transposition has brought both gains and losses. In this essay Hardy projects both the nostalgically backward-looking pastoral view and the forward-looking sociological view.

The conjunction of the two views is expressed when Hardy, after

speaking of all that has been lost by the new generation of
Dorsetshire labourers, says in Darwin's manner that 'new varieties
of happiness evolve themselves like new varieties of plants'.

> Thus, while their pecuniary condition in the prime of life is
> bettered, and their freedom enlarged, they have lost touch with
> their environment, and that sense of long local participancy which
> is one of the pleasures of age.

The feudal obligation to maintain the aged labourer is lessened
now that the labourer's youthful strength

> has often been expended elsewhere. The sojourning existence of
> the town masses is more and more the existence of the rural
> masses, with its corresponding benefits and disadvantages. With
> uncertainty of residence often comes a laxer morality, and more
> cynical views of the duties of life. Domestic stability is a factor in
> conduct which nothing else can equal. On the other hand, new
> varieties of happiness evolve themselves like new varieties of
> plants, and new charms may have arisen among the classes who
> have been driven to adopt the remedy of locomotion for the evils
> of oppression and poverty – charms which compensate in some
> measure for the lost sense of home.[5]

Hardy's novels might be ranged along a continuum, with at one
end the relative stability of *Under the Greenwood Tree* and at the other
the increasing locomotion in *Mayor of Casterbridge, Tess* and, most
notably, *Jude*.

To understand Hardy's achievement in *The Return of the Native*
(1878), we must now turn back to the two more purely pastoral
novels that preceded it – *Under the Greenwood Tree* (1872) and *Far
from the Madding Crowd* (1874). In these earlier novels nature is
always beautiful and in harmony with the characters, though
nature can be dangerous in *Madding Crowd*. The problems that turn
up in a small way in *Greenwood Tree* and in a much bigger way in
Madding Crowd (which contains much violence) can still be resolved
to promote the happy endings of pastoral comedy. The problems
in *Return of the Native*, instead, lead to tragedy in the main plot
with the happy ending reserved problematically for Thomasin and
Venn. After *Greenwood Tree* Hardy always exceeds the limits of
pastoral, so that pastoral becomes a useful taking-off point rather
than a determining principle of my discussion.

Hardy's first published novel, *Desperate Remedies* (1871), is not pastoral; it is a curiously sophisticated even decadent work, involving suggestions of lesbianism – hardly the debut to be expected from a young man of humble country origins. Between the pastoral novels *Under the Greenwood Tree* and *Far from the Madding Crowd* Hardy published *A Pair of Blue Eyes* (1873), which is not pastoral though it takes place mainly in the country with some high-society scenes in London. *A Pair of Blue Eyes* is a powerful novel of manners in which the principal characters, except for the socially rising hero, are upper class and in which class distinctions take on an importance (in this novel a bitterly tragic importance) they do not have in the more pastoral novels. The novel is so successful (it was Tennyson's favourite) that if it does not count as major, it is probably because Hardy never does quite as well with novels of manners as with novels that emerge from pastoral.

I cite these two non-pastoral novels to emphasise that Hardy was not a country bumpkin who had inevitably to write pastoral, but that he wrote or did not write pastoral as a deliberate literary choice. In the August 1871 letter to Macmillan accompanying the manuscript of *Greenwood Tree*, Hardy wrote that he turned to rural life because in his previous novel *Desperate Remedies* 'the rustic characters & scenery had very little part yet to my surprise they were made very much of by the reviews' (*Letters*, I: 11). Nevertheless, he did approximately alternate between the novels that are pastoral or allude to pastoralism and other kinds of novels; the alternation approximately corresponds to the alternation between major and minor novels. Like much of the verse the minor novels tend to be obviously intellectual and as highly intelligent novels of ideas have an enduring interest of their own.[6]

Hardy's next major novel, *The Mayor of Casterbridge* (1886), alludes to pastoralism, but takes place in a market town rather than the country and deals with trading, indeed speculating, in wheat rather than with its production. In *The Woodlanders* the following year, Hardy returns directly to pastoral in order to subvert it. Hardy alludes again to pastoral in *Tess of the d'Urbervilles* (1891), especially in his portrayal of the idyllic Talbothays dairy farm where Tess and Angel meet and fall in love. But the pastoral experience proves illusory and destructive; the couple do not, to quote *Madding Crowd*, know 'the rougher sides of each other's character' before marrying. The antipastoral Flintcomb-Ash farm, with its devilish harvesting machine and cash-nexus relation to labour, seems truer than

Talbothays to modern reality. In *Jude the Obscure* (1896), nature hardly appears at all, appearing when it does in its cruellest aspects. *Jude* takes place in towns through which the by now rootless characters wander. Yet the pastoral tradition is indirectly recalled in this novel as a measure of all that has been lost.

Under the Greenwood Tree, Hardy's third but first artistically successful novel, is a masterpiece of pastoral comedy. The fragility and deftness of its art ('the work is so delicate as not to hit every taste', wrote the publisher's reader) gives evidence enough to refute those who consider Hardy a clumsy bucolic genius with little craft. There has been an invidious mixture of social and literary condescension in the judgement of Hardy – as in Henry James's 'The good little Thomas Hardy has scored a great success with *Tess of the d'Urbervilles*, which is chock-full of faults and falsity and yet has a singular beauty and charm.' Some reviewers, however, linked Hardy to George Eliot for 'philosophic thought', to Meredith for 'serious . . . thought and intention' and to Thackeray for having 'raised the standard of workmanship'.[7]

What is so impressive artistically about *Under the Greenwood Tree* is Hardy's attention to the requirements of his chosen genre. His original title *The Mellstock Quire* refers to the novel's account of the village's old-fashioned instrumental choir and its dissolution. The insertion of the phrase from a song in Shakespeare's pastoral comedy *Much Ado About Nothing* – making the title *Under the Greenwood Tree or The Mellstock Quire* – calls attention to the love story, but it also calls attention to the *artfulness* of pastoral as does the subtitle *A Rural Painting of the Dutch School*.[8]

The first sentence establishes a criterion for judging character which will inform all the pastoral novels. 'To dwellers in a wood almost every species of tree has its voice as well as its feature.'[9] The most worthy characters are sufficiently steeped in nature to detect the subtle variety of its signals. In *The Return of the Native*, Thomasin trusts 'for guidance to her general knowledge of the [heath's] contours, which was scarcely surpassed by Clym's or by that of the heath-croppers themselves' (v, viii: 283). And in *The Woodlanders* Grace says that Marty and Giles, the book's two noblest characters, '"could speak in . . . the tongue of the trees and fruits and flowers themselves"'.[10] Even in *Greenwood Tree*, where harmony

with nature is taken for granted, the hero Dick Dewy stands out
by being late for his wedding because his bees 'swarmed' and had
to be tended to. His instinct is right since 'swarming' bees on a
wedding day are a good omen, clearly an omen of fertility.

The opening of *Greenwood Tree* continues:

> At the passing of the breeze the fir-trees sob and moan no less
> distinctly than they rock; the holly whistles as it battles with
> itself. . . . And winter, which modifies the note of such trees as
> shed their leaves, does not destroy its individuality. (I, i: 39)

This lovely passage on the individuality of tree species throws light
on Hardy's principles of characterisation in the pastoral novels. We
are told of Grandfather William Dewy, the book's model character,
that 'to his neighbours he had no character in particular' (I, iii: 50),
that they see him as changing according to their own changing
perceptions – as, in other words, the way they see a natural object.
We are old the same thing about Gabriel Oak in *Far from the Madding
Crowd*: 'when his friends and critics were in tantrums, he was considered rather a bad man; when they were pleased, he was rather
a good man; when they were neither, he was a man whose moral
colour was a kind of pepper-and-salt mixture'.[11] Character, we are
to understand, should not derive from the eccentricity so much
prized in modern literature, but rather from the individuality of the
species, from a deep rootedness that unfolds through fundamental
situations. In *The Return of the Native* Thomasin, in a sentence
Lawrence might have written, is characterised organically: 'An in-
genuous, transparent life was disclosed; as if the flow of her existence could be seen passing within her' (I, iv: 30). Yet this natural
characterisation, which works well for Grandfather Dewy and
Gabriel Oak, makes Thomasin mainly uninteresting, perhaps because she has to compete with Eustacia and Clym who are vividly
individualised and psychologised in the modern manner.

In the purely pastoral *Under the Greenwood Tree*, there is surprisingly little description of nature after the beautiful opening
paragraph. Nature is taken for granted as a background, gorgeous
when described:

> It was a morning of the latter summer-time; a morning of lin-
> gering dews. . . . Fuchsias and dahlias were laden till eleven o'clock
> with small drops and dashes of water, changing the colour of
> their sparkle at every movement of the air. . . . (III, iii: 156)

and the novel is divided according to the four seasons, which correspond to the burgeoning of love and marriage between Fancy Day and Dick Dewy. Nevertheless, the main subject of *Under the Greenwood Tree* is not nature but community – the organic community resulting from the pastoral vision of organic connection between man and nature. The community dealt with is not that of farmers and shepherds, as in the later *Far from the Madding Crowd*, but the village community of artisans and tradesmen, the community of Hardy's family. The main story, about the replacement of the Mellstock choir by what Hardy significantly calls the 'isolated organ', is a fable of organic community and its inevitable dissolution. The choir of village instrumentalists, to which Hardy's father and grandfather belonged, came to an end the year Hardy was born, but he grew up in the ambience of its memory. The family remained musical; Hardy himself played the fiddle at country dances, often in the company of his father as first violinist and his uncle as cellist.

In the novel the choir is a communal enterprise involving not only the musicians but also their relatives and friends, so that there is no division between community and church affairs. 'The displacement of these ecclesiastical bandsmen by an isolated organist', says Hardy in the Preface, 'has tended to stultify the professed aims of the clergy, its direct result being to curtail and extinguish the interest of parishioners in church doings' (33). The novel gives us the sense of an outside world for which the village life portrayed is already anomalous in the 1830s. The regional novel characteristically assures the modern urban reader that in so remotely rural a place as Dorset such a village choir could still have existed so late in time.

In 'The Dorsetshire Labourer', Hardy writes that an urban visitor to backward Dorset would learn that

> wherever a mode of supporting life is neither noxious nor absolutely inadequate, there springs up happiness, and will spring up happiness, of some sort or other. Indeed, it is among such communities as these that happiness will find her last refuge on earth, since it is among them that a perfect insight into the conditions of existence will be longest postponed. (*Personal Writings*, 169)

If we understand the 'perfect insight' to be scientific insight, we understand why regionalism, coinciding in this respect with pastoralism, is indirectly a comment on modern life. (Regionalism coincides partly but not always completely with pastoralism, in that the regional writer is more absorbed than the pastoralist in the particularity of the locale and takes a more 'historical – or even archeological' interest in its 'customs and survivals'.[12] Hardy occupies and exceeds both categories.) Hardy's statement that 'perfect insight into the conditions of existence' can only be postponed suggests the inevitable dissolution of happy organic communities, an inevitability confirmed in *Under the Greenwood Tree* by the choir's curious acquiescence in its own demise. In the 1912 addition to his Preface, Hardy says that he might have treated the dissolution of the choir more seriously, as a symptom we can infer of cultural destruction, but then, he implies, the novel would not have adhered to its chosen genre.

The references in this novel are less to nature than to music, dance and the other arts, the arts being symbols of community. In the first chapter the members of the Mellstock choir appear – in a manner conspicuous in the later novels – as figures emerging from the landscape. But nature soon gives way to art as we meet a man singing a folk song that sets the pastoral tone. Dick Dewy is presented as a kind of archetypal figure against the light sky, 'his profile appearing . . . like the portrait of a gentleman in black cardboard'. The other members of the choir advance 'against the sky in flat outlines, which suggested some processional design on Greek or Etruscan pottery' (I, i: 40).

When we meet these men again at the cottage of Dick's father Reuben, a 'tranter' or carrier, the emphasis is still on artifacts. Each choir member wears the costume or carries the tools of his craft. Mr Penny, the shoemaker, draws forth his last, while William Dewy, a mason, 'wore a long linen apron'. 'His stooping figure formed a well-illuminated picture as he passed towards the fire-place' (I, iii: 51). The lighting recalls the Dutch genre painting alluded to in the novel's subtitle. And indeed such Ruskinian idealisation of craftsmen becomes another version of pastoral, given the typing and innocence of these characters. We are surprised by the quaint spirituality of their conversation about music. '"Strings be safe soul-lifters"', says Mr Spinks. Mr Penny agrees that '"clar'nets were not made for the service of the Lard"'. The tranter objects, '"Angels be supposed to play clar'nets in heaven"' (I, iv: 58–9) and he says later of his father, '"he'd starve to death for music's sake"' (I, viii: 86). This high-mindedness of simple craftsmen recalls the opening carpenter shop scene in *Adam Bede,* where George Eliot also uses Dutch painting as a visual model. *Under the Greenwood Tree* might be considered Hardy's smaller, lighter *Adam Bede,* though it was the anonymous serialisation of *Far from the Madding Crowd* that was attributed by a reviewer to George Eliot.

It is Christmas Eve and the choir circulates in the village singing carols in a rural manner no longer heard, 'embodying a quaint Christianity in words orally transmitted from father to son through several generations' (I, iv: 60). We see signs that the tradition is ending when we see the cool reception given the carol singers by three of the community's most highly placed citizens – the school-mistress Fancy Day, the rich farmer Shiner and the newly arrived vicar Mr Maybold: the three who will replace the choir by the 'isolated organ'.

In the pastoral novels the social range is narrow. In *Under the Greenwood Tree* the farm and village labourers occupy the bottom position; near the top stand the farmers and village tradesmen; while gentry enter only by way of the vicar. Class distinctions are easily bridged; Fancy Day, the daughter of a head gamekeeper and timber-steward on an estate, could have married the vicar. What matters in the pastoral novels is education – whether a character has been educated outside the community and, thus, alienated from it by a self-consciously critical turn of mind. The educated Fancy, Clym and Grace are deferred to by the friends and relatives with whom they grew up. After Dick Dewy's request for Fancy's hand has been haughtily refused by her father, Dick modestly 'turned away wondering at his presumption in asking for a woman whom he had seen from the beginning to be so superior to him' (IV, ii: 182) – superior only in education.

It is a sign of a new social mobility that the fathers of Fancy and Grace, having risen above their peers financially, invest in their daughters' education in order to advance them socially through opportune marriages. In *Greenwood Tree* Mr Penny, the shoemaker, argues against social mobility when he speaks of an inherited stability of foot: even if the boots differ in looks and price, ''tis father's voot and daughter's voot to me, as plain as houses' (I, iii: 54). Social ambition connected with a desire to modernise causes the problems in *Under the Greenwood Tree* and *The Woodlanders.*

Problems which become serious in the later novels are, in a pastoral comedy like *Greenwood Tree,* introduced lightly in order to be quickly resolved. Fancy is only a little separated from the community by her education, which leads her no higher than the job of village schoolmistress. Her education does not prevent her from falling in love with Dick and never shows up in her conversations with him. If she keeps him dangling a while, it is because of the social ambition her father has put into her head but mainly because of female vanity. Vanity, Eve's weakness, is the complication Fancy brings into the Edenic innocence of Dick's world.

This recalls Bruce Johnson's definition of pastoral based on 'the old pastoral opposition of otium [i.e. Dick's contentment] and the aspiring mind [i.e. Fancy's vanity and social ambition]', with pastoral on the side of otium. Johnson applies the contrast to Gabriel Oak's contentment in *Madding Crowd* contrasted with Bathsheba's vanity and aspiration 'to an identity achieved apart from conventional love and marriage'; though Hardy 'rather admires', says Johnson, 'the peculiar nature of her aspiring'.[13]

Despite Fancy's vanity and social ambition, she resists her father's insistence that she marry the rich farmer Shiner, whose claim to superior social status is not accepted because he lacks education. She takes to bed with lovesickness until her frightened father agrees to her engagement to Dick. Mere men are no match for Fancy. Besides this is a benevolent pastoral world in which no one can for long thwart the desires of young lovers.

Hardy's masterly light touch is evident in his portrayal of Fancy's charm and Dick's ardently innocent love-making. Dick falls into a love swoon, disappearing afterwards from the group of carol-singers when Fancy, to thank them, appears as a framed illuminated vision in her window. The courtship is carried on through the elaborately described country dances at the Dewys' Christmas party. Dick makes the most of his turns with Fancy, 'her breath curling round his neck like a summer zephyr that had strayed from its proper date' (I, viii: 83). Never again will Hardy portray a love so sweetly innocent.[14]

Remarkably the choir harbours no resentment against Fancy for playing the instrument that replaces them. Fancy herself does not seek to play the organ in church, but is pushed into it by the vicar Mr Maybold acting at the suggestion of Farmer Shiner because both men are smitten by her charms. The newly arrived Mr Maybold wants also to modernise the church.

Fancy dresses for her debut 'with an audacity unparalleled in the whole history of village schoolmistresses at this date'. When poor Dick, who has to attend a friend's funeral, complains about such dazzling dress for an occasion from which he will be absent, she pouts, '"I do take a little delight in my life, I suppose"' (IV, v: 193– 4). Clothes are a continuing issue between them, an issue showing his moral superiority.

So overwhelmed is Mr Maybold by the proximity to his pulpit of this organ-playing divinity that he resolves to commit the most imprudent act of his life by proposing marriage to one so inferior to himself in station. We have been prepared to expect that Fancy, despite her engagement to Dick, will be unable to resist this temp- tation to climb socially, especially after Maybold has said, '"your natural talents, and the refinement they have brought into your nature . . . are equal to anything ever required of the mistress of a quiet parsonage-house"' (IV, vi: 199). Nevertheless they will move to Yorkshire to obscure her humble origins. In *The Woodlanders*, where social distinctions are taken more seriously, Fitzpiers will suggest a similar move to Grace for the same reason.

Just before Maybold's proposal that evening, Fancy observes a contrast in clothing between Dick, who returned with his black mourning suit dripping wet because he gave away his umbrella to the ladies at the funeral, and Maybold who after Dick's departure appears in the distance as a 'form', dressed elegantly in black and carrying an umbrella. Even before discerning the man, Fancy is attracted to the elegant clothing, whereas in pastoral it is usually the rough appearance that suggests good-heartedness. Fancy's treachery, however, is only momentary. She no sooner accepts Maybold than she begins to reject him when he reaches out to embrace her:

> 'No no, not now!' she said in an agitated whisper. 'There are things; – but the temptation is, O, too strong, and I can't resist it; I can't tell you now, but I must tell you! Don't, please, don't come near me now!' (IV, vi: 200)

As befits pastoral comedy, which repeats the ritual of spring, the spirit of winter, the threat to the lovers' happiness, is introduced so it can be quickly defeated. In the benevolent world of this novel, Maybold himself withdraws when the next day he meets Dick who announces his engagement to Fancy. Maybold's letter to Fancy, chiding her for not telling him of the engagement, crosses hers saying she had no right to accept him. She begs him to keep forever secret what passed between them. The vicar sends an unsigned note, '"Tell him everything; it is best. He will forgive you"' (IV, vii: 204–5). Fancy has too much common sense to follow such advice; as a character in comedy, she does not make Tess's tragic error. The same situation with a different turn becomes dark comedy in *The Woodlanders*, where Fitzpiers tries to keep secret his affairs with other women.

The wedding of Dick and Fancy takes place as spring returns. The novel, organised according to the cycle of the seasons, begins two winters back. The second winter is significantly omitted, perhaps because the spirit of winter was defeated with Maybold's withdrawal at the end of the 'Autumn' section. In the wedding ceremonies nature blends with community. The couple are married in church, a symbol of community, but the wedding procession threads its way 'among dark perpendicular firs, like the shafted columns of a cathedral' (v, i: 219). The wedding festivities, full of song and dance, symbols of community, take place in the shade of 'an ancient tree', symbol of a fertility that makes natural communities:

> Many *hundreds* of birds had been born amidst the boughs of this single tree; *tribes* of rabbits and hares had nibbled at its bark from year to year; quaint tufts of fungi had sprung from the cavities of its forks; and countless *families* of moles and earthworms had crept about its roots. (v, ii: 221; my italics)

Almost as ancient as the tree is the communalising country custom requiring the wedding party to walk in couples around the parish. The educated Fancy balks at the prospect of such an exhibition, but she accedes to tradition, showing her ability to make realistic compromises. Her vanity, however, remains evident. '"I wonder"', says one grandfather to the other, '"which she thinks most about, Dick or her wedding raiment!"' '"Well, 'tis their nature"', the other replies (v, i: 219). The humour, one might protest, is at the woman's expense, except that Fancy triumphs by understanding, with Sancho Panza's realistic comic wisdom, that a little female vanity is necessary to make the world of love go round – so also is a little deceptiveness necessary. '"What was goodness beside love!"' thought Fancy when she set about deceiving her father to make him approve her engagement to Dick (IV, iii: 185).

Now in the novel's final passage, Dick in his happiness bursts out quixotically:

'We'll have no secrets from each other, darling, will we ever? – no secret at all.'

'None from today,' said Fancy. 'Hark! what's that?'

From a neighbouring thicket was suddenly heard to issue in a loud, musical, and liquid voice – 'Tippiwit! swe-e-et! ki-ki-ki! Come hither, come hither, come hither!'

'O, 'tis the nightingale,' murmured she, and thought of a secret she would never tell.   (v, ii: 225–6)

The nightingale is both twitting her deceptiveness and, as the bird of lovers, telling her (the message she hears) to be deceptive for the sake of love.

Fancy's education makes no important difference in her behaviour, which springs ultimately from the laws of biology and of pastoral. (Here she differs from Grace, who is always tied up in educated self-consciousness.) In the Eden where *Under the Greewood Tree* essentially takes place, Fancy remains an Eve who, as a character in pastoral comedy, never goes so far as to bring on the Fall through too much moral scrupulousness.

Far from the Madding Crowd (published two years later in 1874) does not deal with exactly the same problems as *Under the Greenwood Tree, The Return of the Native* and *The Woodlanders*. Education and the impact of modern ideas are not issues. The returned native of *Madding Crowd* is Sergeant Troy, whose alienation from the community comes not from modern education (though we hear he is educated) but from the traditionally rootless, irresponsible life of the soldier. When early in the novel Gabriel proposes to Bathsheba and is refused, she says, '"You are better off than I. I have hardly a penny,"' but '"I am better educated than you"'. There is, however, no evidence that her education has been modernising or that her education rather than her nature has made her a bold, independent, almost feminist woman. It is probably her education that makes her say, conservatively, '"I want somebody to tame me; I am too independent; and you would never be able to, I know"' (IV: 29). To some extent the novel tells a traditionally comic 'taming of the shrew' story. Of all the pastoral novels, *Far From the Madding Crowd*, which is set retrospectively in an unspecified near past, is the most protected from the modern world.

Michael Millgate discusses the social unrest, from the 1830s to the early 1870s, in Dorset, a country 'notorious' for its 'social and economic backwardness' (*Hardy: Career as Novelist*, 98–100). But the novel ignores social problems, portraying a timeless rural existence with its natural hardships. This novel, which introduces the regionalist motif by first using the name Wessex, is so steeped in pastoralism that Hardy, who composed it within and outside his father's house amid the sites he was portraying, later recalled that when he ran out of paper he would continue writing on 'large dead leaves' (*Life*, 96).

Madding Crowd is like *Greenwood Tree* (but unlike *Woodlanders*) in making little of class distinctions. At the beginning Farmer Oak is socially superior to the penniless Bathsheba; later, after he has lost his land and she has become a landowner, she is superior; but at no point is the social distinction between them a bar to their marrying. Nor does Farmer Boldwood's slightly superior station exert much force as a reason for Bathsheba to marry him. As an itinerant soldier and seducer of Bathsheba's servant, Troy is an outsider; so that his marriage to Bathsheba seems socially and sexually outrageous (Hardy makes their relation seem illicit though they are technically married). But even here the class distinction between sergeant and landowner is minimised by the rumour that Troy is the illegitimate son of a nobleman. Class distinctions are bridged by the strong sense of community.

We see this vividly in two episodes. In the first, Bathsheba, in taking over the farm she has inherited, announces at a meeting of the farm labourers that she has dismissed the bailiff and will manage the farm herself. Having amazed every one by asserting her authority in a man's world, Bathsheba calls the payroll, inquiring considerately of each man his name and occupation and adding to his wages a ten shillings gift, thereby winning the men's loyalty and strengthening their sense of community. Gabriel instead, who is employed as her shepherd, is distinctly put in his place: '"You quite understand your duties? – you I mean, Gabriel Oak?"'. Gabriel was 'staggered by the remarkable coolness of her manner'. Nobody would have dreamt that they 'had ever been other than strangers' (x: 67). But Gabriel keeps shifting rank in her regard, depending on her need for his support, so that her pretense of distance enhances their unspoken acknowledgment of the tie between them.

The second episode is the sheep-shearing supper, where all the farm community sit at the same table with one end extended over the sill into Bathsheba's parlour window. They could all sit at the same table just because differences of rank were recognised and absorbed in the sense of community. Bathsheba honours Gabriel by asking him to officiate at the bottom of the table, but when the gentleman farmer Boldwood arrives, she asks Gabriel to yield him the place. Throughout she expresses her sexual interest in Gabriel by teasing him with their difference in rank, while he bears with dignity the necessary torments of the romance hero at the hands of his cruel lady. I employ the model of the long-suffering romance hero to demonstrate Gabriel's strong sexuality throughout, a point often disputed by critics. The model is established by Gabriel's passionate words at the beginning, after Bathsheba has refused his marriage proposal: '"I shall do one thing in this life – one thing certain – that is, love you, and long for you, and *keep wanting you till I die"*' (IV: 29).[15]

The supper is idyllic. All ranks join in communal song, recalling, as Empson points out, 'the essential trick of the old pastoral, which was felt to imply a beautiful relation between rich and poor' (*Some Versions of Pastoral*, 11). In a particularly harmonious moment Bathsheba sings accompanied by Gabriel's flute and Boldwood's bass voice. 'The shearers reclined against each other as at suppers in the early ages of the world' (XXIII: 123). The idyll emerges from the nineteenth-century-long argument for feudal community as opposed to the equality that produces isolation. But the argument is only implied. There is not even so much overt concern with historical change as we find in the yielding of the communal choir in *Greenwood Tree* to the 'isolated organ'.

Yet *Far from the Madding Crowd* is more complex, though less perfect (the Fanny Robin subplot is sentimental melodrama), than *Greenwood Tree* because in *Madding* Hardy gives us, as Ian Gregor says, 'a pastoral world shot through with passion and violence which just manages to contain and subdue these disruptive forces'.[16] When we consider that the novel contains two deaths, one the result of seduction, the other of a murder which sends the murderer to lifetime confinement as insane, we must marvel at the artfulness which makes the novel regain its pastoral composure, though it also contains elements of romance, melodrama, tragedy and modern realism. The final serenity is achieved not only by the happy ending in the long-awaited union of the two lovers, but also because Hardy has minimised our sympathy for Troy and even for Boldwood so that we do not mind seeing them eliminate each other, thus clearing the path for Gabriel and salvaging the novel's main genre, pastoral comedy, in the ritual of which Troy and Boldwood are obstructing spirits of winter for opposite reasons – Troy through a too sensuous relation to Bathsheba, Boldwood through excessive idealisation of her.

The practical Gabriel comes to represent the golden mean between these extremes. We can see that Hardy has overmanipulated the plot in order to achieve the mutual elimination of Gabriel's rivals, but we suspend judgement because Hardy is fulfilling the purpose of pastoral and romance by fulfilling our desire and the lovers'. Even the death of the mawkishly good Fanny Robin might be understood as a death of winter since her main scenes are played out in the snow and since her death brings on the crisis that makes Bathsheba a better woman, preparing her for marriage in the spring. The penultimate chapter begins: 'Bathsheba revived with the spring' (LVI: 297).

Another reason for the re-establishment of pastoral over turbulence is the retrospective view which bathes the novel in an aura of timelessness within which temporary eruptions of passion drop back into the pervading stillness. Timelessness is most clearly evoked in the passage on the Gothic barn where the sheep-shearing takes place, the barn becoming still another emblem of organic community. Echoing Ruskin, Hardy shows that in Gothic there is no distinction between practical and aesthetic–spiritual considerations. Thus, the barn has the same ground plan as the contemporaneous Gothic church nearby, with the advantage over the Gothic church and castle that 'the purpose which had dictated its original erection was the same with that to which it was still applied'. The mind dwelt upon the barn's

> history, with a satisfied sense of functional continuity. . . . Four centuries had neither proved it to be founded on a mistake [like the church] . . . nor given rise to any reaction that had battered it down [like the castle]. . . . The defence and salvation of the body by daily bread is still a study, a religion, and a desire. (XXII: 113–14)

We see here that exaltation of practicality which is the novel's leading moral idea, again reminiscent of George Eliot.[17]

The barn's portrayal as both immediate and permanent leads to Hardy's explicit statement of the novel's time sense. 'Weatherbury was immutable'. The city-dweller's

Then is the rustic's *Now*. In London, twenty or thirty years ago
are old time . . . in Weatherbury three or four score years were
included in the mere present, and nothing less than a century set
a mark on its face or tone.

Hardy also sums up the novel's sense that organic community is as
'natural' as nature: 'So the barn was natural to the shearers, and the
shearers were in harmony with the barn' (XXII: 114). No other Hardy
novel, not even *Greenwood Tree*, is so deliberately 'immutable' as
this one.

Yet *Far from the Madding Crowd* is more complex than *Under the
Greenwood Tree* because turbulence and also psychology intrude into
the 'immutable' pastoral scene. In *Greenwood Tree* there is hardly any
psychology at all, perhaps a little in Fancy's conflict between father
and lover. But the portrayals of Bathsheba and Boldwood are
Hardy's first excursions into the sexual psychology for which he
is distinguished. The treatments of Gabriel and Troy, instead, are
moral rather than psychological.

Hardy hints at sexual problems in earlier novels – Miss Aldclyffe's
possible lesbianism in *Desperate Remedies*, Henry Knight's frigidity
in *A Pair of Blue Eyes* – but he does not develop these problems,
perhaps because he feared censorship or was mainly interested in
plot. Bathsheba and Boldwood, instead, are portrayed in depth as
two people who think themselves invulnerable to sex and are taken
by storm; they have no defences when sexual desire breaks upon
them. We are told of Boldwood, 'The insulation of his heart by
reserve during these many years, without a channel of any kind for
disposable emotion, had worked its effect . . . the causes of love are
chiefly subjective' (XVIII: 97). His love for Bathsheba becomes as
pathologically obsessive as his previous aloofness from women. We
are told of the bold Bathsheba, after Troy has stirred up in her a
mood of masochistic capitulation she was not prepared to recognise
in herself, we are told, 'Capitulation – that was the purport of [her]
simple reply, guarded as it was – capitulation, unknown to herself'
(XXVI: 135).

Bathsheba loved Troy in the way that only self-reliant women
love when they abandon their self-reliance. When a strong woman
recklessly throws away her strength, she is worse than a weak
woman who has never had any strength to throw away.

(XXIX: 147)

Bathsheba is not armed with the strength in passivity of so-called 'weak' women, who in the engagements of love prove stronger than she.

Bathsheba's boldness may seem mannish. But Hardy is profeminist in not stereotyping the sexes as masculine-aggressive, feminine-passive. I can cite as examples the dominating Miss Aldclyffe in *Desperate Remedies*, the expert horsewoman Elfride in *A Pair of Blue Eyes*, who heroically rescues Henry Knight, the significantly named Paula Power in *A Laodicean* and also Ethelberta in *The Hand of Ethelberta*: both Paula and Ethelberta give orders and pay.

Bathsheba can be most fetchingly feminine in her apparently masculine moments, when at the beginning she does acrobatics on horseback unaware that Gabriel is erotically peeping through a loophole of his hut, or later when she trades successfully at the Corn Exchange while the other traders, all men, are smitten with her charms. Her defiant bargaining increases her feminine attractiveness, suggesting 'that there was potentiality enough in that lithe slip of humanity for alarming exploits of sex' (xii: 74). When later her maid Liddy says, '"You would be a match for any man"', Bathsheba asks anxiously, '"I hope I am not a bold sort of maid – mannish?". . . "O no, not mannish; but so almighty womanish that 'tis getting on that way sometimes"' (xxx: 155).

It is because Hardy deals here with the problem of the modern independent woman's femininity that some male critics – notably Henry James, who bridled at her 'wilful . . . *womanishness*'[18] – have disliked Bathsheba and left us wondering whether Hardy intended us to like her. I think he did intend us to like her, but critically. On the whole Hardy is not a feminist even though he makes Bathsheba say, '"I *hate* to be thought men's property"' (iv: 27) and '"It is difficult for a woman to define her feelings in language which is chiefly made by men to express theirs"' (li: 270).

Bathsheba exhibits what Lawrence disapprovingly calls 'female self-sufficiency', in her case enhanced by economic self-sufficiency. After she has begun to regret her marriage to Troy, we are told:

> She had felt herself sufficient to herself, and had in the independence of her girlish heart fancied there was a certain degradation in renouncing the simplicity of a maiden existence to become the humbler half of an indifferent matrimonial whole. (xli: 212)

The feeling is not incompatible with her flirtatiousness where she holds the upper hand, while marriage is in her view submission.

Her early remark to Gabriel, '"I want somebody to tame me"', shows a mistaken understanding of love as a power relationship, which explains her attraction to Troy. For a while it looks as though Troy has 'tamed' her, through his spectacular competence at sword-play, suggesting competence in sex. But Troy loses his dominance when, after their marriage, he proves incompetent at running the farm. Gabriel, who begins as passive compared to Bathsheba (she even rescues him from suffocation), asserts his reliable suppor-tiveness through unfailing competence at work. His name Oak suggests supportiveness, not mastery, and also phallic strength. His first name recalls the 'Chief of th' Angelic Guards' of Paradise in *Paradise Lost* (Bk IV: line 550). Bathsheba learns what other Hardy heroines will have to learn, that the cruel man is not necessarily the sexiest. Her marriage to Gabriel is not, as some critics think, a defeat or submission but an equal partnership in the work of running the farm. Unlike other lovers, they will 'associate . . . in their labours' (LVI: 303).

In *Far from the Madding Crowd* competence at work first emerges as a criterion for judging character, a criterion probably derived from George Eliot. When in the erotic atmosphere of the sheep-shearing Bathsheba impulsively fires Gabriel for not admitting he still loves her, his unique ability to save the sheeps' lives makes her swallow her pride to summon him back by irresistibly feminine means: '"Do not desert me, Gabriel!"' she writes (XXI: 111).

We see the erotic emotions deriving from their working together the night Bathsheba turns against Troy and toward Gabriel on the issue of competence. Troy has just got the farmhands drunk, so that he and they are lying in a stupor when the thunder storm Gabriel has been predicting breaks out, threatening Bathsheba's ricks (wheat stacks). Single-handedly Gabriel tries to save them by thatching, labouring like a hero of romance to serve 'that wilful and fascinat-ing mistress whom the faithful man even now felt within him as the embodiment of all that was sweet and bright and hopeless' (XXXVI: 190). (Bathsheba as modern independent woman merges with the romance figure of the cruel superior lady; Gabriel is both romance hero and hero of modern realistic fiction.) Worried, Bathsheba appears in the dark rickyard carrying a lantern which lights up a recognition scene between them – the first of a series suggesting their increasingly profound discovery of each other. They work together with the repetitive movements that may have influenced Lawrence's ritualised stackyard scene in *The Rainbow*. Almost blinded by a flash of lightning, Gabriel 'could feel Bathsheba's warm arm tremble in his hand – a sensation novel and thrilling' (xxxvii: 194). (One recalls the lightning that finally breaks down the inhibitions of Dorothea and Will in *Middlemarch*.) Their erotic excitement increases as they peep *together* through a chink into the barn where Troy and the farmhands lie snoring. Feeling constrained to account for her marriage, to assure Gabriel that she drove to Bath intending to break off her engagement to Troy, she thanks him for his devotion with new warmth. Her gratitude for his usefulness is undistinguishable from her love, but this does not matter since the reader has been sure of her love and has been waiting for her to discover it. Bathsheba belongs to the line of Jane Austen's Emma and George Eliot's Maggie and Dorothea – headstrong women who have to discover what they really desire.

It is because her emotional life is at the beginning so shallow that Bathsheba can toy with men's emotions without foreseeing the consequences. She is vain like Fancy, but more dangerous because more intelligent and wilful. When Gabriel first beholds her, she is gazing into a hand-mirror, blushing, just as Eve in *Paradise Lost* falls in love with her own reflection in a lake. One might conclude from her narcissism that Bathsheba is developmentally behind Gabriel, but in these early chapters she functions more effectively than he.

In the first four chapters the birth of erotic feeling between Gabriel and Bathsheba is evoked through a remarkable series of lookings and peepings. In their first meeting, Gabriel is aroused by *looking* at the unknown girl *looking* at herself. He recognises her again when, 'putting his eye close to a hole' in a barn, he sees her inside with cows the way 'Milton's Satan first saw Paradise' (ii: 15–16). Bathsheba first appears in the guises of Eve and a pastoral milkmaid. When after her peeped-at acrobatics on horseback she emerges from milking, 'it was with some surprise that she saw Gabriel's face rising like the moon behind the hedge'. All this voyeurism is summed up in Bathsheba's feeling that 'without eyes there is no indecorum . . . that Gabriel's espial had made her an indecorous woman' (iii: 18, 20).[19] Having run after Gabriel in such a way as to elicit has proposal of marriage, she rejects him and Gabriel, after vowing eternal love, adopts the romance hero's strategy of patient selfless service, even to the point of promoting Boldwood's suit in the hope of saving Bathsheba from Troy.

Bathsheba's toying with Boldwood has more serious consequences. Piqued because he refused to look at her in the Corn Exchange, she

jestingly sends him a valentine, affixing to it a red seal which she
realises with a laugh bears the words: '"Marry Me"' (XIII: 79).
Boldwood's stormy reaction is implausible unless we apply Freudian concepts of repression and understand in his reaction Hardy's
criticism of Shelleyan idealism. For Boldwood falls in love with an
idea in his own head, *seeing* Bathsheba only a little better now than
in the Corn Exchange. When after having sent the valentine
Bathsheba again enters the Exchange, we are told of Boldwood:
'Adam had awakened from his deep sleep, and behold! there was
Eve' (XVII: 93). Boldwood beholds an image. We are told of his
courting: 'The great aids to idealisation in love were present here:
occasional observation of her from a distance, and the absence of
social intercourse with her' (XIX: 98).

Neither does Troy *see* her the night they meet in her garden
(recalling Satan in the Garden) by getting entangled in each other's
clothes – she is too sensuously close for visual observation. Only
Gabriel comes to see her as she really is and continues loving her:
he 'was ever regardful of [her face's] faintest changes' (XVIII: 97). As
the mean between extremes Gabriel, as I have suggested, is portrayed morally rather than psychologically. Troy, too, is portrayed
morally because he is given no mitigating inner life – he is simply
the sensualist living in the present with no thought of consequences.
His one trace of inner life, his remorse for the deaths of Fanny
and their baby, is soon wiped out ironically when the rain, running
all night through the mocking jaws of a gargoyle while he sleeps
by Fanny's grave, washes away the flowers he just planted there.
That ends his remorse. He makes for Budmouth where, leaving his
clothes on the beach, he takes the swim in the ocean from which
he does not return, unintentionally giving the impression he has
drowned.

In Bathsheba's portrayal, instead, psychological understanding
mitigates moral judgement, as we can see by the narrator's comment after she has 'unreflectingly' sent the valentine: 'Of love as a
spectacle Bathsheba had a fair knowledge; but of love subjectively
she knew nothing' (XIII: 79). Only after Bathsheba, in the effectively
melodramatic scene over Fanny's coffin, suffers rejection by Troy
does she come to understand love subjectively by suffering the pain
she has so casually inflicted on others.

In the confrontation with Troy over the coffin, Bathsheba 'suffered in an absolute sense' more than Fanny in all her sufferings.
When Troy sinking upon his knees kisses the dead Fanny, Bathsheba

flings her arms round his neck, 'exclaiming wildly from the deepest deep of her heart', a depth she only now discovers in herself, begging him to kiss her too.

There was something so abnormal and startling in the childlike pain and simplicity of this appeal from a woman of Bathsheba's calibre and independence, that Troy, loosening her tightly closed arms from his neck, looked at her in bewilderment. . . . Troy could hardly seem to believe her to be his proud wife Bathsheba.

Bathsheba is brought still lower when Troy, refusing to kiss her, calls Fanny his true wife. '"If she's – that, – what – am I?"' Bathsheba sobs, recalling to our minds the illicit quality of their marriage. She emits 'a wail of anguish' (XLIII: 230–1) that brings back all the wailings in the literature of the past. The moment makes us wonder how much weight we should give to the historical reverberations of the names Troy and Bathsheba. Both names recall cases of illegitimate sexual attraction leading to violence – with in Troy's case the characteristically Greek tragic conclusion; and in Bathsheba's case the characteristically Hebrew providential conclusion, for the Biblical Bathsheba became the mother of Solomon and, thus, of King David's legitimate successors.

Bathsheba descends even lower when she flees to pass the night in a ferny hollow like the hollow where Troy first seduced her with his sword-play. Only this hollow is swampy, exhaling 'the essences of evil things in the earth, and in the waters under the earth' (XLIV: 233). The going under, the passage through evil, is widely recognised as a necessary stage in the experience of rebirth into a less egocentric selfhood.

The rebirth symbolism continues as Bathsheba, after her infernal night, becomes aware the next morning of two saving figures. The first is a passing schoolboy who chants the prayer for 'grace' which applies to her condition. The second, an apparition in the mist, turns out to be Liddy. It is a sign of Bathsheba's spiritual isolation that she warns Liddy not to try crossing the swamp. Nevertheless Liddy, like Jesus walking on the water, crosses to her, creating as she trod, 'irridescent bubbles of dank subterranean breath' that 'burst and expanded away to join the vapoury firmament above' (XLIV: 234). The movement from 'dank subterranean breath' to 'vapoury firmament' signifies rebirth, as does Bathsheba's discovery that she has after the night's exposure lost her voice. Hardy's poems contain no texture of imagery denser than the imagery of this episode. The recollection of the earlier hollow suggests that if Bathsheba has finally matured from girl to woman, it is Troy who began the process by bringing her to life sexually, that Troy paved the way for Gabriel.

Bathsheba goes to the opposite extreme symbolically by ascending from the hollow to her attic, where she imprisons herself in order to hide from Troy. Bathsheba's penitential self-imprisonment corresponds to what Hardy calls Troy's 'romanticism' in hoping to compensate for his crime against Fanny by giving her an expensive tombstone. Troy soon abandons his remorse; whereas Bathsheba continues her moral development, though her rebirth yields at first a listless woman, lacking the sparkle of the bold, self-centred girl. Thus, out of guilt over Boldwood and fear for his sanity, she reluctantly submits to a six-year engagement to him – six years to see whether Troy returns.

With Gabriel receded into the background, the novel becomes perfunctory – kept going by dazzling tricks of plot, such as Troy's return as a performer in a circus show attended by Bathsheba and Boldwood who do not recognise him. Hardy even makes Bathsheba lean so far back against a circus tent that Troy, on the other side, can slip a hand beneath the tent to lift from her fingers a note informing her of his return. Hardy's virtuosity with plot is, as I have said, both a strength and a danger.

The virtuosity and the danger are illustrated by Troy's disguised entrance and unmasking at Boldwood's Christmas party. He has come, he announces, to claim his wife. In a momentary display of subtle psychology amidst the melodrama, Hardy makes Boldwood say, in an unrecognisable voice masking his frustration, '"Bathsheba, go with your husband!"' 'Sudden despair had transformed him' (LIII: 289). It is Bathsheba's scream when Troy touches her that causes Boldwood to shoot and kill him, then rush to the police to give himself up. As I have suggested, we accept the manipulation that eliminates Gabriel's rivals because, as in all good melodramatic romance, this highly theatrical scene brings to fulfilment our desire to see the two lovers married.

There is a return to psychological validity in Bathsheba's suffering over her responsibility for so much disaster. She shows a new generosity of spirit in having Troy buried with Fanny. Outside a church within which children are singing, she weeps copiously,

allowing as never before a release of emotion. She becomes aware
of a waiting presence. It is Gabriel who, having been made farm
manager, tells her he must resign, that he is leaving England. Re-
verting to her earlier feminine appeals, she cries out, '"Now that I
am more helpless than ever you go away!"' Gabriel gives '"that very
helplessness"' (LVI: 299) as his reason for departing. By laying down
this rough ultimatum, Gabriel becomes both the model for and the
agent of Bathsheba's renewal of self-confidence – a renewal which
would not take place were he overgentle with her, as Giles is with
Grace in *Woodlanders*. Earlier Bathsheba had recognised that Oak's
superiority lay in his patience and objectivity:

> What a way Oak had, she thought, of enduring things. Boldwood,
> who seemed so much deeper and higher and stronger in feeling
> than Gabriel, had not yet learnt, any more than she herself, the
> simple lesson which Oak showed a mastery of . . . that among the
> multitude of interests by which he was surrounded, those which
> affected his personal well-being were not the most absorbing and
> important in his eyes. (XLIII: 226)

In envying Oak's adjustment to objective reality, she is advancing
the novel's main moral idea.

Now after Gabriel's ultimatum, Bathsheba

> was aggrieved and wounded that the possession of hopeless love
> from Gabriel, which she had grown to regard as her inalienable
> right for life, should have been withdrawn just at his own pleas-
> ure in this way. She was bewildered too by the prospect of hav-
> ing to rely on her own resources again: it seemed to herself that
> she never could again acquire energy sufficient to go to market,
> barter, and sell. (LVI: 300–1)

Such a passage would seem to confirm Peter Casagrande's argument that Bathsheba makes no moral improvement, that Hardy's
aim is to show 'Woman's prescriptive infirmity': 'Her [egocentric]
irrationality is curbed, not transformed, by the end of the novel'.[20]
If Casagrande is right, the novel mainly tells a traditionally
misogynistic 'taming of the shrew' story – an unlikely stand for a
progressive late-Victorian writer. In a letter of 1874 referring to

Bathsheba, Hardy says he has 'no great liking for the perfect woman of fiction, but this may be for purely artistic reasons' (*Letters*, I: 33). Penny Boumelha is accurate in saying, in *Hardy and Women*, that 'the radicalism of Hardy's representation of women resides . . . in their resistance to reduction to a single and uniform ideological position' (7).[21] Hence Hardy's shifting between apparently feminist and apparently antifeminist positions. Irving Howe cuts through the argument with the fundamental insight that 'as a writer of novels Thomas Hardy was endowed with a precious gift: he liked women' (*Hardy*, 108).

Let us look carefully at the end of *Madding Crowd*. As earlier, Bathsheba pursues Gabriel, this time to his cottage, to elicit his proposal of marriage. Picking up her signal Gabriel, 'tenderly and in surprise' (words that argue against the 'taming of the shrew' reading), says:

> 'If I only knew one thing – whether you would allow me to love you and win you, and marry you after all – If I only knew that!'
> 'But you never will know," she murmured.
> 'Why?'
> 'Because you never ask.'   (LVI: 303)

Accompanying her home happily, Gabriel talks not about love but about his forthcoming tenure of the farm Boldwood left him – an inheritance that equalises them, giving their marriage the social appropriateness required by traditional comic endings.

Many critics consider the marriage of Gabriel and Bathsheba a settling for less, a tragedy of reduced expectations. But the text suggests, instead, a fulfilment of Hardy's advanced ideas about marriage. Hardy's approval of Gabriel's omission of love talk ('pretty phrases and warm expressions being probably unnecessary between such tried friends') suggests a realistic new statement about love and marriage. Hardy concludes with marriage, the required happy ending, but gives us also a critique of traditional marriage. According to Hardy's revision of the old idealising view, it is an advantage that Bathsheba's love of Gabriel is buttressed by self-interest while self-interest is justified by love. In the important view of marriage proposed in the chapter's last paragraph, a view toward which the whole novel has been leading, there is no talk of female submission but rather of 'good-fellowship – *camaraderie*' between the partners in a working and a love relationship, 'romance growing up in the interstices of a mass of hard prosaic reality'.

> Theirs was that substantial affection which arises (if any arises at all) when the two who are thrown together begin first by knowing the rougher sides of each other's character, and not the best till further on, the romance growing up in the interstices of a mass of hard prosaic reality. This good-fellowship – *camaraderie* – usually occurring through similarity of pursuits, is unfortunately seldom superadded to love between the sexes, because men and women associate, not in their labours, but in their pleasures merely. Where, however, happy circumstance permits its development, the compounded feeling proves itself to be the only love which is strong as death . . . beside which the passion usually called by the name is evanescent as steam.   (LVI: 303–4)

Paradoxically this genuine romantic love, 'the only love which is strong as death', endures because the lovers began by knowing the worst about each other. Thus, Bathsheba does not in the end need to be morally perfect in order to be loved and become capable of loving. With the self-confidence that comes from being loved, her competence, it is implied, will return and she will participate with Gabriel in the management of the farm.

Finally we must notice Gabriel's moral development; for of all Hardy's heroes Gabriel comes closest to perfection and serves, therefore, as a model by which the others are to be judged. Gabriel combines, as I have suggested, three modes of heroism: he is a hero of pastoral, of romance and, as he evolves, a hero also of the new realistic mode.

Gabriel is first presented as a pastoral, flute-playing shepherd, who has through past competence worked himself up from shepherd to farmer by leasing a small sheep farm at Norcombe. We see right away a combination of pastoral and realist virtues – a combination reinforced when we are told that Gabriel reads the stars both for their beauty and for practical information, that he is only middling in looks and goodness and is 'Laodicean' (I: 7) or lukewarm in religious conviction (for Hardy an advantage despite the contrary judgments of Revelation 3: 14–16 and Dante). Gabriel's

general attractiveness increases as we see him in *action* in real circumstances over a long period of time.

When the story begins Gabriel seems lacking in competence, for
he falls asleep on two crucial occasions. On the first he falls asleep
with the windows of his shepherd's hut closed, so that he would
have suffocated were it not that Bathsheba – whom he has seen
only once, long enough to have fallen in love with her – exhibits her
competence by saving his life. He awakes to find 'his head was
upon her lap, his face and neck were disagreeably wet, and her
fingers were unbuttoning his collar', a physical intimacy suggesting
that they will become lovers (III: 21). On the second occasion he is
sleeping so soundly that he does not hear his young, inexperienced
sheep dog driving his sheep over a precipice, killing them all. He
is financially ruined.

His total defeat at Norcombe works a great change in Gabriel,
giving him that serene attunement to reality which Bathsheba will
spend the rest of the novel catching up with.

> He had passed through an ordeal of wretchedness which had
> given him more than it had taken away. He had sunk from his
> modest elevation as pastoral king into the very slime-pits of
> Siddim; but there was left to him a dignified calm he had never
> before known, and that indifference to fate which, though it often
> makes a villain of a man, is the basis of his sublimity when it
> does not. And thus the abasement had been exaltation, and the
> loss gain.   (VI: 34)

The 'slime-pits of Siddim' (Gen. 14: 10) parallel the swampy hollow
in which Bathsheba will experience a similar rebirth.

The romance theme continues when Gabriel falls asleep for
the third time, this time beneficially; for the wagon in which he
falls asleep deposits him on Bathsheba's newly inherited farm at
Weatherbury just as her ricks are burning, so he can take charge
and save them. Falling asleep is clearly the means by which Gabriel
follows his destiny, fulfilling his deepest desires. Falling asleep will
work the same way for Tess.

Gabriel's heroic skill leads to an almost magical recognition scene
in which the farmer, a lady on a pony, veiled against the fire, 'lifted
the wool veil tied round her face, and looked all astonishment',
when Gabriel asks, '"Do you happen to want a shepherd, ma'am?"'

'Gabriel and his cold-hearted darling, Bathsheba Everdene, were face to face' (VI: 41).

As Bathsheba's shepherd Gabriel behaves with manly dignity, braving her wrath by telling her the truth about objective circumstances and by refusing to make the declarations of love that would expose him to further rebuffs. Even as he labours alone in the night, like a romance hero, to save Bathsheba's ricks, he calculates, like a hero of realism, the impending loss to her in pounds and shillings. Nor does his serviceableness make him uncritically subservient to Bathsheba as Giles is to Grace. Gabriel learns to treat Bathsheba with loving roughness.

In contrast to Boldwood who because of his hopeless love lets his farm fall into ruin, Gabriel's hopelessness does not interfere with his efficiency. Bathsheba, who for most of the book understands love only in terms of power (either she dominates as with Boldwood or is dominated as with Troy) mistakes Gabriel's gentleness for lack of masculine strength. Having told him he was not the one who could 'tame' her, she is constantly surprised and angered that so faithful a servant can successfully resist her domination. Gabriel finally 'tames' her, to use her inappropriate word, by making himself so quietly supportive that she finally realises she wants to lean on him. Gabriel's is the true masculine strength because it reinforces her feminine strength, suggesting the only kind of sexual competence that can be combined with enduring love and mutual respect.

Because there is no conflict between Gabriel's piety and his competence, he can without loss of integrity win in the end his long sought goal, Bathsheba's hand in marriage, along with unsought for material benefits – Boldwood's farm and Bathsheba's. His combination of country skills with reading and spiritual wisdom contrasts with Clym's regressive pastoralism in renouncing his intellectual ambitions to become a furze cutter, the least skilled of country occupations.

Giles in *The Woodlanders* excels in country skills and is like Gabriel a hero of pastoral and romance; but he cannot take care of himself in the struggle that would advance him economically and socially. Nor can he compete sexually; his courtship of Grace is inept. It is true that Giles is threatened, as Gabriel is not, by characters from the outside modern world (the world of the late 1870s) – by Mrs Charmond who takes his houses and Fitzpiers who takes Grace. This outside world renders the novel's pastoral setting anomalous and Giles's country virtues obsolete. But Gabriel, with his realist virtues, could one feels adapt to modern conditions. He has the ability to survive and that, as we see over and over again, is an ability respected by the Darwinian Hardy.

For all his altruism Gabriel is not an 'idealist', for in him there is no dissociation between the ideal and the real. He stands as a criterion of judgement for Hardy's subsequent studies of failed idealists, beginning with Clym Yeobright. Gabriel is Hardy's model for what Yeats was to call Unity of Being.

4
Diversions from Pastoral

The heath in the opening pages of *Return of the Native* is presented as an expanse of space–time. The heath is both timeless and subject to geological change – a change so slow as to look like permanence:

> The great inviolate place had an ancient permanence which the sea cannot claim. . . . The sea changed, the fields changed, the rivers, the villages, and the people changed, yet Egdon remained.[1]

Even the changes wrought by man fade into the 'permanence' of slow change: 'An aged highway, and a still more aged barrow . . . almost crystallized to natural products by long continuance' (I, i: 5). This combination of motion and stillness, the source of so much romantic imagery, establishes the heath as both real and symbolic, but symbolic of many different things. The symbolic significances are sometimes congruent – night, unconsciousness, the primeval past, the grotesque, the sublime – and sometimes conflicting: the heath is both nurturing and destructive like the maternal principle it symbolises. Hardy uses the heath the way Swinburne uses the sea.

The heath is small – the characters can walk across it. But it is also vast. The walks across the heath seem long and strenuous when they are journeys from one spiritual or psychological location to another. 'A long day's march was before' Clym (III, vi: 165) when he leaves his mother's house, after quarreling with her over his marriage, to find a house for Eustacia and himself. He is moving into a new psychological region, changing allegiance from mother to wife. Later he recrosses the heath, moving from wife back to mother. Before this Mrs Yeobright's journey across the heath to be reconciled with the married couple exhausted and killed her.

Hardy evolves from the heath a new anthropological view of culture, as in his comment on the Guy Fawkes bonfires: 'such blazes as this the heathmen were now enjoying are rather the lineal descendants from the jumbled Druidical rites and Saxon ceremonies [for Thor and Woden] than the inventions of popular feeling about

95

Gunpowder Plot'.[2] The heath folk break into a dance – 'a whirling of dark shapes amid a boiling confusion of sparks' (I, iii: 12, 24) – danced in that place a thousand years ago. Hardy's novels deal with such organic continuity, but they also deal with the rupture of continuity, as in the modern self-conscious attempt to revive ancient customs that have lost meaning – the Christmas pantomime in *Return of the Native* or the May Day dancing in *Tess* or the Midsummer eve festival in *The Woodlanders*.

Yet there are other primitive customs, considered long since dead, that flare up in remote Wessex with unexpected frightening violence – the witchcraft rituals in *Return of the Native* and the skimmity ride in *The Mayor of Casterbridge*.[3] Hardy is a master at exploiting folk customs not as the single cause of events, but as confirming and deepening the other causes. The sudden flare-up of forgotten customs corresponds to the sudden flare-up of the individual unconscious, accounting for the 'explosive' characterisations noted by Lawrence.

Into his rendition of layered organic continuity, Hardy injects a story of modern self-conscious alienation. The self-conscious, alienated Eustacia is given a mythical quality by her initial presentation as emerging from a Celtic barrow and the heath's nocturnal aspect. Even after she has taken on individual lineaments, she remains witch-like in the way she enchants the boy Johnny who makes her bonfire and the way she uses the fire (she is compared to the Witch of Endor) to 'conjure up' Wildeve. Eustacia has more stature than the other characters because she is portrayed realistically with supernatural glimmers around the edges; so that the rumours of her witchcraft are false in one sense and true in another.

Clym, the 'native' of the title, who was 'so inwoven with the heath in his boyhood that hardly anybody could look upon it without thinking of him' (III, i: 132), Clym severed connections with his roots by working for a jeweller in Paris – a place and occupation at the opposite pole from the heath. In returning to the heath Clym unconsciously wants to recover organic connection with his roots. But having acquired radical ideas in Paris, he consciously aims to educate and modernise the heath folk without realising that he would, by making them self-consciously critical destroy the organic community he wants to rejoin. Hardy's ritualised presentation of the heath folk, though often criticised, is a way of portraying a non-thinking society, a society governed by customs and memory rather than ideas. '"You be bound to dance at Christmas"', says one of the heath folk, '"because 'tis the time o' year; you must dance at weddings because 'tis the time o' life"'; but no dancing at funerals (I, iii: 17). Like so many modern intellectuals, Clym wants the best of both worlds – progress together with the survival of a romanticised past.

Clym does not realise, says Hardy with Marx-like disapproval, that intellectual advancement must follow economic advancement. Clym is an 'idealist' (as Gabriel Oak is not), because his idealism is disproportionate to his sense of reality. The novel shows that Clym's idealism accomplished nothing, while incidentally destroying the lives of his mother and wife. Beginning with *The Return of the Native*, Hardy's novels launch a continuing critique of idealists.

Clym's idealism can be best understood by comparing him to Eustacia, Wildeve and Venn, who are significantly similar to and different from him. Like Clym's, Eustacia's idealism derives from reading and is expressed through alienation from the heath. The difference is that Eustacia's reading makes her idealise far-away places; her *imagination* is alienated, while Clym finds imaginative satisfaction in the heath. Wildeve is Eustacia's pale double (pale because he lacks her imaginative power), in that he too is educated, hates the heath and cares 'for the remote' while disliking 'the near': 'He might have been called the Rousseau of Egdon' (III, vi: 170).

Although a relative newcomer to the heath with a vaguely cosmopolitan background (her well-born English mother eloped with a Cypriot bandleader), Eustacia mysteriously knows the heath as well as Clym does. Despite her continually voiced desire to escape (she marries Clym in the hope that he will take her to Paris), Eustacia's life seems even more integrally tied to the heath than Clym's. He has gone away; whereas she refuses the three chances offered her to escape. It is as though she could have no being apart from the heath – emerging as the human figuration of the nocturnal heath and disappearing in the end back into the heath at night. An outsider (therefore in Hardy suspect), Eustacia has fastened upon the heath through the power of hate, hence the rumours of her witchcraft. Hardy, I think, wanted in his portrayals of Clym and Eustacia to contrast two kinds of romantic idealism – the angelic or Shelleyan versus the demonic or Byronic kind.

In Hardy the surprising point of the contrast is that the angelic idealist turns out to be the more destructive of the two. Clym does more harm to others than does Eustacia; Angel Clare does more harm to Tess than does Alex; and the angelic Sue Bridehead, the most extreme case, destroys everyone in sight – herself, Jude, their children, Phillotson. Sue's antagonist Arabella is not demonic because not an idealist. There is in Arabella no diseased imagination – she has no imagination. What we find unattractive is her animal ability to survive in the struggle for existence. But for the Darwinian Hardy, the ability to survive is a virtue not to be discounted as indicated by a quotation in his notebook:

> Science tells us that, in the struggle for life, the surviving organism is not necessarily that which is absolutely the best in an ideal sense, though it must be that which is most in harmony with surrounding conditions.[4]

For all his high-mindedness Venn is not like Clym an 'idealist', but a realist like Oak, as demonstrated by his unfailing competence and his shrewd thwarting of Eustacia's and Wildeve's intrigues against Thomasin. Like Oak's regression from farmer to shepherd, Venn's regression from farmer to reddleman enables him to watch over the lady who has rejected him. In his faithfulness to his lady, Venn like Oak is a hero of romance while also a hero of realism. But he has also a supernatural aura because his nearly obsolete occupation has dyed him satanic red (powerful as reverse symbolism) and because he is almost supernaturally ubiquitous.

Clym instead is not a hero of realism because of the disproportion between his idealism and his sense of reality. Nor is he a hero of romance, because he descends to the lowly occupation of furze-cutter not to advance his love of Eustacia but to withdraw from it. Ignoring Eustacia's horror at their reduced condition of life, he can actually say to her: '"I am much happier. And if my mother were reconciled to me and to you I should, I think, be happy quite"' (IV, ii: 196). In his relation to women Clym assumes, not the active role of a romance hero, but rather a passive, almost infantile role. After his break with his mother and then with his wife, he waits passively for the women to initiate the reconciliation. Clym's reluctance to take the initiative brings on the deaths of the two women.

It might be said that the idealists – Clym, Eustacia and Wildeve – are modern dissociated personalities: dissociated between their thoughts and feelings, their sense of inner and outer reality. Mrs Yeobright is not an idealist, but is excessively rational and wilful. Only Venn and Thomasin exemplify Unity of Being, because all their faculties operate harmoniously. It is difficult to make such harmonious characters interesting though Oak, Hardy's most successful example of Unity of Being, is interesting.

Venn is a supernaturalised Oak and it is questionable whether Hardy did well to introduce so supernaturalised a character into a realistic novel. The issue is pinpointed in the question whether or not Venn should marry Thomasin in the end. As a providence hovering over the action rather than a vulnerable character engaged in it, Venn should not marry Thomasin. But as a romance hero, he should. Hardy indicates – in the footnote to the third chapter of Book Six, introduced in the Wessex edition of 1912 – that he originally intended the first ending. Venn

> was to have retained his isolation and weird character to the last, and to have disappeared mysteriously from the the heath, nobody knowing whither–Thomasin remaining a widow. But certain circumstances of serial publication led to a change of intent. (307n. 5)

The change of intent recognised that the novel's romance element required a happy ending for at least one couple.

We understand the supernatural auras of Eustacia and Venn when we learn from John Paterson's study of the manuscripts that in the original version Eustacia, called Avice, plays 'the witch in a more than merely metaphorical sense', whereas Venn's supernatural qualities were added and then modified in revisions. Eustacia/Avice and her father, Lieutenant Drew, were 'not romantic strangers but natives of the heath' (hence her anomalous familiarity with the heath in the final version). The change from father to indifferent grandfather follows the pastoral pattern by which Hardy's heroines are fatherless or minimally fathered. Eustacia and her grandfather, Captain Vye, were later upgraded socially. In the revisions Eustacia was romanticised from a quasi-supernatural into a metaphorical witch, 'from Satanic antagonist to Promethean protagonist'.

Venn, instead, began as a rude, dialect-speaking peasant, 'the unsuccessful suitor of an entirely countrified Thomasin'.[5] He then became a supernaturalised reddleman, a romantic outcast. He was finally domesticated and elevated socially to a dairy farmer as a way of making acceptable his marriage to a Thomasin whose gentility is established through the social elevation of Mrs Yeobright in the interlineations. The three irreconcileable layers remain in Venn's characterisation.

Clym, too, in the first version, wanders no farther from the heath than Budmouth, where he works as a jeweller's assistant. In speech and manner he is barely distinguishable from the heath folk. Thus, we see that the first draft was more purely than the final version the 'story of country life, somewhat of the nature of "Far from the Madding Crowd"' that Hardy projected in 1877 (*Letters*, I: 50). The theme that in revising Hardy developed through the broadening of spatial references (which originally did not exceed the boundaries of Wessex) and through the social and intellectual elevation of the main characters, especially of Clym and Eustacia, is the theme of modern alienation versus traditional rootedness. The revised *Return of the Native* became a novel that takes the modern world into account, as *Far from the Madding Crowd* does not. Pastoral was enlarged to deal not only with the contrast between country and city, but also with the contrast between traditional and modern modes of life and personality. Valorisations are not entirely on the side of tradition and the country; for even though the intellectualised characters encounter difficulties, their lives seem nobler than the lives of the more rooted heath folk.

Like many Shakespeare plays, *The Return of the Native* is a layered structure in which the remains of earlier versions leave contradictions and ambiguities that create a dense texture suggesting unplumbed profundities. A good example is our uneasy sense that Clym and Thomasin are more than cousins since they grew up under the same roof with Mrs Yeobright, Thomasin's guardian. Mrs Yeobright's desire that they marry seems therefore unnatural (recalling the desire of Hardy's mother that her children never marry but set up houses as brother–sister couples). Sure enough Clym and Thomasin turn out in the original manuscript to have been brother and sister. In the final version, the atmosphere of incest also pervades the unconscious relationship between the fatherless Clym and his mother.

To return to Venn, his natural–supernatural character is amply justified by his role in the boldly imaginative dicing scene, perhaps the most poetic scene in Hardy's verse or prose. Mrs Yeobright, not trusting Wildeve with Thomasin's inheritance (she did her best to prevent their marriage), employs her simple-minded servant Christian Cantle to carry to Clym's wedding party, which she refused to attend, fifty pounds each for Clym and Thomasin. Wildeve, hearing about the money from Christian and incensed that Mrs Yeobright did not entrust him with his wife's money, entices Christian on the heath at nightfall into a dice game in which Wildeve wins the whole hundred pounds.

Christian having run off in despair, Wildeve starts home with his winnings when the ubiquitous Venn, having overheard Christian's hint to Wildeve, appears as if magically. The scene becomes increasingly supernatural when Venn challenges Wildeve to a dice game and wins continually, inevitably, no matter what conditions the increasingly desperate Wildeve sets, until Venn wins back the hundred pounds. The dice game may be the most implausible scene in Hardy, but it is also one of the most successful and memorable scenes. The reason is that the natural setting is sufficiently supernaturalised to admit strange events, yet remains indubitably real so that the reality of the setting gives reality to the events.

Wildeve and Venn play on the heath at night on a flat stone lit by a lantern. At first the game fluctuates. 'The light of the candle had by this time attracted heath-flies, moths, and other winged creatures of night. . . . By this time a change had come over the game; the reddleman won continually.' The animal visitations having affected the game, the magic is reinforced by the ghostliness of the next animal visitors:

> They were surrounded by dusky forms between four and five feet high, standing a few paces beyond the rays of the lantern. A moment's inspection revealed that the encircling figures were heath-croppers [wild ponies], their heads being all towards the players, at whom they gazed intently.

They are like Greek gods who in their animal guises watch over the battles of mortals, taking sides. As if understanding the heath-croppers' hostility to himself, Wildeve chases them away with a shout. But the gods cannot be defied. 'A large death's-head moth advanced from the obscure outer air, wheeled twice round the lantern, flew straight at the candle, and extinguished it by the force of the blow.'

Desperate for matches, Wildeve notices lights dotting 'the hillside like stars of a low magnitude. "Ah – glowworms"', he says. There follows a touch so delicately fantastic as to recall Shakespeare's way with fairies. Wildeve shakes from a foxglove leaf thirteen glow-worms (the number is magical) arranging them so as to cast on the dice 'a pale phosphoric shine'. Ironically Wildeve's delicate inspiration leads to a demonic intrusion into the natural scene.

They are now reduced to a single die, the only one recovered after Wildeve in a fury threw the dice into the darkness. Wildeve demands they play for the lowest number in the hope of changing his luck. But the ghostly return of the heath-croppers suggests to him that his luck will not change. Wildeve 'clenched his teeth upon [the die] in sheer rage'. They both throw aces, but the die splits after Venn's throw. '"I've thrown nothing at all"', says Venn. Insisting Venn has won, Wildeve throws the money at him. Venn withdraws with the money, leaving 'Wildeve sitting stupefied' (III, viii: 182–5).

This conclusion shows Hardy's way of validating the supernatural by psychologising it. Wildeve's self-destructiveness in the end suggests his self-destructiveness throughout; so that the inexorable fall of the dice against him objectifies his deepest wish to lose, perhaps because of his guilt at having spirited away Thomasin's money. Looking up to see a carriage carrying Eustacia and Clym to their wedding at Mistover, he forgets his loss of money so overwhelmed is he by his loss of Eustacia. Wildeve is not, however, sentimentalised. Eustacia's 'preciousness in his eyes', says Hardy sardonically, 'was increasing in geometrical progression with each new incident that reminded him of their hopeless division' (185). Wildeve is like Eustacia in desiring the lovers he cannot have and spurning the ones he can have.

I have already suggested that *The Return of the Native* contains a mixture of genres which makes it exceed the boundaries of pastoral. The mixture of genres – supernaturalism, realism, romance, tragedy – derives from the novel's ambivalent treatment of nature and the psychological complexity of its characterisations. As in Wordsworth the ambivalent forces of nature produce the unconscious life from which the characters draw their vitality. Characterisation points always toward the unconscious life, toward enigma. To supplement the critics who concentrate on formal signs of tragedy in *Return of the Native* (such as unities of time and place), I shall establish the tragic element by analysing the characters' psychological life. In *Return of the Native* projection of the unconscious is best exemplified by the characterisation of Clym. Clym's relation with his mother is a spectacular pre-Freudian treatment of the Oedipus complex – a treatment exceeded in psychological thoroughness only by Lawrence's *Sons and Lovers*. As an Oedipal type Clym is intellectual, idealistic, gentle, attractive to women, but lacking in masculine will and passionate spontaneity.

His return to Egdon Heath is rendered in such a way as to make his motives for returning ambiguous. When he reveals his intention to become a schoolmaster in Budmouth and keep a night school for the heath folk, both his mother and the heath folk think he has made a big mistake. But Clym never does get around to teaching; he prevents himself from achieving that goal by marrying Eustacia, by nearly blinding himself through overreading and by becoming a furze-cutter. All this suggests that 'the native' has returned for deeper reasons than a change of occupation.

Clym repeats the Wordsworthian pattern of a therapeutic return to one's roots in nature after a period of exposure in the city to abstract radical ideas. It is indicative of Hardy's post-Darwinian, ironic rewriting of Wordsworth that Clym's return to nature causes death for his mother and wife and regression rather than development for himself. The difference is that Hardy understood – as Wordsworth did not, at least consciously – the Oedipal implications of the return. The heath represents for the natives (but not for the two outsiders, Eustacia and Wildeve) a nurturing maternal principle. Clym's return to the heath represents an unconscious return to his mother at an age when such a return is dangerous. When near the end Clym comes upon his mother dying on the heath, we are told that 'all sense of time and place left him, and it seemed as if he and his mother were as when he was a child with her many years ago on this heath' (IV, vii: 229).

Clym's first fervent references to Eustacia awaken in his mother an implacable hostility toward this girl whom she has hardly seen. Hardy generalises the conflict as explicitly as Freud might have done: 'Hardly a maternal heart within the four seas could, in such circumstances, have helped being irritated at that ill-timed betrayal of feeling for a new woman.' The words that follow, '"You are *blinded*, Clym. . . . It was a bad day for you when you first set *eyes* on her"' (III, iii: 152, my italics) make sufficient impression on Clym to become self-fulfilling. If we recall that blinding according to Freud can substitute for castration as in the Oedipus myth (*Works*, XIII: 130), we understand why Clym, when he becomes blind, seems to have lost sexual power. Such deep psychological penetration exceeds the boundaries of pastoral. And indeed Hardy suggests in a letter of 1889 that in *Return of the Native* he made the transition from pastoral to tragedy through deep insight into the characters.[6]

In quarrelling with his mother over his choice of poverty on the heath rather than wealth in Paris, Clym strangely feels 'a sickness of heart in finding he could shake [persuade] her' (III, iii: 149). This sentence, according to C. C. Walcutt, 'seems to reveal that Clym *wants* his mother to disapprove of what he is doing ... Clym's growing passion [for Eustacia] is almost matched by the emotional force of his conflict with his mother'.[7] It is almost as though Clym were making love to his mother in reverse by making love to Eustacia. '"You give up your whole thought – you set your whole soul – to please a woman"', says Mrs Yeobright jealously. '"I do"', Clym replies. '"And that woman is you"' (III, v: 161).

As for Mrs Yeobright, she is correct in her low estimates of Wildeve and Eustacia. But her motives are wrong. 'She had a singular insight into life, considering that she had never mixed with it' (III, iii: 149). Her judgements rationalise a hysterical possessiveness. She is intellectually right, but emotionally wrong.

We see an example of Mrs Yebright's intrusion into Clym's sex life when Clym senses Eustacia's kiss as 'something which lingered upon his lips like a seal set there ... it seemed as if his mother might say, "What red spot is that glowing upon your mouth so vividly?"' (III, iii: 151). Mrs Yeobright's subsequent admonition, '"You are blinded, Clym"', begins a series of allusions to Oedipus which eventually become explicit when Oedipus is named. Oedipus blinded himself as self-punishment for having killed his father and slept with his mother. Clym in a deep psychological sense blinds himself as self-punishment for having abandoned his mother by marrying Eustacia.

Clym's near-blindness and consequent turn to furze-cutting maintains even in marriage his allegiance to his mother, since his furze-cutting represents a regressively mindless connection to the womb-like heath:

> His daily life was of a curious microscopic sort, his whole world being limited to a circuit of a few feet from his person. His familiars were creeping and winged things, and they seemed to enrol him in their band. . . . None of them feared him,

because he seemed one of them (IV, ii: 197). Even Wordsworth would agree that such mindless harmony with nature is not desirable at

Clym's stage of life. His near-blindness seems to represent a sexual turning away from Eustacia. It is surprising how little we read about Clym's blindness after his mother's death when, having abandoned Eustacia, he returns to his mother emotionally by settling in her house. The furze-cutting stops.

Clym is even more responsible than Eustacia for the crucial episode in which they do not open to Mrs Yeobright's knocking on their cottage door. He earlier announced to Eustacia his intention of calling on his mother, but laid upon her responsibility for the reconciliation. The tragedy is brought on by Clym's delay in carrying out his impulse toward reconciliation with his mother and later with his wife. Retrospectively in 1912, after correcting proofs for the Wessex Edition, Hardy wrote in his journal: 'I got to like the character of Clym before I had done with him. I think he is the nicest of all my heroes, and *not a bit* like me' (*Life*, 357–8). 'Got to like' indicates that Hardy is not saying what he felt about Clym while creating him in 1877–8. The emphatic disclaimer, '*not a bit* like me', suggests resemblance. Did Hardy write out in Clym certain tendencies in himself he hoped to outgrow?

Clym is certainly 'nice' and our sympathy is with him through two-thirds of the novel, especially in contrast to our adverse judgement of Eustacia. But the narrator is increasingly critical of Clym until in the end, with Eustacia's emergence as a tragic heroine, the reader's sympathy is, by a triumph of art, directed away from him towards her. (We find a similar change from antipathy to sympathy for Henchard when he steps into his tragic role at the end of *Mayor of Casterbridge*.)

To return to the bad timing of Mrs Yeobright's arrival at Clym's door, she reaches the vicinity just when she can look down from her vantage on a hill upon a furze-cutter who 'seemed to be of no more account in life than an insect' (IV, v: 216). Realising with a shock – as she delineates in the Hardyan manner the individual from a distant figure on the landscape – that this furze-cutter is her son, she sees him and later a second man (Wildeve) enter the cottage.

As so often in Hardy, there are the moral and the deep psychological ways of interpreting Eustacia's behaviour in not opening the door to her mother-in-law's knocking. One interpretation should be imposed upon the other. According to the moral interpretation, Eustacia here as elsewhere plays the villain. Her former lover is in the house while her husband sleeps with animal exhaustion on the floor. Although a brother-in-law's visit is technically innocent, there is guilt in the air since Eustacia and Wildeve have not seen each other since their sexually charged chance meeting where their dance together contrasted for Eustacia with the 'arctic frigidity' (IV, iii: 205) of her life with Clym. Eustacia already feels accused by the knocking on the door (recalling the morally portentous knocking in *Macbeth*), but when pushing back the window curtain, she sees her mortal enemy, the woman who suspects her relation with Wildeve, Eustacia panics. She makes Wildeve slip out the back door with the injunction never to return. Hearing Clym in the front room say '"Mother"', she waits for him to open the door and break the ice before calling her. But hearing no further sound, she returns to the front room, finds Clym fast asleep and hastens to open the door. It is too late, Mrs Yeobright has gone.

Eustacia ought at this point to have awakened Clym, told him what happened and sent him in search of his mother. But she cannot bring herself to tell him about Wildeve. Like Tess with Angel, she finds it increasingly difficult to tell the truth because she has not told it immediately. According to the moral reading, Eustacia makes a series of wrong moral choices, beginning with her unwillingness to open the door and let Mrs Yeobright find Wildeve in the house. When later she recognises Clym in the group around Mrs Yeobright's dead body, she hears 'a confused sob' and gasps, '"That's Clym – I must go to him – yet dare I do it? No!"' Again she makes a wrong moral choice. But this time she judges herself morally: '"I am to blame for this. There is evil in store for me"' (IV, viii: 238).

According to the psychological reading, Eustacia is a victim of circumstances. The appearance just after Wildeve's of the mother-in-law who hates her unnerves Eustacia. Since Wildeve calls as a relative, expecting to see Clym in the house, and since Eustacia tells Wildeve never to return, his visit is technically innocent. It is Clym's sleeping that makes the visit illicit. Clym's deep animal sleep, envied by Eustacia and Wildeve, seems an evasion, especially since his utterance of the word '"Mother"' (displaying Hardy's psychological understanding) suggests unconscious awareness of his mother's presence and refusal to wake. Upon waking Clym describes to Eustacia a dream about his mother which shows that he knew in his sleep what was transpiring: '"I dreamt that I took you to her house to make up differences, and when we got there we couldn't get in, though she kept on crying to us for help"' (IV, vii: 227). Eustacia is right to refuse responsibility for the reconciliation and to assume from Clym's utterance that he was awake and able to answer the door. Mrs Yeobright turns away from Clym's cottage brokenhearted, not so much because Eustacia, whom she saw at the window, did not open the door, but because her son, whom she knew to be at home, did not open. In the deep psychological sense Mrs Yeobright is correct; it is Clym who did not open the door.

When Mrs Yeobright turns away from Clym's unopened door to meet her death on the heath, she plays out the tragedy of King Lear, of an aged parent rejected by an ungrateful child.[8] Susan Nunsuch's little son who accompanies Mrs Yeobright playing the Fool to her Lear, later reports her dying words that she was '"a broken-hearted woman and cast off by her son"' (IV, viii: 238). Overhearing this report, Clym, in a passage of major poetry, plays out the remorse of Oedipus who blinded himself. The already purblind Clym blinds himself psychologically a second time: 'his eyes lit by a hot light, as if the fire in their pupils were burning up their substance'. '"I sinned against her, and on that account there is no light for me"', he tells Eustacia (v, i: 239–40). The intensity of his remorse intensifies her sense of guilt, making it increasingly difficult for her to confess.

When Clym later learns from Johnny Nunsuch that a second man entered the house and that Eustacia saw his mother and did not open to her, he loads all the guilt upon Eustacia '"Cast off by my son!' No! ... But by your son's, your son's – May all murderesses get the torment they deserve!"' In the subsequent quarrel with Eustacia, Clym never admits that he too was in the house; nor does he later mention that fact to Thomasin.

The paragraph following the above quotation is a good example of the unexpected and penetrating leaps of imagination that make Hardy a great novelist because a great prose poet. 'The pupils of [Clym's] eyes, fixed steadfastly on blankness, were vaguely lit with an icy shine; his mouth had passed into the phase more or less imaginatively rendered in studies of Oedipus.' But Clym cannot fulfil the tragic role. 'The strangest deeds were possible to his mood. But they were not possible to his situation' (v, ii: 251). Eustacia wants to commit great tragic indiscretions with tragic consequences. But Clym is a reflective modern man incapable of sustaining (as the false rhetoric suggests) the rage of his imprecation, '"May all murderesses get the torment they deserve!"' He is effective only at self-torment.

The next chapter in which Clym rushes wildly home to accuse Eustacia, begins with paralysis:

> A consciousness of a vast impassivity in all which lay around
> him took possession even of Yeobright in his wild walk towards
> Alderworth. He had once before felt in his own person this over-
> powering of the fervid by the inanimate; but then it had tended
> to enervate a passion far sweeter than that which at present per-
> vaded him.   (v, iii: 252)

The vast impassivity of the heath enervated his love as now it
enervates his hatred for Eustacia. His mother, with whom he asso-
ciates the heath, blocks all his emotions. In Eustacia and Clym we
see the contrast between two noble modern types – the romantic
tragic hero and the reflective idealist.

In the quarrel scene our sympathy finally turns away from Clym
toward Eustacia as we see her step into the role of tragic heroine.
She has been restlessly destructive while waiting for this role; the
very traits that earlier seemed villainous now seem tragic. Clym's
accusatory presence is magnified through his appearance in the
mirror toward which her face is turned (a device taken over by
Lawrence for the fatal quarrel between Gerald and Gudrun near
the end of *Women in Love*). Clym loses our sympathy when he
accuses her of adeptness '"in a certain trade"'. Her defence shows
up his moral pretentiousness: '"I have not done what you suppose; but if to have done no harm at all is the only innocence
recognised, I am beyond forgiveness."' Eustacia gains our sympathy when her strength breaks down:

> 'O, O, O!' she cried, breaking down at last; and, shaking with
> sobs which choked her, she sank upon her knees. 'O, will you
> have done! O, you are too relentless – there's a limit to the cruelty
> of savages!'

Earlier she accuses him in words that ring truer than his: '"I have
lost all through you, but I have not complained"' (v, iii: 255–6). In
answer to his demand that she confess all, she remains defiant.

Caught up in passion, Eustacia, with the self-destructive instinct
of a tragic heroine, rushes toward her destiny with no thought for
the next moment, let alone for the settlement of property rights.
Clym, instead, weak in passion, has the self-preserving instinct of
the survivor. He moves to his mother's house, now his, where he
can grieve in comfort, waiting for Eustacia to initiate a reconciliation.

The novel traces Clym's sad non-fulfilment of his god-like

potentiality. In the end, having abandoned his radical ideals, he survives as an itinerant open-air preacher of 'unimpeachable' or conventional morality, who makes no great stir but is everywhere kindly received out of compassion. In the scene portrayed Clym's position on Rainbarrow, where Eustacia first appeared, recalls her vital presence in contrast to his tameness. The text he quotes is 1 Kings 2: 19–20 about King Solomon's acquiescence to his mother, which seems appropriate to Clym's character. But if we read on in the Biblical text, we find that Solomon orders the man his mother petitioned for killed. Does the choice of text reflect Clym's feeling that he appeared to love his mother but actually betrayed her?

Eustacia, we are told, 'had the passions and instincts which make a model goddess, that is, those which make not quite a model woman' (I, vii: 53). This disparity, which makes Clym too good for real life, makes her too bad because she is cut on too large a frame. But she is able in the events leading to her death to *create* the situations in which she can rise to her full stature, so that her corpse 'eclipsed all her living phases. . . . The stateliness of look which had been almost too marked for a dweller in a country domicile had at last found an artistically happy background' (V, ix: 293).

After her directionless departure from the house she shared with Clym, Eustacia rushes directly to her doom. She is in love with her tragic destiny; it is her only real love. Thus, she refuses two offers to leave the designated scene of her tragedy – the heath: it '"will be my death!"' she said earlier to Wildeve (I, ix: 69). Now she refuses the third offer, Wildeve's plan to facilitate her escape to Paris either with or without him. In refusing again to escape, this time to the city of her desires, Eustacia creates her tragic conclusion. She is making her way on a wildly rainy night to meet Wildeve, when suddenly she realizes that she cannot honourably accept his monetary help without eloping with him as his mistress. Then she displays her grandeur:

> 'He's not *great* enough for me to give myself to – he does not suffice for my desire! . . . If he had been a Saul or a Bonaparte – ah! But to break my marriage vow for him – it is too poor a luxury!' (V, vii: 275)

a statement suggesting she has not had sexual relations with Wildeve. Her reason for not accepting his offer is aesthetic rather than moral and would therefore have been impossible in Greek or even in Shakespearean tragedy where the *grandeur* of characters and events is not the problem.

'"Why should I not die if I wish"', she asks the stable boy who hides her grandfather's pistols upon noticing their fascination for her (v, iv: 261). Applying his technique of overdetermination, Hardy portrays her drowning both as suicide and accident. The constant emphasis on poor visibility suggests that the drowning was accidental. On the other hand, the pool in which Eustacia drowns belongs to a roaring dam that would have alerted her to danger.

Eustacia's movement toward death began ten pages back with the universalising cry of protest we will hear again from Henchard, Tess and Jude: '"How destiny has been against me! . . . I do not deserve my lot!"' (v, vii: 276). Characteristically Hardy on the same page suggests still another possible reason for Eustacia's impulse toward death. Susan Nunsuch, convinced that Eustacia has bewitched her ailing son, sticks pins into a wax effigy of her and melts it over the fire. A lesser artist would have made Eustacia catch a glimpse of the terrifying ritual. Instead Eustacia, as she leaves the house for her flight, sees only the 'distant light' from Susan's window – as though *unconsciously* aware of what was happening. The episode shows Hardy's powerful use of folklore to replicate the unconscious and add a mythical dimension to his realistic stories of modern life.

The tragic denouement is brought on by the old device of the mistimed or misplaced letter. Hardy negates his own plot device, however, by saying, as Eustacia steals out of the house, that 'even the receipt of Clym's letter [of reconciliation] would not have stopped her now' (v, vii: 274). Thus, as with the letter of confession Tess slides uselessly under Angel's door, Hardy throws the weight onto the psychological motivation.

As in a play all the main characters turn up at the pool where Eustacia has drowned. We may find particularly staged the arrival of Clym and Wildeve before the others, in time to hear together through the storm the sound of Eustacia's body falling into the pool. The playwright and storyteller must be allowed their devices as long as they pay off; and this one does pay off abundantly, since it presents a surprising new contrast between Clym and Wildeve.[9]

Like Eustacia, but in a paler way, the unattractive Wildeve is justified in the end as he turns into a selfless lover and tragic hero. At the sight of Eustacia's 'dark body . . . slowly borne by one of the backward currents', the impulsive Wildeve cries out, '"Oh my darling!"' and 'leaped into the boiling caldron'. The less impulsive Clym is about to leap in after Wildeve, but thinking of a wiser plan, he rushes around to a lower, more convenient entrance into the pool. He is no more effective than Wildeve at rescuing Eustacia.

It remains for the efficient Venn, who appears soon after, to drag out two men, the one's legs tightly embraced by the other. They turn out to be the two rivals, Clym and Wildeve (recalling ironically the loving embrace of George Eliot's drowned Tom and Maggie). Wildeve is dead; Clym survives. Venn finally comes up 'with an armful of wet drapery enclosing a woman's cold form, which was all that remained of the desperate Eustacia' (v, ix: 288–90). The description in the previous paragraph (echoing Shelley's *Adonais*, 'I am borne darkly, fearfully, afar') animates Eustacia's dead body through its abandonment to the current's movement. This final description instead emphasises the body's inertness, its tragic loss of all Eustacia's wonderful vitality.

In revising away from his original intention, Hardy turned his pastoral novel into the equivalent of a five-act tragedy with epilogue and psychologised the characters to a depth inappropriate for pastoral. Nevertheless, the novel remains a complex pastoral because the heath remains the novel's most powerful presence and because the major events take place outdoors on the heath. Mrs Yeobright, Wildeve and Eustacia die on the heath and even the bookish Clym in the end, after having worked on the heath as a furze-cutter, becomes an 'itinerant open-air preacher' (vi, iv: 315), marking with his ineffectualness a contrast between the unheroic survivor and the tragic heroine.

The Woodlanders (1887), which appeared nine years and five novels after *The Return of the Native*, is the least understood and the most underrated of Hardy's major novels (a few critics even consider it minor). It has not been understood because, with a few exceptions, critics have not been able to define its genre, so have not been able to account for the report in the *Life* that 'in after years [Hardy] often said that in some respects *The Woodlanders* was his best novel' (185). Identification of genre is crucial in order to raise the right expectations for understanding and evaluation, and such identification was already recognised as a problem in *The Spectator* review of 26 March 1887.

This is a very powerful book, and as disagreeable as it is powerful. It is a picture of shameless falsehood, levity, and infidelity,
followed by no true repentance, and yet crowned at the end with
perfect success; nor does Mr Hardy seem to paint his picture in
any spirit of indignation that redeems the moral drift of the book.
He does not impress us as even personally disposed to resent the
good-natured profligacy of his hero; and the letter which Fitzpiers
sends his wife towards the close of the story, – the letter which
opens the way to the renewal of their married life, – has in it an
unashamed air, by which Grace, if she had been all that Mr Hardy
wishes us to believe her, would have been more revolted than
gratified. . . . [Such] indifference to the moral effect . . . lowers the
art of his works.[10]

Skipping to the present, we find that Penny Boumelha, in *Thomas
Hardy and Women* (1985), begins her discussion of *The Woodlanders*
in a similar vein:

It is difficult to say what kind of a novel *The Woodlanders* is;
it draws on genres so widely disparate as to be at times
incompatible. . . . Such disparate formal elements point to the
novel's major characteristic, the uncertainties of genre, rapid sub-
stitutions of points of view and abrupt shifts of tone that make it
unsettling to read.   (98–9)

Another difficulty stems from the novel's clear affinity to pastoral
and yet its problematic antipastoralism. Hence the disappointment
of Michael Squires who, in *The Pastoral Novel*, sees that *The
Woodlanders* possesses a 'tone quite unlike that of [Hardy's] earlier
pastoral novels'. It 'is gloomy and ironic'. He questions the novel's
moral coherence because 'the passion of Mrs Charmond and
Fitzpiers' becomes 'more attractive to the reader than perhaps it
should if we are to remain persuaded by the novel's moral vision',
its 'ethic of man and nature fusing harmoniously' (150, 164, 155).
Squires does not see that Marty and Giles and the pastoral ethic
they represent is itself under critical scrutiny.

Michael Millgate sees Fitzpiers' story as 'ultimately comic' and
Giles's as 'ultimately tragic' (*Hardy: His Career as Novelist*, 258);
whereas I shall argue that Giles's story is at least tragicomic because treated with ironical sympathy. Ian Gregor goes far in seeing
The Woodlanders as, in its sequence to *Mayor of Casterbridge*, 'elegiac,

rather than heroic', a development which 'looks like a loss of power'. Gregor proceeds to establish the novel's power in other terms, in a detachment of authorial consciousness leading, as I shall argue, to the sustained tone of irony that is the book's triumph. Gregor perceives ironies and even at one point a touch of *'comédie noire'*, which I approve, but he fails to perceive 'black comedy' in the hut episode ending in Giles's death. He quotes, as suggesting failed tragedy, Hardy's curious remark that if Grace '"could have done a really self-abandoned, impassioned thing . . . he would have made a fine tragic ending to the book"' (*Great Web*), 139–40, 164, 155). Yet it was Hardy who gave Grace her qualities. The motives of all the characters are not grand but either petty or unrealistically high-minded.

Hardy clearly did not intend tragedy, but rather I think dark comedy on the model of *Measure for Measure* and *Cymbeline*, Shakespeare plays named in this novel. *The Woodlanders* resembles both dark comedies in the general unattractiveness of its characters and situations. Just as in *Measure for Measure* Isabella meets Angelo when she comes to plead for her brother's life, so Grace first meets Fitzpiers when she comes to plead for Gammer Oliver; and Fitzpier's sudden turn from asceticism to lust parallels Angelo's shocking transformation. But *The Woodlanders* is even darker than Shakespeare's comedy because there is no omniscient duke to make all right in the end.

Mary Jacobus, in a perceptive essay, also calls the novel's mood 'elegiac', as manifested by 'its attenuation of vigour into quiescence, passion into elegy'. *The Woodlanders* exhibits, she says, 'the failure of pastoral'.[11] The elegiac mood is certainly present in the depictions of Giles and Marty but subordinate, I think, to an all-encompassing irony which gives the novel a savage energy. In the line of pastoral novels beginning with *Under the Greenwood Tree*, there is a steady complication and darkening of vision which culminates in what I consider to be the antipastoralism of *The Woodlanders*. The most obvious sign is Hardy's view of nature which is, as in *Return of the Native*, Darwinian; but here the descriptions of nature are in a new way mainly ugly and sinister. I shall argue, then, for this novel as antipastoral dark comedy and a triumph in that genre. Once we read it that way, all the details fall into place.

Hardy first projected this novel in the 1870s as a pastoral on the model of *Under the Greenwood Tree*. When he returned to the story in 1885, he took a new view of the country; for while the earlier pastoral novels are retrospective, *The Woodlanders* takes place around

1878–9,[12] so close to the time of writing as to make the pastoral landscape, the woodland of Little Hintock, anachronistic in a world of busy roads, railroads and industry.

In the opening paragraph, the sentimental 'rambler who, for old association's sake', enters this woodland, represents the urban reader who chooses to move backward in place and time. The point of view quickly changes, however, to that of the hard-boiled barber from Abbot's Cernel, a small enough town, who is travelling, in order to buy Marty South's hair for Mrs Charmond, to the minuscule village of Little Hintock. '"Tis such a little small place"', says the coachwoman, '"that, as a town gentleman, you'd need have a candle and lantern to find it if ye don't know where 'tis"' (I: 42).[13] The survival of such a place is anachronistic as is the barbaric custom of hair selling, which is somewhat less shocking than the wife selling that opens *The Mayor of Casterbridge*. Especially anachronistic is the barber's bland assumption in addressing Marty that she has no choice but to obey the lady of the manor and sell her hair on terms fixed by the barber. The modern world impinges when we learn that the recently arrived lady is no lady and has no feudal rights, her now defunct industrialist husband having bought Hintock House for cash.

The remoteness and enclosure of pastoral is established by such phrases as 'It was one of those sequestered spots outside the gates of the world' (I: 44). But in this novel pastoral is introduced only to be subverted. For example, Chapter XIX begins with 'flowers of late April' and 'the rush of sap in the veins of the trees' (183). Caught up in a pastoral mood, the outsider Fitzpiers thinks of settling here with Grace as he listens to the sound of tree barking. Then we are abruptly reminded that 'each tree [is] doomed to the flaying process' like an 'executioner's victim' (184). Fitzpiers and Grace meet on this idyllic landscape, but Grace walks away with Marty 'between the spectral arms of the peeled trees' (192).

In order to show the movement away from the pastoralism of the earlier novels, let me begin with the question of fathers. There are no fathers in *Far from the Madding Crowd* and *Return of the Native* and the father in *Under the Greenwood Tree* is pliant. It is a sign of antipastoralism that in *The Woodlanders* Grace is dominated by an authoritarian, intrusive father; for pastoralism is associated with a non-authoritarian maternal principle. To be sure there are no proper mothers either in these novels; there are only Fancy's and Grace's stepmothers and Mrs Yeobright who tries to exert authority but is disobeyed. In the first three pastoral novels, nature serves as the maternal principle.

Not so in *The Woodlanders*, where nature is too brutally engaged in the Darwinian struggle for existence to seem maternal. The Darwinism of *Return of the Native* is different; it suggests ubiquitous fertility: 'independent worlds of ephemerons were passing their time in mad carousal, some in the air, some on the hot ground and vegetation, some in the tepid and stringy water of a nearly dried pool' (IV, v: 215–16). Here instead is nature in *The Woodlanders*: 'the creaking sound of two overcrowded branches in the neighbouring wood, which were rubbing each other into wounds' (III: 54). This recalls the nature descriptions in the poems, as does this:

> Here, as everywhere, the Unfulfilled Intention, which makes life what it is, was as obvious as it could be among the depraved crowds of a city slum. The leaf was deformed, ... the lichen ate the vigour of the stalk, and the ivy slowly strangled to death the promising sapling.   (VII: 93)

In other words, the country is no better than the city – the reverse of the pastoral message.

Later we read, 'Except at midday the sun was not seen complete by the Hintock people, but rather in the form of numerous little stars staring through the leaves' (XX: 193). It has not been sufficiently noticed that the novel is played out either in nocturnal darkness or in daytime semi-darkness.[14]

On the pastoral side there are the idyllic scenes in which Giles and Marty figure as nature spirits:

> Winterborne's fingers were endowed with a gentle conjuror's touch in spreading the roots of each little tree ... 'How they sigh directly we put 'em upright,' ... said Marty. ... She erected one of the young pines into its hole, and held up her finger; the soft musical breathing instantly set in.   (VIII: 106)

There is an exaggerated gulf, not found in the earlier pastoral novels, between nature as brutal and nature as superidyllic – a gulf which drains the superidyllic of vigour. Despite the sexual symbolism of erecting the pine into its hole, Giles and Marty seem curiously sexless – a decline from the nymphs and satyrs of classical pastoral or even from the sexiness of Dick and Fancy in *Greenwood Tree* and the lovers in *Madding Crowd*.

In *The Woodlanders* the satyr turns out to be the intellectual outsider Dr Fitzpiers, who began as an austere follower of Idealist
philosophers. I have already alluded to the scene in which Fitzpiers
discovers sexual desire; it is an extraordinary scene of lovers' meeting, disturbing in its use of an almost perverse voyeurism. Grace is
shown into Dr Fitzpier's reception room and finds him asleep on
the sofa. She 'stood gazing in great embarrassment', as though she
had caught him in bed. Turning her back upon him, she sees in a
mirror 'that the eyes of the reflected image were open, gazing
wonderingly at her'. An 'indescribable thrill passed through her'.
But when she turns she finds him 'asleep' as before (xviii: 175–6). The
disorienting sexual vibrations set up by this scene characterise their
subsequent meetings, meetings in which Grace feels more fear than
love of him.

Only Fitzpiers understands the true meaning of the 'old Midsummer eve' ritual,[15] in which under moonlight maidens cast spells to
get a glimpse of their future husbands, the young bachelors having
obligingly taken up positions in the shadows surrounding the
moonlit maidens. In another example of erotic voyeurism, Hardy
shows Fitzpiers 'intently observing Grace, who was in the full rays
of the moon' (xx: 194–5). Excitedly pushing aside Giles, who makes
no protest, Fitzpiers catches Grace in his arms, who 'rested on him
like one utterly mastered' (198). The sado-masochism looks toward
Tess's relation with Alec. Fitzpiers then transfers his attention to
the village girl Suke Damson whom satyr-like he chases across the
countryside – a chase as erotic as anything in Lawrence, ending in
intercourse. The outsiders Fitzpiers and Mrs Charmond may not
know about trees, but they understand better than the pastoral
characters the fundamental sexual force in nature.

Giles' lack of protest shows how Giles and Marty give up all too
easily in the sexual contest. Marty, who refused to sell her hair
because she loves Giles, sells it after hearing Melbury say he in-
tends Grace for Giles to repay a moral debt he owes Giles's dead
father. Afterward the shorn Marty works beside Giles as though
she were another man. Giles seems unaware of her love since
she never presents herself as a woman. In the same way Grace, as
the novel suggests, might have married Giles had he pursued her
more aggressively.

Giles renounces his claim to Grace after Melbury indicates that
he no longer considers him suitable. But even earlier, when Melbury
as a sign of favour sends him to meet Grace on her return from

boarding-school, he carries with him a specimen apple tree to sell and is so 'fixed to the spot by his apple-tree' that he 'could not advance to meet her' (v: 77). Later Giles is up in South's tree pruning it, when Grace passing beneath calls up to him that her father is probably right in breaking off their engagement. ' "Very well," he answered in an enfeebled voice.' His high perch in the tree enfeebles him for sexual pursuit.

> She added with emotion in her tone. 'For myself I would have married you – some day – I think.' . . . He made no reply. . . . Thus he remained till the fog and the night had completely inclosed him from her view.

Such isolating fogs develop the antipastoral theme of modern isolation which pervades the novel. 'Had Giles', Hardy asks, 'immediately come down from the tree to her, would she have contined in that filial, acquiescent frame of mind?' (xⅢ: 141). The tree, a traditional symbol of fertility, becomes in this novel a block to sexuality.

On South's death, Giles loses lifehold leases to his cottages because he has postponed renewing them in order to prune the tree that was threatening South's sanity. Giles, we are told, does not allow the loss of his cottages and of Grace to 'affect his outer conduct' (142). Although Giles is highly competent at his pastoral tasks, his incompetence at love and business and his stifling of normal emotional response to loss are not admirable – especially if we compare his specialised competence to the all-round competence of Gabriel Oak.

Marty instead is competent in the manner of Venn. She is ubiquitous and very good at doing things for the right people, even if not for herself. She helps bring Fitzpiers back to Grace by writing to him about the origin of Mrs Charmond's luxuriant hair, and she takes Grace, in time to save her from dying of Giles's disease, the medicine Fitzpiers left for her in Giles's hut.

I said earlier that class distinctions do not much matter in pastoral, but in *The Woodlanders* we encounter an ugly economic and social situation. Giles's cottages revert to Mrs Charmond's estate which demolishes them. Again in *Tess* and in his essays, Hardy complains about the demolition of cottages and the consequent break-up of village communities. The feudal obeisance to Mrs Charmond shows how far by 1878–9 the contradiction had swung between symbol and reality, for she is not aristocratic and has no sense of feudal obligation. She lives in Hintock House in meaningless isolation, knowing neither the local gentry nor the villagers and escaping to the Continent as often as she can.

Melbury, who crawls before her, has better 'blood' than she. For that matter Melbury and Giles are equal socially; they are separated only by money. Money counts most in this apparently pastoral environment. Money creates the social mobility that caused Melbury to send Grace to an elegant boarding-school to advance her socially. The portrayal of conflict in class and manners – through Grace's snobbish worship of Mrs Charmond and Giles's defeat because of his uncouth Christmas party – belongs to comedy of manners not pastoral. The model for pastoral is Bathsheba's long supper table where all kinds of manners have their proper place in an integrated community. Hence the verse epigraph to *The Woodlanders*, composed by Hardy, which says that it takes not only trees but also the right kind of hearts to make pastoral.

There can be no more grovelling instance of snobbery in the English novel than Melbury's wishful vision of the day when Grace as Mrs Fitzpiers, relative to defunct nobility, will drive by him in her carriage:

> 'If you should ever meet me then, Grace, you can drive past me, looking the other way. I shouldn't expect you to speak to me, or wish such a thing – unless it happened to be in some lonely private place where 'twouldn't lower 'ee at all.'   (XXIII: 213)

The triumph of class division in *The Woodlanders* signals its antipastoral direction. Its plot parallels that of *Under the Greenwood Tree*, where Fancy Day's boarding-school education and her father's social ambition temporarily block the consummation of the love between her and simple warmhearted Dick Dewey. But in *Greenwood Tree* class division swiftly crumbles before the general benevolence; not so in *Woodlanders*, where there is little benevolence.

If as I have suggested *Under the Greenwood Tree* is a pastoral fable about organic community, *The Woodlanders* is an antipastoral fable about modern isolation. In his Introduction to the Penguin edition, Ian Gregor discusses the 'profound isolation' at the novel's heart

(16). Mrs Charmond sits alone in her huge house. Fitzpiers begins by seeking isolation. Grace is a returned native, isolated like Clym by her education. She feels herself, writes Gregor beginning with Hardy's words, '"in mid-air between two storeys of society," ill at ease in the world of the woodlanders, disenchanted with the world of her husband'(18).

In his book *The Great Web*, Gregor argues that beneath these isolations there remains a fundamentally unifying 'great web', as suggested by Hardy's memorable poetic passage on Giles and Marty:

> Hardly anything could be more isolated or more self-contained than the lives of these two walking here in the lonely hour before day.... And yet their lonely courses formed no detached design at all, but were part of a pattern in the great web of human doings then weaving in both hemispheres from the White Sea to Cape Horn. (Hardy, III: 59; quoted 144–5)

The passage applies better to a later work *The Dynasts* than to *The Woodlanders*, the action of which does not develop this sense of global pattern. The solitary lives of Giles and Marty connect them with the natural environment, but this very connection isolates them from the other characters and society, from 'human' as distinguished from natural 'doings'.

If we recall the novels dealing with failed idealists, Fitzpier's case becomes ironic. For his idealism has to do with Idealist epistemology rather than conduct: '"I am in love"', he says to Giles, '"with something in my own head, and no thing-in-itself outside it at all"' (XVI: 165). He talks like a modern intellectual as Clym never does. Fitzpiers' solipsism frees him for an unscrupulous sexuality that contrasts ironically with the sexual ineffectiveness of such sentimental idealists as Boldwood, Clym, Angel and Giles. Was this novel originally entitled *Fitzpiers at Hintock* because Hardy's main purpose was to satirise a new kind of idealist, a destructive intruder with a mind opposite to that of the pastoral community?

The most savage satire on idealism occurs as Fitzpiers rides to join Mrs Charmond on the mare Giles gave Grace, with his wife Grace watching, knowing where he is heading; as Fitzpiers rides he murmurs to himself, of all inappropriate things, lines from 'Epipsychidion', Shelley's poem on Platonic love. Grace turns for relief to Giles, who has just appeared, and finds him looking and smelling 'like Autumn's very brother' – another damaging idealisation which blocks her 'sudden impulse to be familiar with him'. Grace's attempt to solve her problem by lapsing back into pastoralism – 'she became the crude country girl of her latent early instincts' (XXVIII: 261) – is self-deceptive.

If we recall such bold fatherless heroines as Bathsheba, Eustacia and even Thomasin, we must recognise that Grace's portrayal as a snobbish prig pathologically obedient to a domineering father reverses Hardy's pattern so blatantly as to indicate a satirical intent. There is something ridiculous in the way Grace, like a rubber ball, lets herself be bounced by her father first to Giles, then to Fitzpiers, then back again to Giles after Fitzpiers' infidelity, then back again to Fitzpiers after the divorce suit fails. It is ridiculous and pathological that Grace, after her father's meddling has messed up her life, should still follow his advice, 'reverently believing in her father's sound judgment and knowledge, as good girls', says Hardy with unmistakable satire, 'are wont to do' (XXXVIII: 341). The portrayals of Grace and Giles combine satire with depth psychology.

While hope for the divorce suit is alive, Grace on her father's instructions encourages Giles to the point where he holds her hand. Her remonstrance to him is zany: '"I think we have gone as far as we ought to go at present – and far enough to satisfy my poor father that we are the same as ever"' (344). For once Giles acts unscrupulously, withholding from her the news that the divorce suit has failed so he can claim the passionate kiss he waited for so long. '"Giles"', she says afterward, '"if you had only shown half the boldness before I married that you show now, you would have carried me off for your own, first instead of second"' (XXXIX: 356). Again we are reminded that cruelty is a necessary element in love and that Grace has been a victim of Giles's lack of masculine aggressiveness. Giles's immediate remorse – 'the feeling of his cruelty mounted higher and higher' (356) – may account for his overcompensation in the disastrous episode at his cottage.

The paternal voice returns melodramatically: '"Take out that arm! . . . Giles, don't say anything to me, but go away!"' (357). Fitzpiers, it turned out, did not do Grace '"*enough* harm"' (358) to justify divorce even under the new law of 1878.[16] He can legally, after his break on the Continent with Felice Charmond and her subsequent murder by a disappointed lover, reclaim his marital rights. Hardy is mocking both marriage and the divorce laws.

Like Giles, Grace lacks adequate emotional response:

Her jealousy was languid even to death. . . . In truth, her ante-
nuptial regard for Fitzpiers had been rather of the quality of awe
towards a superior being than of tender solicitude for a
lover.   (xxviii: 258)

From the start her attraction to Fitzpiers was, as we have seen,
masochistic: 'he seemed to be her ruler' (xxiv: 219). Like other
Hardy heroines, Grace is excited sexually by the scoundrel rather
than by the gentle friend. It is not certain that she has come to 'love'
Fitzpiers even in the end when she returns to him. Perhaps Hardy
is leaving in question the definition of 'love'.

Upon news of Fitzpiers' imminent arrival after the failure of the
divorce suit, Grace in a panic flees into the dark wood where the
whole action has taken place. But now, because the darkness is
intensified by lush summer foliation, the dark wood seems to symbolise her erotic unconscious. Although she ostensibly flees to join
a girlfriend, her unconscious leads her to Giles's cottage: 'It was the
place she sought' (xl: 364).

Here begins the weirdest and most memorable episode in the
novel. Yet its wild implausibility has set many critics against it.
Once more there has been a failure to perceive genre and tone – a
tone continually changing, mixing admiration and pity with scorn.
We cannot help admiring Giles's chivalry. But how much does Hardy
intend us to admire it? 'No one, neither man nor dog, should have
to be that loyal', says Irving Howe with annoyance (*Thomas Hardy*,
104). Though admirable Giles's 'final act of self-sacrifice', says
Michael Millgate, perceiving the mixture, 'has often been regarded
as excessive, as almost comic in its strict observation of the propri-
eties' (*Hardy: Career as Novelist*, 257–8). Giles's chivalry has, I think,
gone berserk because it supports conventions Hardy clearly wants
us to scorn. Plausibility is not the appropriate criterion by which to
judge a scene where exaggeration is necessary for the satire and
psychological penetration.

It is Giles (this has not been sufficiently noticed) who sets up the
absurd scenario for the protection of Grace's virtue. It is he who
decides that she will inhabit the cottage alone, lock herself in and
pass him food through the window, while he, already gravely ill,
sleeps outside in the rain. Grace remains uneasy with this arrangement, which is not what she unconsciously desired in making her
way here. But as always she is too passive to break through the
arrangement or to ascertain where Giles is sleeping. '"Appearance

is no matter"', she says on arriving, '"when the reality is right"' (XL: 365). But he insists on preserving appearances where there is no one to witness them.

It is Grace who declares her love. '"Why should I not speak out? You know what I feel for you – what I have felt for no other living man"'. She continues with words full of sexual innuendo: '"I am a woman, and you are a man. I cannot speak more plainly. I yearn to let you in, but . . . "'. When Giles has failed to answer, she calls out, '"O, come in – come in!"' . . . '"I don't want to keep you out any longer. . . . *Come to me, dearest! I don't mind what they say or what they think of us any more*"' (XLI: 372–3, 375). But in response to this passionate invitation, 'a feeble voice reached her, floating upon the weather as though a part of it. "Here I am – all right!"' (375). We recall the feeble voice that earlier floated down to Grace from the tree-top when Giles did not descend to claim her. Paradoxically harmony with nature produces in Giles idealised disembodiment.

Nevertheless Grace takes the whole blame upon herself when with 'dreadful enlightenment' she cries out, '"Can it be that cruel propriety is killing the dearest heart . . . !"' (379). She has learned that in emergencies propriety can become immoral – a lesson that will later enable her to separate herself from her skirt to get free of the man-trap. Now she abandons propriety when, after conveying home the feverishly unconscious Giles, she removes his wet clothes, bathes and kisses him. It is typical of this novel's method that our growing admiration for Grace is undercut by a comparison at this point with an earlier scene in which Mrs Charmond, not worrying about appearances, hid the wounded Fitzpiers in her house, nursing him back to health, whereas Grace's nursing comes too late.

Abandoning discretion, Grace goes so far as to fetch her husband to treat Giles. When Fitzpiers, having announced Giles's imminent death, asks Grace whether he is to draw from the situation '"the extremest inference"', she replies defiantly, '"Yes," . . . "the extremest inference"' (XLIII: 388). The denouement brings to the surface all that Grace throughout this episode has repressed in the way of capacity for sexual feeling and heroic action. It is the intensity of Grace's and Giles's repression that gives the scene the perverse eroticism whereby sickness and a love-death substitute for consummation. Far from being a failure, the cottage episode concentrates the novel's conflicting tones and values as does no other single episode.

Grace's new decisiveness has actually been prepared for in two earlier sections. In the first, a showdown about Fitzpiers with Mrs Charmond, the older woman feels herself 'dominated mentally and emotionally by this simple school-girl', who tells her, '"*you* will suffer most"', for '"you *love* him!"' (xxxiii: 297). In a scene remarkable for its inventiveness, the two rivals get lost in the woods where again the younger woman takes charge. They spend the night locked in each other's arms from which position Mrs Charmond whispers in Grace's ear that Fitzpiers has '"had"' her. Grace is 'thunderstruck', but remains solicitous (xxxii: 302).

In the second section, word of Fitzpiers' accident has got out before he returns home. Suke Damson and Mrs Charmond appear at the house to inquire anxiously after him (Mrs Charmond will later find him at her window). Realising that their 'relations with him were as close as her own *without its conventionality*', Grace conducts them to his empty bedroom, saying with uncharacteristic wit, '"Wives all, let's enter together!"' (xxxv: 321; my italics). This scene represents a big step in Grace's maturing.

After Giles's death, Grace returns to pastoralism by joining Marty to strew flowers regularly on his grave. '"He ought to have married *you*, Marty"', she says. '"You and he could speak in a tongue that nobody else knew . . . the tongue of the trees and fruits and flowers themselves."' Marty demurs: '"The one thing he never spoke of to me was love; nor I to him"' (xliv: 399) Marty's and Grace's asexual relation to Giles is criticised in the narrator's statement: 'As no anticipation of gratified affection had been in existence while he was with them there was none to be disappointed now that he had gone' (398).

As a counterpoint to the pastoral theme, Fitzpiers at the same time woos Grace with obstinate persistence against all the odds. His persistence contrasts with Giles's readiness to surrender. It is brilliantly ironic and psychologically right that Fitzpiers becomes sexually excited by Grace's avowal of cohabitation with Giles (though Marty, who regularly passed by the cottage, later confirms Grace's virtue to Melbury and Fitzpiers).

Fitzpiers is now portrayed as contrite and accommodating. Only a few statements like the following cast doubt on his sincerity: 'A subtlist in emotions' (xlv: 406), he was enjoying for a time the masochistic pleasures he had inflicted upon Grace and took 'almost also an artistic pleasure in being the yearning *innamorato* of a woman he once had deserted' (xlvi: 417). Like all great seducers, he seems more interested in the game of seduction than in its object, and we sense that in a relation based from the start on power the tables might turn after his victory.

Significantly Grace does not consult her father before agreeing to meet Fitzpiers, guiltily keeping their meetings secret from him. But when Fitzpiers asks her whether she might return to him, she reverts to her pastoral idealism, indicating that she will continue to '"go with Marty to Giles's grave"'. Fitzpier's suggestion, '"I think you might get your heart out of that grave"' is right. The sign of this is the description of Grace's mind as having 'returned to poor Giles's "frustrate ghost"' (XLVI: 415–16) – a quotation from Browning's 'The Statue and the Bust', in which the lovers are, as I have said, chided for *not* consummating their adulterous union.

The impasse between the pastoral and seduction themes is broken by the clever contrivance of the man-trap set by Suke's jealous husband to catch Fitzpiers. Rushing in the direction of a woman's scream, Fitzpiers finds Grace's skirt in the trap's cruel jaws and fears the worst. His grief is sincere and affecting. But his skirtless wife soon appears from the bushes and his next act, which is to embrace and kiss her passionately, is 'irresistible' to this skirtless Grace, who 'made no further attempt at reserve' (XLVII: 427, 429).

The symbolism of Grace's skirtlessness is appropriately comic since the Grace–Fitzpiers story ends comically with a marriage renewed. Although Grace wraps her skirt around her, it is a psychologically skirtless Grace who proceeds to the end. She does not say no to Fitzpiers' proposal that she join him in the Midlands where he has bought a practice, nor to his proposal that she spend the night with him in a hotel. When her father appears with a search party, Grace refuses his offer to take her home. Melbury is angry because he has not been told earlier what was happening. The filial bond has at last been cut.

Melbury's reflections afterwards are full of nasty sexual predictions:

> 'Let her take him back to her bed if she will! . . . But let her bear in mind that the woman walks and laughs somewhere at this very moment whose neck he'll be coling next year as he does hers to-night; and as he did Felice Charmond's last year; and Suke Damson's the year afore! . . . It's a forlorn hope for her; and God knows how it will end!' (XLVIII: 435)

His prediction is confirmed by the rustics accompanying him, a sign that Hardy wants us to understand that Fitzpiers probably will return to philandering. In a letter of 1889, Hardy wrote about *The Woodlanders*, 'You have probably observed that the *ending* of the story, as hinted rather than stated, is that the heroine is doomed to an unhappy life with an inconstant husband' (*Letters*, I: 195). Happy ending? As much as is possible in the 'real' world of black comedy. Would a lifetime of worshipping at Giles's grave, or of filial obedience, have made Grace happier? *The Woodlanders* seems particularly modern in the open-endedness of the Grace–Fitzpiers story.

But the novel ends with Marty, and is that conclusion open-ended? The answer depends on our judgement of Marty and our interpretation of the last two paragraphs. Marty is certainly the novel's most attractive character and since she speaks the novel's last and most beautiful words, many readers come away with the feeling that the pastoral values she enunciates, and has represented throughout, are the book's final univocal message, yielding a closed ending.

The rustics, after hearing Melbury's unpleasant prediction, bring back the pastoral theme by beholding, as they pass the graveyard, 'a motionless figure standing by the gate' (XLVIII: 437). Marty has been waiting patiently for Grace to keep their appointment, but gathering from the rustics' talk what has happened she proceeds alone to the grave where she speaks the novel's final paragraph:

> 'Now, my own, own love,' she whispered, 'you are mine, and only mine; for she has forgot 'ee at last, although for her you died! But I – wherever I get up I'll think of 'ee, and whenever I lie down I'll think of 'ee again. Whenever I plant the young larches I'll think that none can plant as you planted; .... If ever I forget your name let me forget home and heaven! ... But no, no, my love, I never can forget 'ee; for you was a good man, and did good things!' (439)

The previous paragraph, however, raises doubts about Marty's pastoral values when it says of her that 'the contours of womanhood [are] so undeveloped as to be scarcely perceptible in her'. In the moonlight 'she touched sublimity at points, and looked almost like a being who had rejected with indifference the attribute of sex for the loftier quality of abstract humanism' (438–9). She possesses nobility at the price of sexuality. By one set of values this is admirable. But by an antithetical set of values we ought to wonder if the price is not too high, since we were expected to disapprove of repressed sexuality in Grace and Giles and even to sympathise a bit with foolish, vain Felice Charmond because she loved unreservedly.

We may even be inclined to question Marty's last statement. Giles was undoubtedly 'a good man', but did he always do 'good things'? Giles, after all, caused Marty's desexualisation by not looking upon her as a woman. It could be argued that Giles, by not wooing Grace more aggressively, harmed her more than Fitzpiers did. In Hardy's continuing critique of idealism, Giles is in a class with Clym and Angel – idealists who fail their women. Barnet, in Hardy's sardonic short story 'Fellow-Townsmen' (*Wessex Tales*), continually fails his women; he may seem an idealist, but his high-mindedness masks a lack of guts leading to a life of mediocre non-fulfilment.

The Woodlanders is, I am arguing, dialectical and, therefore, open-ended, in giving almost equal weight to two opposing sets of values – sexuality that goes with moral ambiguousness and the ability to survive in this flawed antipastoral world, and asexuality that goes with a nobility that by the late 1870s can survive only in the remote, protected circumstances of pastoral. Only in this partly antipastoral novel is sexuality cut off from pastoral. The novel tilts, I think, toward the antipastoral solution arrived at by Grace when she chooses her potent if imperfect husband over Giles's dead perfection and by Grace and Fitzpiers who are leaving the rustic enclosure for the industrial Midlands. Marty's final pastoral perfection, instead, depends on a stasis so posed – 'this solitary and silent girl stood there in the moonlight, a straight slim figure, clothed in a plaitless gown' (438) – as to remind us of a funerary statue.

Such ironic complexities, such shifts in tone and criteria of judgement, such revaluations of values through subjection of pastoral values to critical scrutiny, such discords between pastoral and antipastoral, comedy and dark comedy must be discerned in order to earn for *The Woodlanders* a secure place among Hardy's major novels, though it is entirely different from the other novels. It is different not because it mixes genres (most of the novels, as I have shown, mix genres), but because of the genres mixed and the jarring nature of the mixture – the surprising way in which one genre subverts the other.

5

The Minimisation of Sexuality

Exceptional in Hardy, the minimisation of sexuality is apparent in *The Mayor of Casterbridge* (1886) and in Hardy's last novel *The Well-Beloved* (1897). A few critics have recently noticed something special about Hardy's treatment of sexuality in *The Mayor of Casterbridge*. To take only two examples, J. Hillis Miller, in *Hardy: Distance and Desire* (1970) speaks of the book as 'a nightmare of frustrated desire', of sexual desire mixed with desire for possession (148); while T. R. Wright, in *Hardy and the Erotic* (1989), describes Henchard's relationship with Farfrae as 'never an avowedly homosexual relationship, but Henchard's manliness is clearly more complex than he cares to admit' (78). I would like to qualify these perceptions by noting a minimum of sexual feeling in the novel as a whole and almost an absence of it in the main character Henchard; so that talk of frustrated desire or homosexual desire is not entirely applicable. Ian Gregor describes *The Mayor* as 'one of the very few major novels ... where sexual relationships are not ... the dominant element' (*Great Web*, 119). This turn away from sexuality in the novel as a whole is unusual in Hardy and may explain why Lawrence in his *Study of Hardy* says little about *The Mayor of Casterbridge*.

To be sure the idealists, Clym, Giles and Angel seem low in sexual drive and Hardy's criticism of them seems to include a criticism of their low sexuality, even though the 'villains' – Wildeve, Fitzpiers and Alec – are better endowed sexually. But Henchard presents a different case in that he is not an idealist, is even something of a 'villain', and has the energy and aggressiveness which would lead us to expect a vigorous sexuality. Yet it is difficult to believe on the evidence shown that Michael Henchard can ever have been in love with his wife Susan, and we know that he fell into a probably sexual relationship with Lucetta (explicitly sexual in the manuscript[1]) not out of love or lust but out of gratitude to her for having saved his life when he was ill in Jersey. In the novel we see only his desire to escape these women. When later he decides to marry Lucetta, a

127

project interrupted by his need to remarry Susan, his motive in both cases is pure moral obligation without anticipation of sexual pleasure. (His pursuit of Lucetta becomes more heated when he has to compete with Farfrae.) Henchard's lack of sexual feeling throws the emphasis on his moral obligation to these women, while the minimisation of sexuality in the novel as a whole emphasises moral and public questions and indeed the novel's tragic dimensions.

Susan figures on her reappearance as a ghost ('Mrs Henchard was so pale that the boys called her "The Ghost"'), which she is in two senses. She is the ghost of a past crime, the wife sale, but she is also ghostly in her lack of sexual vitality. 'He pressed on the preparations for his union, or rather reunion, with this pale creature', feeling 'no amatory fire'.[2] But this pale creature is deceiving him since she is remarrying only for the sake of her daughter whom she passes off as the Elizabeth-Jane he gave away. Only after Susan's death does he learn from a letter she leaves that his daughter died and that this Elizabeth-Jane is Newson's daughter.

The wife sale scene at the beginning sets the tone. Henchard's mind is entirely on the economic drag of wife and daughter: '"if I were a free man again I'd be worth a thousand pound before I'd done o't"' (I: 7). We see also his tragic flaw, his lack of moderation, in the explosive drunken action which he regrets the next day, a pattern he will repeat even when not under the influence of liquor. The wife sale itself is not given the erotic colouring it might have had. Newson's motive in purchasing Susan might be kindness no less than sexual interest, as shown by his gentle considerateness.

Hardy's foreshortening of time, so that Susan's return with the grown-up Elizabeth-Jane follows upon Henchard's penitential oath the day after the wife sale, shows that the consequences of the crime begin immediately and will have no end. In revising, Hardy made the wife sale particularly outrageous by deleting precedents for wife selling which Henchard cites in his defence.[3] The wife sale cannot be laid entirely to impulse, for Michael has, says Susan, '"talked this nonsense in public places before"' (I: 8). Clearly Henchard has chosen the pursuit of money and power over the pleasures of sexuality. His penitential oath to avoid alcohol for twenty-one years furthers his chosen pursuit, as does his abstinence from women with the exception of Lucetta. '"No wife could I hear of in all that time"', he tells Farfrae, '"and being by nature something of a woman-hater, I have found it no hardship to keep mostly at a distance from the sex"' (XII: 60).

Henchard's asceticism proves useful for the accumulation of money and is notably a bourgeois characteristic, as described by Max Weber in his seminal work *The Protestant Ethic and the Spirit of Capitalism*.[4] Yet Henchard hardly seems bourgeois, what with his country mentality ('he had . . . received the education of Achilles', that is, no education; XII: 58), his rough, irregular ways of doing business and his feudal relation to his employees. 'We have little sense of the class to which Henchard has risen', says a socially oriented critic like John Goode (*Hardy: Offensive Truth*, 82). Of the two, Donald Farfrae, who has a normal if tepid sex life, is the bourgeois. Perhaps we are seeing two phases of capitalism, the early heroic and the developed.

It is difficult to believe that a man so virile in body and in superabundance of energy should show so little sexual interest. At the time of his fall, every one marvelled at 'how admirably he had used his one talent of energy to create a position of affluence out of absolutely nothing' (XXXI: 169). His violently explosive behaviour might be attributed to sexual repression. But that Freudian concept does not seem to apply, largely because we are not given a sense of charged-up sexual energy and because Henchard's two soaring expressions of love, for Farfrae and Elizabeth-Jane, are not apparently directed toward physical gratification though they might have been portrayed that way. As Dale Kramer points out, neither readers nor other characters in the novel think of sexual implications when the forty-year old Henchard goes on living with the twenty-year old Elizabeth-Jane after discovering that she is not his daughter.[5]

Henchard's sudden passion for Farfrae, which is striking after his coolness toward women, suggests homosexuality on his side (Farfrae's response never exceeds cool affection). But their relation does not develop in a way that bears out this hypothesis; for it quickly turns into male power rivalry once Farfrae breaks out of Henchard's proprietorship. Another sign is that the wrestling match between them is not, like the match between Gerald and Birkin in *Women in Love*, given a homosexually erotic colour. For one thing they wrestle with their clothes on, whereas Gerald and Birkin strip naked. After an initial homo-erotic detail – Henchard 'gazed upon the lowered eyes of his fair and slim antagonist' – the details lead our thoughts away from eros toward power: 'the pair rocking and writhing like trees in a gale'. There is no complete body contact – 'this part of the struggle ended by his forcing Farfrae down on his knees by sheer pressure of one of his muscular arms' – until the Scotsman, to save himself from the precipice, 'for the first time locked himself to his adversary' (xxxviii: 209). The initiative is Farfrae's and the emphasis is on the danger to Farfrae's life. The fact that Henchard wrestles with one hand tied emphasises the test of physical power.

In Henchard the desire for power replaces sexuality; he seeks to possess completely the people he loves or is unable to distinguish the pleasure of love from the pleasure of proprietorship. Early in the novel Elizabeth-Jane observes 'Henchard's tigerish affection for the younger man, his constant liking to have Farfrae near him, now and then resulted in a tendency to domineer' (xiv: 69). And in the period when Henchard thinks Elizabeth-Jane is his daughter, he provides her with money and clothing but seeks to dominate every aspect of her life, blowing up with fury when she slips into dialect.

In portraying Henchard's love of Farfrae, Hardy suggests if not homosexuality at least the inevitable homo-erotic element in male bonding. We read of Farfrae's slight stature compared to Henchard's bulk and of Henchard's prolonged 'holding [of] the young man's hand' as he tries to persuade him not to go to America: '"Come bide with me – and name your own terms. I'll agree to 'em willingly and 'ithout a word of gainsaying; for, hang it, Farfrae, I like thee well!"' Henchard's enthusiasm for Farfrae contains but also exceeds business considerations, for 'this man of strong impulses declared that his new friend should take up his abode in his house' (ix: 49–50) and they become inseparable though Farfrae declares that they ought to separate if he was to be valuable 'as a second pair of eyes' (xiv: 69).

The example which best points toward homo-eroticism comes from Elizabeth-Jane's observation of them at a time when she is feeling the first stirrings of her own fragile sexuality in response to signs of Donald's admiration. She envies 'Friendship between man and man; what a rugged strength there was in it, as evinced by these two' (xv: 74). Elizabeth-Jane keeps her eye on Farfrae as though she were competing with Henchard for his affection.

Homo-eroticism but also power hunger shows itself in Henchard's extravagantly irrational reaction when Farfrae steps out of the passive role assigned him to challenge Henchard's authority in the disciplining of Abe Whittle. By dismissing Farfrae Henchard encourages him to set up a rival firm, and in all the subsequent acts of rivalry, always initiated by Henchard, Farfrae wins. These self-destructive hostilities – self-destructiveness is the key to Henchard's character – are ways of remaining in contact with Farfrae, who continues to dominate Henchard's consciousness. This self-destructive way of remaining in contact reaches a climax through the body contact of the wrestling match, which follows the powerful scene in which Henchard is publicly humiliated by Farfrae, who is now Mayor of Casterbridge, before the Royal visitor. Henchard by appearing in his oldest clothes and trying to pre-empt the City Council's welcome is asking for such public humiliation. What matters is Farfrae's *physical* dislodgment of Henchard.

> He seized Henchard by the shoulder, dragged him back, and told him roughly to be off. Henchard's eyes met his, and Farfrae observed the fierce light in them despite his excitement and irritation. For a moment Henchard stood his ground rigidly; then by an unaccountable impulse gave way and retired. (xxxvii: 204)

The test of body contact and will shows that the power relation between them has been reversed. The 'unaccountable impulse' will cause Henchard again to surrender after he has won the wrestling match.

Henchard seeks to restore the balance by asserting his superior physical strength in a wrestling match to the death. But we know from the start that he will not be able to kill Farfrae, for Farfrae enters the barn singing the song he sang when Henchard first met him. 'Nothing moved Henchard like an old melody. He sank back. "No; I can't do it!" he gasped' (xxxviii: 208). Henchard's susceptibility to music, one of his endearing characteristics, signifies here his continuing love of Farfrae. He finally brings Farfrae to the point where he can say to him: '"Your life is in my hands."'

> 'Then take it, take it!' said Farfrae. 'Ye've wished to long enough!'
> Henchard looked down upon him in silence, and their eyes met. 'O Farfrae – that's not true!' he said bitterly. 'God is my witness that no man ever loved another as I did thee at one time. . . . And now – though I came here to kill 'ee, I cannot hurt thee!' (xxxviii: 210)

The cadences of that declaration suggest continuing love. '"My heart is true to you still"', he declares later, when Farfrae does not believe

his warning of the danger to Lucetta (XL: 219). His capacity to love
Farfrae and Elizabeth-Jane, together with his susceptibility to music
and his inability (after the initial blunder of the wife sale) to carry
through any ruthless design – all these virtues make Henchard,
despite his blunders, a tragic hero rather than a villain who gets his
just deserts.

Henchard's change after his self-defeat in the wrestling match
is strikingly pictorialised. 'So thoroughy subdued was he that he
remained . . . in a crouching attitude, unusual for a man, and for
such a man. Its *womanliness* sat tragically on the figure of so stern
a piece of virility' (XXXVIII: 210, my italics). 'Womanliness' presents
a stunning reversal of Henchard's characterisation so far. Virility
has been the main point of his characterisation (making remarkable, as I have said, his lack of sexual feeling). Susan, when she
catches her first glimpse of him since their separation sees signs of
a temperament, which having cut all ties with women, has become
thoroughly male, 'a temperament which would have no pity for
weakness, but would be ready to yield ungrudging admiration to
greatness and strength' (V: 26). Dale Kramer argues that the ges-
tures and language which might suggest Henchard's latent homosexuality actually reflect his worship of male power and his 'scornful
opinion of women as weak'. But after suffering humiliation and
defeat he 'transfers his affection from Farfrae to Elizabeth-Jane:
"Above all things what he desired now was affection from anything that was good and pure"' (*Hardy: Forms of Tragedy*, 87–8). The
fact that 'womanliness sat tragically' upon him suggests, given his
values, a reduction of stature. Now, however, there has taken place
within him an enrichment of values.

The novel traces a process of 'unmanning' that marks Henchard's
decline, according to his values, but also the acquisition of feminine
values which makes him capable of tragic sympathy with suffering.
The word 'unmanned' is first used when in the Roman theatre he
gives up his desire for revenge over Lucetta, agreeing to return her
letters, because he is reminded 'of another ill-used woman [Susan]
who had stood there'. But he harbours still 'his old feeling of super-
cilious pity for womankind in general' (XXXV: 192) when actually he
is deceived by Lucetta, who has dressed in a way to induce his pity,
and by Susan, who not only made the wife sale go through but
keeps up her sleeve the revelation about Elizabeth-Jane (these in
addition to the furmity woman who directly causes his downfall).
It is in his return to Elizabeth-Jane, whom he cast out after learning

she·was not his daughter, that his feminisation is complete, for 'he schooled himself to accept her will . . . as absolute and unquestionable' (XLII: 232).

In her brilliant feminist essay, 'The Unmanning of the Mayor of Casterbridge', Elaine Showalter writes:

> Henchard's efforts, first to deny and divorce his passional self, and ultimately to accept and educate it, involve him in a pilgrimage of 'unmanning' which is a movement towards both self-discovery and tragic vulnerability. It is in the analysis of this New Man, rather than in the evaluation of Hardy's New Women, that the case for Hardy's feminist sympathies may be argued.[6]

Hardy himself describes the change in Henchard more ambivalently: 'the dependence upon Elizabeth's regard into which he had declined (or, in another sense, to which he had advanced) – *denaturalized* him' (XLII: 233, my italics). 'Denaturalized' suggests that Hardy does not abandon 'declined' for 'advanced', but maintains both possibilities.

I do not not find in Hardy's text any sign that 'the effigy which Henchard sees floating' after the skimmity-ride is, as Showalter puts it, 'the symbolic shell of a discarded male self' (Kramer, ed., *Critical Approaches to Fiction of Hardy*, 112). Hardy does not use the word 'effigy', but makes Henchard perceive 'with a sense of horror that it was *himself*. Not a man somewhat resembling him, but one in all respects his counterpart, his actual double, was floating as if dead' (XLI: 227). In this partly objective, partly subjective self-perception, Henchard's manliness would seem to remain intact. But I do agree with Showalter's argument that

> the nature and intensity of Henchard's need is [not] sexual. It is an absence of feeling which Henchard looks to others to supply. . . What he wants is a 'greedy exclusiveness,' a title; and this feeling is stimulated by male competition.   (Kramer, ed., 106)

Thus, he shows himself to be the same old Henchard when, on an impulse triggered by his proprietary love for Elizabeth-Jane, he informs her father Newson, who comes looking for her, that she is dead. Worst of all and most fundamentally characteristic of him is the self-destructive impulse that makes him, after he sees in his telescope the face of Newson returning, announce to Elizabeth-Jane that he will leave Casterbridge. Wiping out all he has accomplished, dressing the way he began as a hay trusser, with a hay trusser's tools, he flees both Newson and the need to attend Elizabeth-Jane's wedding to Farfrae. Hardy speaks of Henchard's 'own *haughty* sense that his presence was no longer desired' (XLIV: 245, my italics). His haughtiness and self-destructive decision are signs of the pride and impulsiveness which are his tragic flaws. A few pages later Hardy quotes Shelley's *Revolt of Islam* (canto VIII, st.VI: 1.2) to say that Henchard 'stood like a dark ruin, obscured by "the shade from his own soul upthrown"' (XLIV: 249).

The irony is that Newson was not planning to interfere in the relation between Henchard and Elizabeth-Jane. Had Henchard rationally stayed on to face the consequences of Newson's return and Elizabeth-Jane's wedding, all would have gone well. But if Henchard were rational, he would not be a tragic hero – a character who, as Hardy sees here, *creates* like Eustacia his own tragedy. It was his destiny to break every tie of love, to will himself into a condition of loneliness and alienation. 'Susan, Farfrae, Lucetta, Elizabeth – all had gone from him', he reflects, 'one after one, either by his fault or by his misfortune' (XLI: 226). By his fault, we are to understand, for it is truer of *Mayor* than of the other major novels that, in the remark of Novalis cited here, 'Character is Fate' (XVII: 88). 'A Man of Character' in the novel's subtitle may refer to a man who has determined his own destiny despite the coincidences of the plot. In the Preface Hardy calls this story 'more particularly a study of one man's deeds and character' than any of his others (1).

As he takes his lonely way out of Casterbridge, Henchard dramatises his plight self-consciously: '"I – Cain – go alone as I deserve – an outcast and a vagabond."' In contrast to Cain, who in Genesis 4: 13 says, '"My punishment is greater than I can bear"', Henchard says, '"But my punishment is *not* greater than I can bear!"' (XLIII: 239). Now he understands the cause of his tragedy – he had let concern for money replace love (the love–money antithesis is largely the book's point). 'But his attempts to replace ambition by love had been as fully foiled as his ambition itself' (XLIV: 243). Henchard begins to triumph over circumstances as he gains a glimpse of the whole scheme.

So we see how through self-punishment Henchard generates his own tragedy and, as with all Hardy's tragic heroes, Henchard's display of imaginative and emotional resources too large for success in life makes him tragic. That is his distinction over Farfrae

who has the right balance of resources for success. Hardy's skilful feat here (as in his characterisation of Eustacia) is to portray
Henchard as mainly unattractive and then to turn our sympathies
toward him in the end when he becomes a tragic figure.

In a conversation with Farfrae early in the novel, Henchard, in
describing the mood he was in when he met Lucetta, shows where
he wants to end up. '"I sank into one of those gloomy fits I sometimes suffer from . . . when the world seems to have the blackness
of hell, and, like Job, I could curse the day that gave me birth"'
'"Ah, now, I never feel like it"', says the well-adjusted Farfrae (XII:
60). In the end Henchard, having refused to attend Elizabeth-Jane's
wedding, bungles his return to the wedding in such a way as to
bring upon himself even more pain through her rejection of him.
He neglects to give her the caged bird he brought as a gift, but
finding it dead a few days later, Elizabeth-Jane extends its pathos
to Henchard, so that 'her heart softened towards the self-alienated
man', always 'one of his own worst accusers' (XLV: 251). And finally
he fulfils his deepest wish in the terrible Job-like epitaph he pre-
scribes for himself as his will: '"& that I be not bury'd in conse-
crated ground. / . . . & that no man remember me"' (XLV: 254). By
obeying his directions, Elizabeth-Jane allows Henchard his tragic
ending undiluted with sentimentality.

> She knew the directions to be a piece of the same stuff that his
> whole life was made of, and hence were not to be tampered with
> to give herself a mournful pleasure, or her husband credit for
> large-heartedness. (XLV: 255)

To return to my original argument about Henchard's lack of sexual
feeling, he finds little to interest him sexually in Susan and Lucetta,
his love of Farfrae is at most homo-erotic for a while before it turns
into bitter rivalry masking a love that grows increasingly spiritual;
while his eventual love for Elizabeth-Jane is paternal and spiritual,
with no sexual component suggested. Indeed Henchard demonstrates a large capacity for asexual love; the sign of this is the implied comparison with the initiation into love of King Lear, a man
too old for sexual emotions. Having been rejected by his 'daughter',
Henchard like Lear wanders alone attended only by his faithful
fool (Abel Whittle). One finds the pattern of the Lear–Cordelia
story in Henchard's rejection of the loving Elizabeth-Jane when he
learns she is not his biological daughter and when their subsequent

reconciliation is followed by his final heartbreak after she, in an analogue to Cordelia's death, rejects him.

How sexual are the other major characters? Both Donald Farfrae and Elizabeth-Jane are cool sexually, or at least their sexual emotions do not interfere with the clarity of their thinking. The only sexually passionate character in the novel is Lucetta, who dies because her unreserved passion for Farfrae gets mixed up through exposure in the skimmity-ride with the consequences of her earlier unreserved passion for Henchard. '"I'd let people live and love at their pleasure!"' says the amorous Lucetta (xxiii: 124).

Farfrae's character is exemplified by his ability to bring tears to the eyes of himself and others with songs of his native Scotland even though he has no intention of returning there. '"It's well you feel a song for a few minutes"', he says to Elizabeth-Jane after his performance at The Three Mariners,

'and your eyes they get quite tearful; but you finish it, and for all you felt you don't mind it or think of it again for a long while. O no, I don't want to go back! Yet I'll sing the song to you wi' pleasure whenever you like.' (xiv: 72)

Such shallow emotions are an advantage for succeeding in the acquisition of money and power; and this aspect of Farfrae's character is displayed again at the end, when Henchard from the street hears Donald at his wedding singing 'a song of his dear native country that he loved so well as never to have revisited it' (xliv: 247). The repetition, through the ears of the fallen Henchard, discredits Farfrae in comparison with Henchard whose lack of moderation, of control over his emotions, is one of the flaws that make him a tragic hero. 'Character is Fate, said Novalis, and Farfrae's character was just the reverse of Henchard's' (xvii: 88).

Most revealing of all is Lucetta's analysis of Farfrae's character. Speaking of Scotsmen generally, she says on first meeting him, '"We common people are all one way or the other – warm or cold, passionate or frigid. You have both temperatures going on in you at the same time."' The narrator speaks of the curious mixture in Farfrae of 'the commercial and the romantic' (xxiii: 122–3). Sure enough Farfrae interrupts his first meeting with Lucetta to attend to a customer, but not before he has pleased Lucetta and himself by hiring a young carter with his old father so as to keep the carter in the vicinity near his sweetheart. Farfrae is both practical and sentimental, a not unusual combination among people who do not let the sentimental get in the way of the practical.

Farfrae's coolness is shown by his notable lack of response to Henchard's warm feelings for him of love and rivalry. He easily drops his courtship of Elizabeth-Jane after Henchard indicates displeasure over it; and after Henchard drops his objection, he comes to court Elizabeth-Jane but turns to Lucetta instead, showing in his susceptibility to her blandishments little understanding of women. After his wife Lucetta's death, there is no emphasis on his grief for her and their unborn child, but only on his swift recovery so he can turn his attention back to Elizabeth-Jane. Farfrae has the right amount of sexual feeling for success in life, since he is attracted to women as Henchard is not, but sex does not interfere with his other faculties. In Henchard, instead, the powerful passionateness that displaces sexual feeling does interfere with his other faculties.

Elizabeth-Jane's case is more complicated, for though her sexuality is measured and moderate, she does fall in love with Farfrae almost at first sight and she remains steadfastly in love with him. She begins, however, as a colourless, priggish maiden with a quite unromantic rage for respectability. 'Elizabeth-Jane', Hardy wrote in a letter, 'was, of course, too estimable to be piquant' (21 October 1897, *Letters*, II: 180). In fact Elizabeth-Jane *discovers* her womanliness, her sexuality evolves in the course of the novel. If *The Mayor of Casterbridge* is, on the one hand, about the moral 'feminisation' of Henchard, it is, on the other hand, about the biological feminisation of Elizabeth-Jane.

Under the secure shelter of Henchard's financial support, Elizabeth-Jane's womanliness begins to blossom. 'With peace of mind came development, and with development beauty' (XIV: 66). In her newly acquired finery, she begins to draw admiration, including Farfrae's. 'Sex', we are told, 'had never before asserted itself in her so strongly, for in former days she had perhaps been too impersonally human to be distinctively feminine.' Yet she still doubts whether she is sufficiently feminine to justify such frivolous clothing: '"Good Heaven"', she whispered, '"can it be? Here am I setting up as the town beauty! . . . If they only knew what an unfinished girl I am. . . . Better sell all this finery and buy myself grammar-books and dictionaries and a history of all the philosophies!"' (XV: 74). There remains throughout her story the obstacle to feminisation which Hardy calls her impersonal humanity and we might call her introspective intellectuality. At first 'her budding beauty' went unregarded, for 'when she walked abroad she seemed to be occupied with an inner chamber of ideas' (xv: 73). When at a dance Farfrae alludes to a question he would like to ask her that very night, 'instead of encouraging him she remained incompetently silent'. Wondering later how permanent was the impression she had made on him, she thought that 'by this time he had discovered how plain and homely was the informing spirit of that pretty outside' (xvii: 84, 86). Hardy takes a cue from George Eliot's Dorothea in portraying a beautiful woman who does not *feel* beautiful and compensates with intellectuality.

Elizabeth-Jane's asexual intellectuality is developed through contrast with Lucetta, who, when Elizabeth-Jane settled into her house, deposited herself on the sofa in the pose of Titian's Venus. Instead, 'Elizabeth's mind ran on acquirements to an almost morbid degree. "You speak French and Italian fluently, no doubt", she said. "I have not been able to get beyond a wretched bit of Latin yet"' (xxii: 116). We can hear Elizabeth-Jane's unspoken criticism when later Lucetta asks for help in choosing her new wardrobe. '"I wouldn't think so hard about it"', says Elizabeth-Jane. Depending on your choice, Lucetta explains, '"You are that person" (pointing to one of the arrangements), "or you are *that* totally different person" (pointing to the other)'. She finally decided to be 'the cherry-coloured person at all hazards' (xxiv: 127). As a result Farfrae 'passed from perception of Elizabeth into a brighter sphere of existence than she appertained to' (xxiv: 130) – he saw only the cherry-coloured Lucetta. Hardy, however, gives us with Elizabeth-Jane a heroine in whom beauty and goodness triumph in reconciliation with intellectuality. When Farfrae courts her again in the end, he presents her with many books, thus recognising her difference from Lucetta.

There is another reason for Elizabeth-Jane's intellectuality and sobriety. These are appropriate qualities for her other function as the novel's observer, Hardy's nearest approach so far to a Jamesian central intelligence (he will go even farther in *The Well-Beloved*). 'The position of Elizabeth-Jane's [back] room – rather high in the house . . . afforded her opportunity for accurate observation of what went on' in the hay-stores and granaries where Donald was running Henchard's business. 'Her quiet eye' (xiv: 69) – she is called

'that silent observing woman' (XVII: 85) – expresses the quality of
her observation throughout. After Donald's dismissal, she moves to
a front chamber overlooking the street. And when she moves in
with Lucetta, she is afforded windows 'looking out upon the market' (XXII: 117) where Donald and Henchard do business. Although
her eye is mainly on Donald out of love for him, her erotic voyeurism does not, as in the earlier novels, disturb the accuracy of her
observation. This may be one reason Hardy makes her erotic tem-
perature run low.

The quality of Elizabeth-Jane's love is described in the following
passage:

> Thus she lived on, a dumb, deep-feeling great-eyed creature,
> construed by not a single contiguous being; quenching with pa-
> tient fortitude her incipient interest in Farfrae, because it seemed
> to be one-sided, unmaidenly, and unwise. (XX: 102)

'Unwise' is the key word, showing that her emotions are never
allowed to exceed the boundaries of reason (we hear only of her
'incipient interest in Farfrae'). Her erotic watching, as she moves
from one point of obervation to another, is pursued emotionally but
calmly.

Thus, she fulfils her dual function of lover and observer. Even in
dealing with her rival Lucetta, where her own vital love interest is
at stake, she can be remarkably perspicacious. From the data at
hand she can divine a meeting between Donald and Lucetta she has
not attended, the first in which sparks flew, so that the scene 'could
be held as witnessed' (XXIV: 131), the way the author would witness
it. And 'surveying ... from the *crystalline sphere of a straightforward
mind*, [Elizabeth-Jane] did not fail to perceive that her father, as she
called him, and Donald Farfrae became more desperately enamoured of her friend every day' (XXV: 137, my italics). Henchard is
not really enamoured but stimulated by competition; Elizabeth-Jane
is perceptive but not omniscient. Note the contrast between the
serenity of her perceiving mind and the passionate material perceived, material especially relevant to Elizabeth-Jane's own desire.

Elizabeth-Jane's detachment can be maintained because she can
assimilate her disappointment at losing Donald to the lesson of
renunciation she had long since learned. And just as Donald took
with relative equanimity his early loss of her and his later loss of
Lucetta, 'so she viewed with an approach to equanimity the now

cancelled days when Donald had been her undeclared lover, and wondered what unwished-for thing Heaven might send her in place of him' (xxv: 137). But we see in the following passage another reason for her detachment. At a moment of tension among Lucetta, Henchard and Farfrae, 'Elizabeth-Jane, being out of the game, and out of the group, could observe all from afar, like the evangelist who had to write it down' (xxvi: 139). Through much of the book she acts as surrogate for the author.

Even when after Lucetta's death she marries Donald, Elizabeth-Jane takes this turn of fortune with only a little livelier equanimity than her earlier misfortune, absorbing it into her philosophy of endurance. Henchard is surprised to find her dancing at her wedding; for she 'had long ago appraised life at a moderate value' and knew 'that marriage was as a rule no dancing matter' (xliv: 248).

> As the lively and sparkling emotions of her early married life cohered into an equable serenity, the finer movements of her nature found scope in discovering to the narrow-lived ones around her the secret (as she had once learnt it) of making limited opportunities endurable. (xlv: 255)

These are not the views of a heroine whom love has taken by storm. Such views are expanded in the novel's final sentence in which Elizabeth-Jane, in the midst of her happiness, shows a clear-eyed understanding that 'happiness was but the occasional episode in a general drama of pain' (xlv: 256). One is reminded of the choruses in *Oedipus Rex*. As the author's surrogate Elizabeth-Jane expresses the tragic view of life which accounts for and makes endurable the spectacle of Henchard's fall. Hardy thought tragedy inherent in the nature of things and not an aberration.[7]

Elizabeth-Jane might, with her colourless sobriety, be considered a dull heroine (Hardy describes her as 'our poor only heroine', xliii: 236) were it not for her perceptive intelligence and consistent dignity (her 'countenance whose beauty had ever lain in its meditative soberness', xli: 255). George Eliot's Dorothea seems by comparison colourful and romantic. The nearest precedent might be Jane Austen's Fanny Price in *Mansfield Park*, whose stance for morality and respectability is not swept away by erotic emotion. But Elizabeth-Jane is more intellectual and more tragic-minded than Fanny, because of her role as observer and author's surrogate; she emerges therefore as a new kind of heroine.

Hardy's intention to write a tragic novel may explain the reversal of his usual concern with sexuality. He minimises the sexuality of his major characters, except for Lucetta, in order to throw the emphasis on moral judgement, since Eros creates its own laws of judgement, making us forget moral questions as we sympathise with love for its own sake. (The erotic Lucetta is, compared to the other major characters, too trivial to command such sympathy.) Hardy reveals his tragic intention in his journal where, two days after noting that he has finished the last page of *The Mayor of Casterbridge*, he writes: 'The business of the poet and novelist is to show the sorriness underlying the grandest things, and the grandeur underlying the sorriest things' (*Life*, 171).

The minimisation of sexuality goes even farther in what in its book form is Hardy's last novel, *The Well-Beloved* (1897). Sexuality is minimised for different reasons than in *Mayor*; first, because this last novel, in its serialised form, *The Pursuit of the Well-Beloved* (1892), was written for Tillotson & Son after they had rejected the serialisation of *Tess* (called then *Too Late Beloved*) for moral reasons. *The Well-Beloved* is the 'something light'[8] which Hardy offered Tillotson in place of *Tess*. Hardy always insisted on the sexlessness of *The Well-Beloved*. 'There is more fleshliness in *The Loves of the Triangles* than in this story', he wrote when the novel came out in book form (*Life*, 286). And in the prospectus for Tillotson he wrote: 'There is not a word or scene in the tale which can offend the most fastidious taste' (Purdy, 95).

Hardy exaggerates in that the novel contains many allusions to sexuality whether consummated or not. For example Avice Caro, the first Avice, does not meet Jocelyn the evening before his departure for fear that he will take advantage of the island custom which encourages pre-marital intercourse of engaged couples. Jocelyn abandons Avice after falling in love with Marcia while drying her underclothes over a fire at an inn; they elope to London where they live together at a hotel while awaiting marriage papers delayed because of Jocelyn's error. (A frequent device in Hardy, delayed marriage papers usually indicates the man's doubt about marrying.) The enmity between their families causes them to quarrel and Marcia returns to her father who, 'a born islander', does not consider that her pre-marital intercourse with Jocelyn necessitates marriage.[9] It is apparently only with Marcia that Jocelyn has intercourse and that is delicately alluded to.

The novel is all about love, but about the Platonic–Shelleyan kind – another reason that sexuality is minimised. Hardy sketched the novel many years before its serialisation, 'when I was comparatively a young man, and interested in the Platonic Idea, which, considering its charm and its poetry, one could well wish to be interested in always'. He adds that '*The Well-Beloved* is a fanciful exhibition of the artistic nature' (*Life*, 286–7). Hardy came to see the danger of the Platonic Idea while maintaining his sense of its attractiveness, for *The Well-Beloved* amounts in the end to a critique of idealisation in love and art. Thus, Hardy's last novel brings to a climax the attraction to and criticism of idealism which I have been tracing through most of the novels. The connection of the Platonic Idea with 'the artistic nature' suggests a certain kind of idealising artistic temperament (hence the novel's subtitle, *A Sketch of a Temperament*) which accounts for the sublimated sexuality that causes Jocelyn to care more for his ideal Well-Beloved than for the various women in whom, like a 'goddess', the Well-Beloved embodies herself one after another. He remains faithful to his 'goddess', even if unfaithful to her various embodiments.

As a sculptor it is his 'goddess' whom he portrays in desexualized versions of love goddesses such as Venus and Astarte. The presentation of love along with its desexualisation make Jocelyn Pierston's art popular for reasons he doesn't understand. Sexual inhibition and sublimation account for the creativity of Jocelyn and presumably all idealising artists. Critics have insufficiently emphasised the psychological analysis in this novel of art and artists, a theme I shall attend to. I shall also follow in the footsteps of the essays that have been for me the most influential in calling my attention to this neglected novel – J. Hillis Miller's '*The Well-Beloved*: The Compulsion to Stop Repeating' and Michael Ryan's 'One Name of Many Shapes: *The Well-Beloved*'.[10]

My own argument for the importance of *The Well-Beloved* will appear in the course of this discussion, in which I hope to demonstrate a complexity and consistency in the texture of imagery, action and characterisation – a texture in which characterisations, especially of the three Avices, become imagery. Although I would not rank *The Well-Beloved* with Hardy's greatest novels, it deserves more attention than it has received if only because of its position in Hardy's canon, wrapped as it is around the scandal-making *Jude the*

Obscure: Well-Beloved was serialised in 1892, *Jude* serialised in 1894–5 and published in book form in 1895 and *Well-Beloved* published in book form in 1897. In addition, Hardy has made in *The Well-Beloved* innovations of technique and psychology that make it comparable, as I shall show, to the work of James and Proust.

The genesis of *The Well-Beloved* as a reaction to the withdrawal of *Tess* causes Michael Ryan to read the novel as a bitterly ironic attack on the editors and reading public which prefer such idealised pap to the moral and physiological realism of *Tess* and later on *Jude*. Ryan connects the tone he finds in *The Well-Beloved* with Hardy's bitter critical essay 'Candour in English Fiction' (1890), which calls 'our popular fiction' a 'literature of quackery' and insists that the novel criticise life as a 'physiological fact' and that 'its honest portrayal must be largely concerned with, for one thing, the relations of the sexes' (Kramer, ed., 172–3). Ryan's argument is persuasive until we reread *The Well-Beloved* and simply do not find the irony that heavy, though there is undoubtedly a light irony as reflected in the jauntiness of the chapter titles. But mainly Ryan's argument suggests that Hardy is devaluing *The Well-Beloved* as an example of what fiction should not be; whereas there is reason to believe that he took the novel and wanted it to be taken quite seriously. His letter of thanks for Swinburne's appreciation suggests as much:

> I must thank you for your kind note about my fantastic little tale which, if it can make, in its better parts, any faint claim to imaginative feeling, will owe something of such feeling to you, for I often thought of lines of yours during the writing.   (*Life*, 287)

Hardy's remarks about the 'fantastic' nature of *The Well-Beloved* and its affinity to poetry may explain why critics of Hardy have ignored where they have not condemned his last novel. Critics have expected it to fulfil the realistic conventions of the other novels, but its supernatural suggestions and concentrated narration, without subplots and digressions, relate it rather more to the short stories than the other novels. If Hardy in 'Candour in English Fiction' argues for realistic *content*, he argues in the *Life* against realistic *form*: 'Art is a disproportioning ... of realities. ... Hence "realism" is not Art' (229). Hardy, like James and Proust, combines an atmosphere of fantasy, deriving from Pierston's point of view with its psychological projection and a realistic comparison of manners on the island and in London.

In its relation to the short stories, *The Well-Beloved* shows a remarkable affinity to 'An Imaginative Woman', a poetical short story written at about the same time. In this story an unsuccessful poetess rents, with her husband and children, the rooms at a seaside resort of a successful poet, Robert Trewe, whose poetry she adores. She never lays eyes on him, but the experience of inhabiting his bedroom and sleeping in his bed takes on for her, although she is pregnant, a kind of sexual intimacy. One evening when her husband goes out, she lies in Robert Trewe's bed, with his photograph and volume of verses at the bedside and his

> half-obliterated pencillings on the wallpaper beside her head . . . it seemed as if his very breath, warm and loving, fanned her cheeks from those walls. . . . And now her hair was dragging where his arm had laid when he secured the fugitive fancies; she was . . . immersed in the very essence of him permeated by his spirit as by an ether.[11]

In the end she dies in childbirth, but the boy she produces resembles the man she had never seen: 'the dreamy and peculiar expression of the poet's face sat, as the transmitted idea, upon the child's' (25); so much so that his biological father, after discovering the poet's photograph, repudiates him.

Ironically Robert Trewe, on his side, commits suicide because he never met the ideal woman to whom he has addressed his poetry. 'She, this undiscoverable, elusive one, inspired my last volume; the imaginary woman alone', he explains in the letter he leaves behind. 'There is no real woman behind the title. She has continued to the last unrevealed, unmet, unwon' (20). Both Trewe and the poetess pursued ideal figures comparable to Jocelyn's Well-Beloved. The story shows the destructive effects of idealisation in love and art, a major theme in the novel.

The supernatural element in the novel lies first of all in the projection of so mysterious an essence as the Well-Beloved: 'God only knew what she really was; Pierston did not. She was indescribable.' When Jocelyn, after meeting Avice Caro, recalls the many individualities – 'known as Lucy, Jane, Flora, Evangeline, or whatnot' (I, ii: 16)[12] – through whom the Well-Beloved has already passed, we should see him as a Platonic Don Juan. Don Juan abandoned each woman after satiating his lust; whereas Pierston's spiritual satiation is suggested by the Well-Beloved's initiative in entering and abandoning each woman.

What Hardy calls 'this fantastic tale of a subjective idea . . . the theory of the transmigration of the ideal beloved one, who only exists in the lover, from material woman to material woman – as exemplified by Proust many years later', this story is also told in a poem called 'The Well-Beloved' written at about the same time as the novel's publication in volume form (*Life*, 286). In the poem a goddess, near a place where once stood a Temple to Venus, informs a rapt bridegroom, hurrying to his bride, '"Thou lovest what thou dreamest her; / I am thy very dream!"' Convinced, the lover proposes to the goddess only to hear, as she vanishes, '"I wed no mortal man!"' His bride's 'look', when he arrives, 'was pinched and thin, / As if her soul had shrunk and died' (*Poetical Works*, I: 169–70).

The novel makes the supernatural suggestion that a single family face is maintained through three generations of Avices; so that Jocelyn, by falling in love with all three as though they were one, seems to make time stand still. Hardy tries to rationalise this resemblance in Darwinian terms by attributing it to 'the immemorial island customs of intermarriage and of prenuptial union' – the latter is not relevant; nor is the following born out in the novel:

> under which conditions the type of feature was almost uniform from parent to child through generations; so that, till quite latterly, to have seen one native man and woman was to have seen the whole population of that isolated rock.   (III, ii: 153)

'Till quite latterly' must explain why it is only the three Avices who share the family face. Marcia looks quite different and there is no indication that Pierston resembles anyone else. But the notion of an *island* face suggests an original unity symbolised by the island.

The Avices' story is projected in a journal entry of February 19, 1889: 'The story of a face which goes through three generations or more, would make a fine novel or poem of the passage of Time. The differences in personality to be ignored' (*Life*, 217). The poem 'Heredity', which emerged from this note, begins with the lines, 'I am the family face; / Flesh perishes, I live on' (*Poetical Works*, II: 166). The poem's title recalls Darwin. Hardy chararacteristically combines Platonism with Darwinism and, indeed, as Norman Page has written, gives to this novel 'classified for the 1912 collected edition as a fantasy and referred to in the 1912 preface as "frankly imaginative". . . a substantial realistic and even scientific under-pinning' (letter to me, 2 January 1992). According to J. O. Bailey's note to the poem 'Heredity' (in *Poetry of Hardy: Handbook and Commentary*), Hardy in 1890 read an English translation of August Weissmann's Darwinian *Essays upon Heredity* which argue the im-mortality of the germ plasm even though its bearers are mortal.[13] 'Love,' says Plato in the *Symposium*, 'is neither mortal nor immortal, but in a mean between the two.' Love desires generation and birth because 'the mortal nature is seeking as far as is possible to be everlasting and immortal'.[14]

In the journal entry quoted above Hardy says that in the story of the family face 'differences in personality [are] to be ignored'. Jocelyn sees that the three Avices differ in personality, but largely ignores the differences, making the three women identical, in other words, as an act of imagination. Thus, he assimilates Avice II, for all her differences, to Avice I: 'He could not help seeing in her all that he knew of another, and veiling in her all that did not harmonize with his sense of metempsychosis' (II, vi: 90). There emerges as a theme the subjectivity, indeed the artistry, of romantic love, that the lover *shapes* the object of his love as the sculptor shapes his statue. In a journal entry of July 1926, Hardy notes 'that the theory exhibited in *The Well-Beloved* in 1892 has been since developed by Proust still further' and he quotes Proust to the effect that in the love object '"la plupart des éléments sont tirés de nous-mêmes"' (*Life*, 432). Proust, who read and admired *The Well-Beloved* in 1910, probably modelled after it, according to Miller in *Fiction and Repetition*, the late scene which 'brings together in Odette, Gilberte, and Mlle de Saint-Loup the mother, daughter, and granddaughter whom Marcel has loved or may yet love' (172).

There is a nice ambiguity in the novel, however, between the presentations of the idealistic and realistic views. This shows up especially in the treatment of time – the treatment that is of age which, on the one hand, seems to make time stand still and, on the other, inevitably moves it forward. The ambiguity is illustrated in the titles of the three parts: 'A Young Man of Twenty', 'A Young Man of Forty' and 'A Young Man of Sixty.'[15] Jocelyn is often re-ferred to as looking young or unchanged, while it is also made clear that he is ageing. He presumes to court the daughter and finally even the granddaughter of Avice Caro, as though age does not count, yet disparity in age stands between them.

His meeting with Avice Caro's daughter is presented in such a
way as to foster the illusion of stilled time. Jocelyn has returned
from London for Avice Caro's funeral, which Hardy beautifully
makes him behold from a distance to suggest a spiritual rather than
physical participation, which blurs the ugly finality of moved time.
He seemed that evening

> to see Avice Caro herself, bending over and then withdrawing
> from her grave in the light of the moon. She seemed not a year
> older, not a digit less slender, not a line more angular than when
> he had parted from her twenty years earlier. (II, iv: 78)

Looking through her cottage window, he sees again 'the Avice he
had lost' and though he has been told that she is Avice's only
daughter, he nevertheless, when she opens the door, addresses her
tenderly as '"Avice Caro!" even now unable to get over the strange
feeling that he was twenty years younger, addressing Avice the
forsaken' (79–80).

So far time seems to have stood still. The recognition of reality
begins when the girl tells him her name is Ann, her second name
Avice. '"You are Avice to me"', he says, but he perceives the
difference in personality between mother and daughter. 'The voice
truly was his Avice's; but Avice the Second was clearly more
matter-of-fact, unreflecting, less cultivated than her mother had
been'. When she tells him her age, almost nineteen, about the age of
Avice I when he last knew her, he recalls sharply that he was now
forty. 'She before him was an uneducated laundress, and he was a
sculptor and a Royal Academician. . . . Yet why was it an unpleasant
sensation to him just then to recollect that he was two score?' (81).
Nevertheless, despite her imperviousness, 'in his heart he was not
a day older than when he had wooed the mother at the daughter's
present age' (II, vi: 91). So he oscillates between the illusion that
time stands still and the painful awareness of its movement.

Despite these differences, he pursues Avice II with more passion
than he gave to the pursuit of her mother. Yet the pursuit never
involves the flesh. Even when he brings her to his house in London
as a servant, living alone with her there, he never tries to seduce
her. And when finally she admits that she is already married to
another Pierston, whom she hates, Jocelyn strangely insists that she
rejoin her husband, promising to set him up financially. He will do

this again for Avice III and the young man for whom she deserts him, insisting that ' "she shan't be separated" ' when after her marriage she threatens separation (III, viii: 204). Jocelyn's lack of jealousy shows moral fineness, but also a curious lack of sexual intensity, as though unconsciously he wanted to lose these women to other men.

Bitterest of all for Jocelyn is the moment when Avice II reveals that she would have accepted his marriage proposal were she not already married. 'Pierston sighed, for emotionally he was not much older than she. That hitch in his development, rendering him the most lopsided of God's creatures, was his standing misfortune.' That lopsidedness – along with other deficiencies to be discussed – helps make him an artist.

He defies time most extremely when at sixty he presumes to court Avice Caro's granddaughter. Summoned after twenty years by her mother to encourage the match, he is greeted by the words, ' "why – you are just the same!" '. She instead is 'the sorry shadow of Avice the Second'. His 'inability to ossify with the rest of his generation', he reflects sadly, threw him out of proportion with the time (III, i: 144). Nevertheless he is careful to meet Avice III only in the evening to conceal his age.

Once at daybreak 'a movement of something ghostly' turns out to be himself in the looking-glass: 'The person he appeared was too grievously far, chronologically, in advance of the person he felt himself to be'. When later that morning Avice III sees him for the first time in sunlight, 'she was so overcome that she turned and left the room'. He confesses, when she re-enters, 'visibly pale', how very old he is, the lover of her mother and her grandmother. Her response makes the issue of his age uncanny: ' "My mother's, and my grandmother's," said she, looking at him no longer as at a possible husband, but as a strange fossilized relic in human form. . . . "And were you my greatgrandmother's too?" ' (III, iii: 166–7). After this exchange Jocelyn considers the engagement over, but Avice II, ill with heart disease and anxious to see her daughter settled, tearfully joins their hands and renews the engagement.

Avice III elopes on the wedding day, however, with young Henri Leverre. Avice II dies of the shock, but Jocelyn all too readily acquiesces. Indeed Jocelyn has unconsciously furthered the elopement by helping an unknown sick young man on his way, even offering him his walking-stick and not occupying the bed prepared for Jocelyn in Avice's house – the bed to which Avice III half-carried her sick lover so she could spend the night nursing him. Seeing his walking-stick in the house, Jocelyn says, as if aware of the phallic symbolism, '"I gave it to him. 'Tis like me to play another's game!"' '"Really, sir"', says an old servant, '"one would say you stayed out o' your chammer o' purpose to oblige the young man with a bed!"' (III, vi: 185).

The issue of age takes on new meaning when in the end Marcia returns, first to announce herself as Henri's widowed stepmother, then to appear – when Jocelyn regains consciousness from a fever caught at Avice II's funeral – as his nurse. These meetings seem miraculous only in a psychological sense; Hardy makes them perfectly explicable, maintaining the ambiguity between idealism and reality.

As his nurse Marcia appears heavily veiled and when Jocelyn, who is preoccupied with age, asks to see her face, he is vexed to find her 'remarkably good-looking, considering the lapse of years. . . . "*You* won't do as a chastisement, Marcia!"' he says impatiently. She describes her skill in the use of make-up, offering to show herself the next morning as she really is. '"Remember I am as old as yourself; and I look it."' The next morning he beholds 'an old woman, pale and shrivelled, her forehead ploughed, her cheek hollow, her hair white as snow'. She vows never again to use make-up and he, accepting the terms of a friendship with her based on a mutual recognition of age, says, '"Thank Heaven I am old at last. The curse is removed"' (III, viii: 199–202).

The recognition of his age relates to a loss through the illness of his aesthetic sense. His idealising art was also devoted to making time stand still. Now he has broken through in life and art to a recognition of quotidian reality. Marcia's renunciation of make-up corresponds to Jocelyn's loss of creativity and the aesthetic sense. The fact that Marcia, when they marry, goes to the altar in a wheelchair may be comic, but it also represents an advance in their attunement to reality.

The island – technically a peninsula but psychologically an island and called so, as Hardy points out – represents stillness in a spatial dimension. Not only does the action mainly take place there, but it remains a force even in the London scenes. The sense of place is crucial to *The Well-Beloved*, though we may wonder what the island

represents. A bleak rock in the sea, it partakes of the sea's timelessness, even if a little younger than the sea because composed of
'infinitely stratified walls of oolite'[16] and the 'long thin neck of
pebbles "cast up by rages of the sea"', which connects the island
with the mainland. Hardy never uses the island's modern name
Portland, but makes Pierston, as he returns from London in the
beginning, use its ancient names to indicate its changelessness:
'More than ever the spot seemed what it was said once to have
been, the ancient Vindilia Island, and the Home of the Slingers' and
makes him see 'the unity of the whole island as a solid and single
block of limestone four miles long' (I, i: 9).

Hardy makes Pierston see the place as a rock, which is apparently unchanging but is really like the oolite 'stratified'. The
stratification parallels the pattern of Pierston's ageing, a pattern of
stillness and forward movement, but in this case the movement
collapses back into apparent stillness. The stratification recalls to
Hardy Shelley's lines: 'The melancholy ruins / Of cancelled cycles'
(*Prom. Unb.*, Act IV, lines 288–9) which indicate temporal movement
that looks static (I, i: 9). It suggests what Miller in *Fiction and Repetition* calls 'the totality of biological life' (166) from which, I would
add, the action departs but always returns. Identity is also stratified
in that the island lingers in the fundamental consciousness of all
island characters no matter how sophisticated they become. This
explains the 'groundwork of character' that Pierston looks for in
island women (II, iii: 74). It is only with island women – the Avices
and Marcia – that he has profound relations.

Socially, too, the island represents stillness as a small apparently
unchanged community, so intermarried as to figure almost as a
family and, therefore, a contrast to modern anonymity. (Yet change
is represented by the education of Avice Caro and Pierston.) The
coincidence of Pierston's surname with that of Avice II's husband
was hardly noticed in a community where there are 'only half-a-
dozen surnames' (II, xii: 129). The island serves as a matrix of identity for Jocelyn. The very stone he carves is quarried from the island
by his father, and the father's quarrying of 'the crude original' stone
is valued over the son's 'chipping [of] his ephemeral fancies into
perennial shapes' (II, i: 55), shapes which are departures from the
island's original unity.

No matter how much he achieves in fame, wealth and aristocratic
connections, Jocelyn can never get away from the island. Its force
is exemplified by the scene at the aristocratic London dinner table

where, with the woman he currently loves in view, Jocelyn opens a letter he has neglected to read, a letter from the island announcing the death of Avice Caro.

> By imperceptible and slow degrees the scene at the dinner-table receded into the background, behind the vivid presentment of Avice Caro, and the old, old scenes on Isle Vindilia which were inseparable from her personality. The dining-room was real no more, dissolving under the bold stony promontory and the incoming West Sea.   (II, iii: 70)

The three Avices are always associated for Jocelyn with the island and with all that is fundamental in his own nature. Like his own, Avice Caro's

> family had been islanders for centuries. . . . Hence in her nature, as in his, was some mysterious ingredient sucked from the isle. . . . Thus, though he might never love a woman of the island race, for lack in her of the desired refinement, he could not love long a kimberlin – a woman other than that of the island race, for her lack of this groundwork of character.   (II, iii: 73–74)

Jocelyn's perception of the island's stillness and the Avices' similarity is partly objective and partly a product of his creative imagination. The ambiguity is projected through a device never used before to this extent in Hardy's novels – the controlled use throughout, with very little exception, of a single point of view. Stemming from the Browningesque dramatic monologue and developed in the novel by Henry James, the single point of view is the best device for projecting ambiguous objectivity; for we both sympathise with the point of view and judge it sceptically.[17] And indeed James's central intelligences like Hardy's Pierston often contain in their own minds a certain amount of scepticism or indecisiveness about their view of objectivity. It is not only Hardy's use of point of view, but also his study of a character who combines moral refinement with minimal sexuality that invites comparison with James – an innovation in Hardy who was usually critical of James's fiction.

Jocelyn oscillates between 'unifying' moods, in which the Avices' differences in personality are ignored and an 'honest perception' of these differences. In regard to Avice I and II, 'his unifying mood of the afternoon was now so intense that the lost and the found Avice seemed essentially the same person' (II, v: 85, 83). But even when Avice II's 'lineaments seemed to have all the soul and heart that had characterised her mother's', he asked himself whether 'in this case the manifestation was fictitious' (II, vi: 88). 'Honest perception had told him that this Avice, fairer than her mother in face and form, was her inferior in soul and understanding. Yet the fervour which the first could never kindle in him was, almost to his alarm, burning up now' (II, v: 85). The fervour was not sexual but idealising: 'he was powerless in the grasp of the idealising passion' (II, ix: 112). 'Nobody', he reflects,

> would ever know the truth about him; *what* it was he had sought that had so eluded, tantalised, and escaped him . . . It was not the flesh; he had never knelt low to that. Not a woman in the world had been wrecked by him, though he had been impassioned by so many. (III, vii: 191)

The questions of idealisation, sex and artistic creativity are intertwined. It is a sign of their interdependence that Jocelyn's relation to all three Avices is unsatisfactory. He proposed to Avice Caro without certainty that his Well-Beloved had really lodged in her. His love of her developed later out of memory and regret: 'He loved the woman dead and inaccessible as he had never loved her in life' (II, iii: 72). He looks in Avice II for her mother's features, ignoring her individuality: 'Well he knew the arrangement of those white teeth . . . he knew of the same mark in her mother's mouth, and looked for it here. . . . The subject of her discourse he cared nothing about. . . . He took special pains that in catching her voice he might not comprehend her words' (II, vii: 94–5). And on beholding Avice III, 'Pierston stood as in a dream. It was the very she, in all essential particulars, and with an intensification of general charm, who had kissed him forty years before' (III, i: 147). He is moved not by sexual but by 'genealogical passion – by the aesthetic need to complete the historical 'continuity through three generations' (III, iv: 165), to give the story of the Avices 'an artistic and tender finish' (III, vi: 179). Jocelyn's relation to the three Avices, and doubtless to his other women as well, is spoiled by the excessive imagination and inadequate sexuality which make him unable to attend sufficiently to the individual woman before him.

In his analysis of artists, Hardy relates Jocelyn's deficiencies to his artistic talent. I have already cited the passage on Jocelyn's

emotional lopsidedness. After grieving over Avice II's condemnation of the unnamed young man who 'proved false' to her mother,
Jocelyn concludes that his waywardness accounts for his standing 'in the ranks of an imaginative profession. . . . It was in his
weaknesses as a citizen and a national-unit that his strength lay as
an artist' (II, vii: 98–9).

In his statues of pagan love goddesses, Jocelyn tries to embody
that Well-Beloved which can never long stay embodied in human
forms. The paganism of his art signals its aestheticism, but also,
exemplifying stratification, its roots in the island's past: 'in this last
local stronghold of the Pagan divinities, where Pagan customs lingered yet, Christianity had established itself precariously at best' (I,
ii: 18).[18] To explain Jocelyn's burst of creativity after Marcia abandons him, Hardy advances a theory of sexual sublimation. 'Jocelyn
threw into plastic creations that ever-bubbling spring of emotion
which, without some conduit into space, will surge upwards and
ruin all but the greatest men.' In this period when he sublimated
into art his undirected sexual energy, he prospered most as an artist
and made 'the study of beauty . . . his only joy for years onward' (I,
ix: 50). This is the highly aesthetic period he repudiates after the
illness in which he lost his aesthetic taste along with desire for his
Well-Beloved – along with the sexual desire he had idealised and
sublimated into art.

We can best understand Hardy's elaboration of the aesthetic theme
by considering how he revised the ending for the book version. In
the serialised version, Jocelyn married Marcia in the course of their
elopement to London. After four years' of quarrels originating in
their families' enmity, they separated, acknowledging the right of
each to remarry. Jocelyn later marries Avice III, probably without
consummation: they are, we are told, 'the mock-married couple'
(*Illustrated London News*, 17 December 1892, XXXI: 773). But after Avice
II's death he discovers Avice III's love for young Henri Leverre and
also her intention to remain faithful to her husband Jocelyn. Characteristically Jocelyn seems almost too ready to bring the young
lovers together. He recalls the possibility of annulling his marriage
to Avice by pretending to resuscitate his marriage to Marcia whom
he considers dead (he even advertises for her). 'Since his marriage
with [Marcia] was a farce, why not treat it as a farce by playing
another to match it?' (XXXI: 773–4). To be certain of freeing Avice,
he tries to drown himself by taking an oarless boat and allowing
the currents to carry him into the fatal waters of the Portland Race

where, after a collision against a hard object, he is rescued by men from the lightship (some of these details are used to describe the lovers' elopement in the book version). He falls into a grave illness from concussion of the head and on recovering consciousness he hears in his nurse's voice the sounds of Marcia's. With his eyes still closed he pictures Marcia as she was forty years ago. When finally he opens his eyes – and this is far more a surprise, a recognition scene, than in the book version where Marcia appeared shortly before his illness – he is shocked to see 'the face of Marcia forty years ago, vanished utterly. In its place was a wrinkled crone, with a pointed chin, her figure bowed, her hair as white as snow' (she had answered his advertisements). As in the book version he expresses his relief at being able to acknowledge his own old age.

A telegram arrives to inform not him but *her* of the annulment of Jocelyn's marriage to Avice, a telegram answering *her* petition. This is not in the book version; nor is the following. The sight of Marcia beside a photograph of Avice

> brought into his brain a sudden sense of the grotesqueness of things. His wife was – not Avice, but that parchment-covered skull moving about his room. An irresistible fit of laughter, so violent as to be an agony, seized upon him. . . . He laughed and laughed, till he was almost too weak to draw breath. . . .
>
> 'O – no, no! I – I – it is too, too droll – this ending to my would-be romantic history!'

And the narrator joins in the laughter, making the novel's final sounds, 'Ho – ho – ho!' (xxxiii: 775).

The serialised version repudiates only idealised notions of time's stillness and the youthful beauty of lovers. We do not find here Marcia's art of make-up and her repudiation of it. Nor do we find its parallel in Jocelyn's loss of his aesthetic sense and his turn toward utilitarian values. In the book he pays to close the island's old natural fountains in order to supply piped water, and to replace romantic old Elizabethan cottages with hygienic new ones. We do not find in the first version the repudiation of art and the aesthetic sense with which the book version ends. How are we to interpret this repudiation of art? Is it Hardy's or just Jocelyn's? Hardy pursued after this last novel a career as poet for more than a quarter of a century. This hardly seems a repudiation of art.

It is Jocelyn, I think, who is repudiating the wrong kind of art, the idealising, Shelleyan kind. Shelley has been on Hardy's mind throughout his career, but is particularly a haunting presence in *The Well-Beloved* which begins with an epigraph from *The Revolt of Islam*, contains quotations from and allusions to Shelley and deals with a Shelleyan protagonist.[19] There has been a subtle critique throughout of Jocelyn's self-centred idealisations of life (with his belief in time's stillness) and of love (with his fidelity to his self-created wraith of the Well-Beloved). There has also been criticism of Jocelyn's idealised art, his desexualised statues of pagan love goddesses. When his system of idealisation collapses – as it must when he confronts the reality of time and the reality of women as individuals in their own right, individuals who dispel his self-serving illusion of the Well-Beloved – when his system collapses, it is understandable that he runs to the other extreme by paying homage only to utilitarian values. But Hardy, the inveterate tourist and attender of museums, would not expect us to agree with Jocelyn when he loses his taste for the famous paintings in the National Gallery and can see no difference between them and the productions of street painters. If Jocelyn seems in some respects to resemble Hardy, it is because like Clym he represented for Hardy a potentiality in himself which he successfully avoided.

In *The Well-Beloved* Hardy weaves a beautifully gauzy Shelleyan fabric only to reject it in the end, not in favour of mere materialism but of a proper balance between the ideal and the real. This balance has been the point of his greatest novels, and it remains the point of the poems he will write in the years following the publication of *The Well-Beloved*. The search for that balance places Hardy squarely in the nineteenth-century tradition but with a critical stance toward its idealism that he has passed on to the twentieth century. When we consider how extensively his poetry has influenced recent poetry, how his innovations in fiction reach through Lawrence into the twentieth century, how his critique of marriage and his portrayals of women have entered into current controversies over feminism, how his social criticism, humanitarianism and interest in science meet our concerns as does his treatment of nature and of the unconscious and sexuality, we realise that Hardy remains a commanding presence in our time.

Notes

Notes to the Preface

1. Florence Emily Hardy, *The Life of Thomas Hardy 1840–1928* (London and Basingstoke: Macmillan, 1982), p. 185. Quotations from this text of Hardy's disguised autobiography, with Hardy's second wife as the long-accepted ostensible author, have been checked against the more recent version edited by Michael Millgate as Thomas Hardy, *The Life and Work of Thomas Hardy* (Athens, Ga: University of Georgia Press, 1985), in which some presumably authentic passages have been omitted because not originally intended for inclusion by Hardy. I have retained such passages as valid because of Mrs Hardy's participation in the authorship of the book bearing her name. For example, the sentence quoted on p. x from Florence Hardy 185 is omitted in Millgate 192 but makes a valuable addition to the journal entry in both texts: 'Finished *The Woodlanders* . . .' Mrs Hardy adds to the document what she remembers Hardy having often said.
2. See F. R. Leavis, *The Great Tradition* (London: Chatto and Windus, 1948) and *D. H. Lawrence: Novelist* (London: Chatto and Windus, 1955), which 'carries on from *The Great Tradition*' (p. v).
3. E. T. [Jessie Chambers], *D. H. Lawrence: A Personal Record* (Cambridge: Cambridge University Press, 1980), p. 105.

Notes to Chapter 1: Hardy and Lawrence

1. Harold Bloom, *The Anxiety of Influence* (New York: Oxford University Press, 1973), p. 141.
2. D. H. Lawrence, *Study of Thomas Hardy* (1914), first published in *Phoenix: The Posthumous Papers of D. H. Lawrence 1936*, ed. Edward D. McDonald (New York: Viking Press, 1968), p. 480. See Mark Kinkead-Weekes, 'Lawrence on Hardy', in *Thomas Hardy After Fifty Years*, ed. Lance St John Butler (London and Basingstoke: Macmillan, 1977).
3. *The Letters of D. H. Lawrence*, ed. James T. Boulton, 6 vols (Cambridge: Cambridge University Press, 1984), III: 41.
4. 'My book on Thomas Hardy,' he wrote Amy Lowell on 18 December 1914, 'has turned out as a sort of *Story of My Heart*: or a Confessio Fidei' (*Letters*, II: 243).
5. In *Hardy and the Erotic*, T. R. Wright quotes John Fowles' claim that Hardy was 'the first to break the Victorian middle-class seal over the supposed Pandora's box of sex' (New York: St Martin's Press, 1989), p. 4.

6. Mark Kinkead-Weekes, 'The Marble and the Statue: The Exploratory Imagination of D. H. Lawrence', in *Imagined Worlds: Essays in Honour of John Butt*, ed. Maynard Mack and Ian Gregor (London: Methuen, 1968), p. 380.

7. See Charles L. Ross, *The Composition of 'The Rainbow' and 'Women in Love'* (Charlottesville: University Press of Virginia, 1979), pp. 28–31.

8. D. H. Lawrence, *The Rainbow* (Harmondsworth: Penguin, 1975), ch. I, pp. 9, 8.

9. Thomas Hardy, *Tess of the d'Urbervilles*, ed. Scott Elledge, 2nd edn (New York and London: Norton, 1979), Phase III, ch. xxiv, p. 125. I shall quote from excellent editions of the novels that are easily available – Norton Critical Editions, otherwise Penguin or Oxford. I cite chapter with page number so the reader can use any edition.

10. D. H. Lawrence, 'The Blind Man', *The Complete Short Stories*, 3 vols (New York: Viking, 1967), II: 347.

11. Michael Millgate, *Thomas Hardy: A Biography* (New York: Random House, 1982), p. 295.

12. For an explication of Lawrence's system in the *Study*, see H. M. Daleski, *The Forked Flame: A Study of D. H. Lawrence* (Madison: University of Wisconsin Press, 1987), ch. I.

13. See Judith Ruderman, *D. H. Lawrence and the Devouring Mother* (Durham, N.C.: Duke University Press, 1984), p. 11.

14. In his *Essay on Hardy*, John Bayley praises the inconsistency of Hardy's characterisations, using as a prime example Angel's sight of Tess's yawn when they are still in their idyllic phase: 'She was yawning, and he saw the red interior of her mouth as if it had been a snake's.' Bayley comments: 'Success with Hardy usually goes with anomaly' (Cambridge: Cambridge University Press, 1978), pp. 103–4. See also James R. Kincaid, 'Hardy's Absences', in *Critical Approaches to the Fiction of Thomas Hardy*, ed. Dale Kramer (London and Basingstoke: Macmillan; New York: Barnes and Noble, 1979), essay 12.

15. Thomas Hardy, *Far from the Madding Crowd*, ed. Robert C. Schweik (New York and London: Norton 1986), ch. xxii, p. 115.

16. Thomas Hardy, *The Return of the Native*, ed. James Gindin (New York: Norton, 1969), Book IV, ch. iii, p. 205.

17. Quoted in Richard D. McGhee, '"Swinburne Planteth, Hardy Watereth": Victorian Views of Pain and Pleasure in Human Sexuality', in *Sexuality and Victorian Literature, Tennessee Studies in Literature*, vol. 27, ed. Don R. Cox (Knoxville: University of Tennessee Press, 1984), p. 84. For Hardy's most extreme treatment of sadomasochism, see the short story (which shocked T. S. Eliot) 'Barbara of the House of Grebe' in *A Group of Noble Dames*.

18. John Lucas, 'Hardy's Women', *The Literature of Change* (Sussex: Harvester; New York: Barnes and Noble, 1977), p. 120.

19. According to some feminist critics, the 'plot as [Tess's] punishment' is 'almost sadistically enjoyed' by the male 'author–narrator' – an unprovable idea given the structure which is designed to engage in sympathy for Tess the author–narrator along with male and female

readers, all of whom suffer *with* Tess and not at her expense. See Patricia Ingham, 'A Survey of Feminist Readings of Hardy', *Thomas Hardy* (New York and London: Harvester Wheatsheaf, 1989), p. 2.

20. Thomas Hardy, *Tess* [inserted over cancelled *A Daughter*] *of the D'Urbervilles*, The Printer's Manuscript (British Library Additional MS. 38 182), f. 253. Facsimile in the *Thomas Hardy Archive: I*, 2 vols, ed. Simon Gattrell (New York and London: Garland, 1986), 1: 227. In revising Hardy made Tess less sensual and more subjectively intellectual. For example, in speaking of Angel's 'waxing fervour of passion', Hardy crosses out 'for the seductive Tess', leaving 'for the soft & silent Tess' (f. 210; Garland, p. 177); while a left-margin insert reads: 'To carry out her once fond idea of teaching in a village school was now impossible' (f. 137; Garland, p. 107).
21. D. H. Lawrence, *Women in Love*, ed. Charles L. Ross (Harmondsworth: Penguin, 1982), ch. xiv, p. 237.
22. See, for example, Lascelles Abercrombie's *Thomas Hardy* (New York: Russell and Russell, 1912) which says: If we 'allegorize the story, then Tess will be the inmost purity of human life, the longing for purity which has its intensest instinct in virginity; and Alec d'Urberville is "the measureless grossness and the slag" which inevitably takes hold of life, however virginal its desires' (149). This is the critical book Lawrence borrowed, along with Hardy's novels, when he was planning his book on Hardy.
23. Thomas Hardy, *Jude the Obscure*, ed. Norman Page (New York: Norton, 1978), Part vi, ch. 2, p. 263.
24. Elaine Showalter, *Sexual Anarchy: Gender and Culture at the Fin de Siècle* (New York: Viking, 1990), p. 40.
25. Penny Boumelha, *Thomas Hardy and Women* (Madison: University of Wisconsin Press, 1985), pp. 143–4.
26. Florence Emily Hardy, *The Life of Thomas Hardy*, p. 272. Also in Thomas Hardy, *Collected Letters*, 7 vols, ed. Richard L. Purdy and Michael Millgate (Oxford: Clarendon Press, 1978–88) ii: 99.
27. Rosemarie Morgan, *Women and Sexuality in the Novels of Thomas Hardy* (London and New York: Routledge, 1991), pp. 123, 124, 137.
28. Kaja Silverman, 'History, Figuration and Female Subjectivity in *Tess of the d'Urbervilles*', *Novel* (Fall 1984), 7, 9.
29. Elizabeth Langland, 'Becoming a Man in *Jude the Obscure*', in *The Sense of Sex: Feminist Perspectives on Hardy*, ed. Margaret R. Higonnet (Urbana and Chicago: University of Illinois Press, 1993), p. 37.
30. Irving Howe, *Thomas Hardy* (New York: Macmillan; London: Collier-Macmillan, 1967), pp. 134–5.
31. Thomas Hardy, *A Laodicean: A Story of To-day* (London: Macmillan, 1975), Book i, ch. 14, p. 136.

Notes to Chapter 2: The Issue of Hardy's Poetry

1. Donald Davie, *Thomas Hardy and British Poetry* (New York: Oxford University Press, 1972), pp. 3–4.

2.   *The Complete Poetical Works of Thomas Hardy*, ed. Samuel Hynes, 3 vols to date (Oxford: Clarendon Press, 1982–5), II, 319, 324.

3.   W. H. Auden, 'A Literary Transference', in *Hardy: A Collection of Critical Essays*, ed. Albert J. Guerard (Englewood Cliffs, NJ: Prentice-Hall, 1987), pp. 136, 142.

4.   Ezra Pound, *Selected Letters 1907–1941*, ed. D. D. Paige (New York: New Directions, 1971), p. 218. In the Appendix to his anthology *Confucius to Cummings* Pound traces a succession from Browning, through Hardy and Ford, to himself (ed. with Marcella Spann, New York: New Directions, 1964), pp. 326–7.

5.   Thomas Hardy, 'A Singer Asleep', elegy for Swinburne, *Poetical Works*, ed. Hynes, II, 31.

6.   R. P. Blackmur, 'The Shorter Poems of Thomas Hardy', in *Southern Review*, Hardy Centennial Issue (Summer 1940), 44, 28, 20.

7.   W. B. Yeats (ed.), *Oxford Book of Modern Verse 1892–1935* (London: Oxford, 1936), Introduction, p. xiv.

8.   Eugenio Montale, 'A Note on Hardy the Poet' with translations into Italian by Montale and others, *Agenda* 10: 2–3 (Spring–Summer 1972), 77, 79.

9.   J. O. Bailey, *The Poetry of Thomas Hardy: A Handbook and Commentary* (Chapel Hill: University of North Carolina Press, 1970), pp. 274–9.

10. Ezra Pound did not ignore Hardy's novels. '20 novels', he wrote, 'form as good a gradus ad Parnassum as does metrical exercise', *Guide to Kulchur* (New York: New Directions, 1970), p. 293.

11. W. H. Auden (ed.), *19th Century British Minor Poets* (New York: Delacorte Press, 1966), Introduction, p. 15.

12. In her influential book *Poetic Closure* (Chicago and London: University of Chicago Press, 1968), Barbara Herrnstein Smith uses the felicitous phrase 'the sense of a lingering suspension' (p. 245) to describe the endings of successful modern poems. I am arguing that that sense, or an enigmatic suggestiveness, characterises major lyrics, even when their closures and symmetries are relatively formal.

13. T. S. Eliot, 'Rudyard Kipling', *On Poetry and Poets* (New York: Farrar, Strauss and Cudahy, 1957), pp. 294, 274–5.

14. Philip Larkin, 'Wanted: Good Hardy Critic', *Critical Quarterly* 8: 2 (Summer 1966), 179.

15. J. Hillis Miller, 'Hardy', *The Linguistic Moment: From Wordsworth to Stevens* (Princeton: Princeton University Press, 1985), p. 269.

16. Harold Bloom, *A Map of Misreading* (New York: Oxford University Press, 1975), pp. 9, 19.

17. Christopher Ricks (ed.), *The New Oxford Book of Victorian Verse* (Oxford and New York: Oxford University Press, 1987), Introduction, p. xxx.

18. Dennis Taylor, *Hardy's Poetry, 1860–1928* (London and Basingstoke: Macmillan, 1981), pp. xiv–xv, also ch. 1 and Epilogue. See also Taylor's *Hardy's Metres and Victorian Prosody* (Oxford: Clarendon Press, 1988).

19. Samuel Hynes, 'The Question of Development', *The Pattern of Hardy's Poetry* (Chapel Hill: University of North Carolina Press, 1961), p. 131.

20. According to Trevor Johnson, Hardy read *The Waste Land* from 1922 on, making 'extracts and notes upon it for his commonplace book',

A Critical Introduction to the Poems of Thomas Hardy (Basingstoke and London: Macmillan, 1991), p. 7. *The Literary Notebooks of Thomas Hardy* show extracts from 'Prufrock' (pp. 226–7) and 'Miss Helen Slingsby' (p. 441, where Hardy expresses preference for Eliot over Pound and the other *vers libre* poets), ed. Lennart A. Bjork, 2 vols (New York: New York University Press, 1985), vol. 2.

21.   See Patricia O'Neill, 'Thomas Hardy: Poetics of a Postromantic', *Victorian Poetry*, 27: 2 (Summer 1989), 129–45. Although Paul Zietlow, in *Moments of Vision: The Poetry of Thomas Hardy* (Cambridge: Harvard University Press, 1974), shows how Hardy's realism sometimes opens out to epiphany, Hardy is not notably an epiphanic poet.

22.   C. M. Bowra, 'The Lyrical Poetry of Thomas Hardy', *Inspiration and Poetry* (London: Macmillan; New York: St Martin's Press, 1955), p. 220.

23.   For details see Peter J. Casagrande, 'Hardy's Wordsworth: A Record and a Commentary', *English Literature in Transition* 20: 4 (1977), 210–37. Casagrande writes of Hardy's enthusiasm for Gosse's review, 'Mr. Hardy's Lyrical Poems', in the *Edinburgh Review* of April 1918, in which Gosse, after describing Hardy as a follower of Wordsworth, says that Hardy nevertheless 'differs from Wordsworth in being insensible . . . to the imagined sympathy of Nature'. Hardy's poetry, Gosse concludes, is a 'violent reaction against the poetry of egotistic optimism which had ruled the romantic school in England for more than a hundred years' (p. 226). See also Dennis Taylor, 'Hardy and Wordsworth', *Victorian Poetry*, 24: 4 (Winter 1986), 441–54.

24.   William Wordsworth, *Selected Poems and Prefaces*, ed. Jack Stillinger (Boston: Houghton Mifflin, 1965), p. 115.

25.   Cecil Day Lewis, 'The Lyrical Poetry of Thomas Hardy', in *Proceedings of the British Academy*, vol. 37 (London: Oxford University Press, 1951), p. 160.

26.   Robert Browning, 'One Word More', *The Poems*, 2 vols, ed. John Pettigrew and Thomas J. Collins (New Haven and London: Yale University Press, 1981), I, 743.

27.   See Robert Langbaum, *The Poetry of Experience: The Dramatic Monologue in Modern Literary Tradition* (Chicago and London: University of Chicago Press, 1985).

28.   James Richardson, 'Other Lives: Hardy and Browning', *Thomas Hardy: The Poetry of Necessity* (Chicago and London: University of Chicago Press, 1977), pp. 59–60.

29.   Ross C. Murfin, 'New Words: Swinburne and the Poetry of Thomas Hardy', *Swinburne, Hardy, Lawrence and the Burden of Belief* (Chicago and London: University of Chicago Press, 1978), p. 83.

30.   Peter M. Sacks, *The English Elegy: Studies in the Genre from Spenser to Yeats* (Baltimore and London: Johns Hopkins University Press, 1985), p. 231. For further comment on Hardy's elegies, see Jahan Ramazani, 'Hardy's Elegies for an Era: "By the Century's Deathbed"', *Victorian Poetry* (Summer 1991), 131–43 and 'Hardy and the Poetics of Melancholia: Poems of 1912–13 and Other Elegies for Emma', *ELH*, 58 (1991), 957–77.

31. First published in full as *Some Recollections*, a little book edited by Evelyn Hardy and Robert Gittings (Oxford and New York: Oxford University Press, 1979). The scenes in 'During Wind and Rain' are imaginative developments of a few passages in Emma's manuscript.

32. Trevor Johnson, in *Critical Introduction to the Poems of Hardy*, reproduces the manuscript as frontispiece and offers a useful analysis of Hardy's revisions (pp. 167–9). See also *Complete Poetical Works of Hardy*, ed. Hynes, II, 239–40 notes.

Notes on Chapter 3: Versions of Pastoral

1. Thomas Hardy, *The Return of the Native*, ed. James Gindin (New York: Norton, 1969) Book I, ch. ii, pp. 8–9. Full citations of novels after interruption of ch. 2; subsequently abbreviated citations.

2. In writing to Swinburne, for example, Hardy praises his translation of Sappho's line in 'Anactoria': ' "Thee, too, the years shall cover" ', saying 'Those few words present, I think, the finest *drama* of Death and Oblivion, so to speak, in our tongue' (*Life*, p. 287).

3. See, for example, W. W. Greg in his classic *Pastoral Poetry and Pastoral Drama*: 'What does appear to be a constant element in the pastoral as known to literature is the recognition of a contrast ... between pastoral life and some more complex type of civilization' (London: A. H. Bullen, 1906), p. 4. William Empson was revisionist in discovering also non-rural versions of pastoral (*Some Versions of Pastoral*, 1935, rpt Norfolk, Conn.: New Directions, 1950). Michael Squires regards 'the pastoral novel as a variation ... of traditional pastoral' in combining 'realism with the pastoral impulse', *The Pastoral Novel: Studies in George Eliot, Thomas Hardy, and D. H. Lawrence* (Charlottesville: University Press of Virginia, 1974), p. 2. Also relevant to Hardy is Annabel Patterson's demonstration of the extent to which pastorals since Virgil have been used for political and social criticism, *Pastoral and Ideology: Virgil to Valery* (Berkeley and Los Angeles: University of California Press, 1987).

4. Raymond Williams, *The Country and the City* (New York: Oxford University Press, 1973), p. 208. Douglas Brown, 'The Agricultural Theme', *Thomas Hardy* (London: Longmans Green, 1961). For a comprehensive survey of the economic, social and literary aspects of the country background, see Merryn Williams, *Thomas Hardy and Rural England* (London and Basingstoke: Macmillan, 1972).

5. Thomas Hardy, 'The Dorsetshire Labourer', *Personal Writings*, ed. Harold Orel (Lawrence: University of Kansas Press, 1966), p. 182.

6. For detailed discussions of the minor novels, see Norman Page, *Thomas Hardy* (London and Boston: Routledge & Kegan Paul, 1977) and Michael Millgate, *Thomas Hardy: His Career as a Novelist* (New York: Random House, 1971).

7. *Thomas Hardy and His Readers: A Selection of Contemporary Reviews*, ed. Laurence Lerner and John Holmstrom (New York: Barnes and Noble, 1968), pp. 17, 85, 162–3.

8.   In his study of the manuscript, Simon Gatrell finds an 'earliest version of the narrative' in which 'the affairs of the choir were predominant' and the latest version in which the love story (the *Under the Greenwood Tree* theme) predominates, *Thomas Hardy and the Proper Study of Mankind* (Basingstoke: Macmillan; Charlottesville: University Press of Virginia, 1993), pp. 11–12.

9.   Thomas Hardy, *Under the Greenwood Tree or The Mellstock Quire: A Rural Painting of the Dutch School*, ed. David Wright (Harmondsworth: Penguin, 1978), p. 39.

10. Thomas Hardy, *The Woodlanders*, ed. James Gibson, intro. Ian Gregor (Harmondsworth: Penguin, 1981), ch. XLIV, p. 399.

11. Thomas Hardy, *Far from the Madding Crowd*, ed. Robert C. Schweik (New York and London: Norton, 1986), ch. 1, p. 7.

12. See W. J. Keith, 'A Regional Approach to Hardy's Fiction', in *Critical Approaches to Fiction of Hardy*, ed. Kramer, p. 36. See also David Havird, *Thomas Hardy and the Aesthetics of Regionalism* (unpub. diss., Charlottesville: University of Virginia, 1986). Carl J. Weber dates the action of Hardy's novels in *Hardy of Wessex* (New York: Columbia University Press, London: Routledge and Kegan Paul, 1965), p. 224.

13. Bruce Johnson, *True Correspondence: A Phenomenology of Thomas Hardy's Novels* (Tallahassee: University Presses of Florida, 1983), pp. 10–11, 43.

14. In *Anatomy of Criticism*, Northrop Frye characterises pastoral and romance through '*the analogy of innocence*' (Princeton: Princeton University Press, 1957), p. 151. My ideas about genre have inevitably been influenced by this seminal work. See also Alastair Fowler, *Kinds of Literature: An Introduction to the Theory of Genres and Modes* (Oxford: Clarendon Press, 1982).

15. See Susan Beegel's persuasive argument for Gabriel's 'potent, life-affirming sexuality' in 'Bathsheba's Lovers: Male Sexuality in *Far from the Madding Crowd*', in *Sexuality and Victorian Literature, Tennessee Studies in Literature*, vol. 27, ed. Don R. Cox (Knoxville: University of Tennessee Press, 1984), p. 116.

16. Ian Gregor, *The Great Web: The Form of Hardy's Major Fiction* (London, Boston: Faber and Faber, 1982), p. 34.

17. In *Adam Bede*, for example, where Adam replies to his pious brother Seth by saying that the man who '"scrats at his bit o' garden and makes two potatoes grow istead o' one, he's doing more good, and he's just as near to God, as if he was running after some preacher and a-praying and a-groaning"' (George Eliot, *Adam Bede*, ed. John Patterson (Boston: Houghton Mifflin, 1968), p. 10).

18. 'We cannot say that we either understand or like Bathsheba. She is a young lady of the inconsequential, wilful, mettlesome type . . . the type which aims at giving one a very intimate sense of a young lady's *womanishness*' (Henry James's review in *The Nation*, 24 December 1874; reprinted in *Hardy and His Readers*, p. 33). In her study of changes from the manuscript to the *Cornhill* serialisation of *Far from the Madding Crowd*, Rosemarie Morgan shows how Hardy in revising softened Bathsheba's wilfulness, especially her anger, to make her

more conventionally feminine (*Cancelled Words: Rediscovering Thomas Hardy* (London and New York: Routledge, 1992), pp. 124–8).
19. Freud writes that 'in scopophilia [erotic looking] ... the eye corresponds to an erotogenic zone'. 'The eye is perhaps the zone most remote from the sexual object, but it is ... liable to be the most frequently stimulated by the particular quality of excitation whose cause, when it occurs in a sexual object, we describe as beauty' (Sigmund Freud, *The Standard Edition of the Complete Psychological Works*, 24 vols, tr. James Strachey with Anna Freud (London: Hogarth Press and Institute of PsychoAnalysis), vol. VII, pp. 169, 209). In *Thomas Hardy: Distance and Desire*, J. Hillis Miller skilfully treats *watching* in Hardy as an epistemological stance, a 'detachment of consciousness' (9), without noting the erotic quality of watching (Cambridge, Mass.: Harvard University Press, 1970), especially ch. I, 'The Refusal of Involvement'.
20. Peter J. Casagrande, 'A New View of Bathsheba Everdence', in *Critical Approaches to Fiction of Hardy*, ed. Kramer, pp. 69, 57.
21. Boumelha sounds ideological, however, in saying later that 'the only freedom granted' Bathsheba and Paula Power, despite inherited wealth and absent fathers, 'is the freedom to choose a man' and so resubject themselves 'to the patriarchal structures' (p. 40). Hardy became increasingly critical of marriage as an outmoded burden upon both men and women.

Notes on Chapter 4: Diversions from Pastoral

1. This passage is echoed in E. M. Forster's great passage on the Marabar Caves ('They are older than anything in the world') in ch. XII of *A Passage to India*.
2. For an account of the anthropology available to Hardy, see George W. Stocking, Jr, *Victorian Anthropology* (New York: Free Press, 1987).
3. For an account of the folklore used by Hardy, see Ruth A. Firor, *Folkways in Thomas Hardy* (Philadelphia: University of Pennsylvania Press, 1931).
4. *The Literary Notebooks of Thomas Hardy*, ed. Lennart A. Bjork, 2 vols, I, 40 n.392.
5. John Paterson, *The Making of 'The Return to the Native'* (Berkeley and Los Angeles: University of California Press, 1960), pp. 18, 39, 42, 48.
6. To John Addington Symonds, April 14, 1889. 'The tragical conditions of life imperfectly denoted in The Return of the Native & some other stories of mine I am less & less able to keep out of my work. I often begin a story with the intention of making it brighter & gayer than usual; but the question of conscience soon comes in; & it does not seem right, even in novels, to wilfully belie one's own views. All comedy, is tragedy, if – you only look deep enough into it' (*Letters*, I: 190).
7. Charles Child Walcutt, *Man's Changing Masks: Modes and Methods of*

Characterization in Fiction (Minneapolis: University of Minnesota Press, 1966), pp. 168–9.

8. In his 1895 Preface to *The Return of the Native*, Hardy writes: 'It is pleasant to dream that some spot in the extensive tract whose south-western quarter is here described, may be the heath of that traditional King of Wessex – Lear' (p. 1).

9. In his essay 'The Storytellers', Walter Benjamin writes: 'It has seldom been realized that the listener's naive relationship to the storyteller [his 'willing suspension of disbelief', in Coleridge's phrase] is controlled by his interest in retaining what he is told' (*Illuminations*, ed. Hannah Arendt, tr. Harry Zohn (New York: Shocken, 1976), p. 97). Hardy himself thought that fiction gives 'pleasure by gratifying the love of the uncommon in human experience', though the psychology of the characters must be valid: 'the uncommonness must be in the events, not in the characters' (*Life*, p. 150).

10. *Hardy and His Readers: Contemporary Reviews*, ed. Lerner and Holmstrom, pp. 55–6.

11. Mary Jacobus, 'Tree and Machine: *The Woodlanders*', in *Critical Approaches to Fiction of Hardy*, ed. Kramer, pp. 119–20.

12. Carl J. Weber, in his useful datings of the actions of ten Hardy novels, dates *The Woodlanders*' action 1876–9 (*Hardy of Wessex*, p. 224). I would date the action no earlier than 1878 because of the reference the new divorce law of 1878.

13. Quotations from the Penguin edition of Hardy's *The Woodlanders* have been checked against Dale Kramer's critical edition of *The Woodlanders* (Oxford: Clarendon Press, 1981).

14. In a Marxist analysis John Goode says that 'the obscurity generated by the exploitation, whether we are talking about the slums which are generated by capitalist industry, or the woods which are the site of capitalist agriculture (for Melbury is not the same as Oak or Bathsheba despite his memory of work), is always threateningly there' (*Thomas Hardy: The Offensive Truth* (Oxford: Blackwell, 1988), p. 98).

15. 'Old' refers to old Midsummer customs, two of which are described in a June 1871 entry in Thomas Hardy's *Personal Notebooks*, edited with introductions and notes by Richard H. Taylor (London and Basingstoke: Macmillan, 1987), p. 10.

16. The lawyer Beaucock confuses two laws, a sign of his incompetence. The 'new law' cited (20 & 21 Vict., cap. 85) was passed not 'last year' (p. 333) but in 1857. This law first facilitated divorce by establishing a national divorce court, taking away jurisdiction from ecclesiastical courts and special acts of Parliament favouring the rich. The grounds for divorce are stipulated as 'Adultery, or Cruelty, or Desertion without Cause for Two years and upwards'. The new 1878 law, the one passed 'last year' (p. 333) amends the 1857 law by emphasising as grounds for divorce a husband's 'aggravated assault' upon his wife, imperiling 'her future safety'. Thus, Fitzpiers 'had not been sufficiently cruel' (p. 353) to justify divorce. (See *A Collection of the Public General Statutes, Passed in the 20th Year of the Reign of Her Majesty, QV. 1857*, printed by Eyre and Spottiswoode, London: Queen's

Printing Office, 1857, pp. 637, 639. See also *The Law Reports: Public General Statutes*, vol. xiii, 1878, printed by Eyre and Spottiswoode for London: William Clowes, 1878, p. 194.)

Notes on Chapter 5: The Minimisation of Sexuality

1. In an earlier draft Henchard has recently married Lucetta, but annuls the marriage after Susan's reappearance (MS, f. 112, 114); a still earlier version suggests an illicit sexual relation with Lucetta (MS, f. 167). Hardy's revisions minimise the sexual element in Henchard's relation with Lucetta. (Manuscript in Dorset County Museum, Dorchester).

2. Thomas Hardy, *The Mayor of Casterbridge*, ed. James K. Robinson (New York: Norton, 1977), ch. xiii, p. 63.

3. In published novel and in manuscript Henchard says: ' "It [wife selling] has been done elsewhere – and why not here?" ' (10). Excised after 'elsewhere' in the manscript: ' "Why, Jimmy Clay, sold his wife, didn't he, for thirty shillings? And wasn't it done at Southampton the year before last?" ' (MS, f. 17). Hardy read about actual wife sales in old issues of the *Dorset County Chronicle*.

4. Max Weber, *The Protestant Ethic and the Spirit of Capitalism* (1904–5; 1920), tr. Talcott Parsons (New York: Scribner's, 1958). See especially Ch. v: 'Asceticism and the Spirit of Capitalism'.

5. Dale Kramer, *Thomas Hardy: The Forms of Tragedy* (Detroit: Wayne State University Press, 1975), pp. 86–7.

6. Elaine Showalter, 'The Unmanning of the Mayor of Casterbridge', in *Critical Approaches to Fiction of Hardy*, ed. Kramer, pp. 101–2.

7. Commenting on Hegel's rationalism in May 1886, the month *Mayor* appeared in volume form, Hardy wrote: 'These venerable philosophers seem to start wrong; they cannot get away from a prepossession that the world must somehow have been made to be a comfortable place for man' (*Life*, p. 179).

8. See Richard L. Purdy, *Thomas Hardy: A Bibliographical Study* (Oxford: Clarendon Press, 1979), pp. 94–5.

9. Thomas Hardy, *The Well-Beloved: A Sketch of a Temperament*, ed. Tom Hetherington (Oxford and New York: Oxford University Press, 1986), Part i, ch. viii, p. 47.

10. J. Hillis Miller, '*The Well-Beloved*: The Compulsion to Stop Repeating', *Fiction and Repetition* (Cambridge, Mass.: Harvard University Press, 1982), ch. 6; Michael Ryan, 'One Name of Many Shapes: *The Well-Beloved*', in *Critical Approaches to Fiction of Hardy*, ed. Kramer, essay 10. See also T. R. Wright, *Hardy and the Erotic*, ch. 9; and Michael Millgate, *Thomas Hardy: His Career as a Novelist*, Part Five, ch. 3. For an example of negative commentary, see Albert J. Guerard, who calls the novel 'trivial', *Thomas Hardy* (New York: New Directions, 1964), pp. 66–8.

11. Thomas Hardy, 'An Imaginative Woman', *Life's Little Ironies* (Stroud,

Gloucestershire: Alan Sutton, 1990), p. 13. Originally published in *Wessex Tales* (Osgood, McIlvaine, 1896), where it is dated 1893 but may derive from earlier work (Purdy), 60).

12.   In the serialisation Jocelyn attempts to burn love letters from these earlier embodiments of the Well-Beloved. He proposes to Avice Caro after she has seen him burning these letters. '"I see – I see now!" she whispered. "I am – only one – in a long, long row!"' (*Illustrated London News*, 1 October 1892, ch. III, p. 426). *The Pursuit of the Well-Beloved* was published in twelve weekly instalments from 1 October to 17 December 1892.

13.   August Weismann, *Essays upon Heredity*, ed. E. B. Poulton, tr. A. E. Shipley and S. Schonland (Oxford: Oxford University Press, 1899).

14.   Plato, *Symposium, Dialogues*, tr. B. Jowett, 2 vols (New York: Random House, 1937), I, 328, 332.

15.   *The Life* speaks of Hardy's 'lateness of development in virility, while mentally precocious. He himself said humorously in later times that he was a child till he was sixteen, a youth till he was five-and-twenty, and a young man till he was nearly fifty' (p. 32).

16.   Oolite: 'A sedimentary rock usually a limestone, sometimes an iron-stone, resembling in texture the roe of a fish, composed, entirely or largely, of small rounded concentrically *layered* grains (ooliths)' (Challinor's *Dictionary of Geology*, 6th edn, p. 213; my italics).

17.   For an expansion of this idea, see Robert Langbaum, *The Poetry of Experience: The Dramatic Monologue in Modern Literary Tradition*, especially Ch. II, 'The Dramatic Monologue: Sympathy versus Judgment' and Ch. IV, 'The Dramatic Element: Truth as Perspective'.

18.   Pierston sometimes dreamt that his Well-Beloved was '"the wile-weaving Daughter of high Zeus" in person, bent on tormenting him [Pierston] for his sins against her beauty in his art – the implacable Aphrodite herself' (Part I, ch. II, p. 16). The sentence echoes Swinburne's aesthetic neopaganism.

19.   Shelley's comments on his Platonic poem *Epipsychidion* throw light on Pierston's character as man and artist: 'The *Epipsychidion* is a mystery – As to real flesh & blood, you know that I do not deal in those articles'. Less than a year later Shelley reports loss of interest in the lady idealised in the poem, explaining: 'I think one is always in love with something or other; the error, and I confess it is not easy for spirits cased in flesh and blood to avoid it, consists in seeking in a mortal image the likeness of what is perhaps eternal' (letters to John Gisborne, 22 October 1821, 18 June 1822, *The Letters of Percy Bysshe Shelley*, 2 vols, ed. Frederick L. Jones (Oxford: Clarendon Press, 1964), II, 363, 434). Certain passages in the *Epipsychidion* suggest a possible source for *The Well-Beloved*: 'There was a Being whom my spirit oft / Met on its visioned wanderings, far aloft' (lines 190–1); 'If I could find one form resembling hers, / In which she might have masked herself from me' (lines 254–5); 'In many mortal forms I rashly sought / The shadow of that idol of my thought' (lines 267–8), *The Complete Poetical Works of Percy Bysshe Shelley*, ed. Thomas Hutchinson (London, New York: Oxford University Press, 1947), pp. 416–17.

Index

Ross, Charles, *The Composition of 'The Rainbow' and 'Women in Love'*, 4–5, 157 n.7
Rousseau, Jean Jacques, 97
Ruderman, Judith, *D. H. Lawrence and the Devouring Mother*, 8, 157 n.13
Ruskin, John, 73, 81
Ryan, Michael, 'One Name of Many Shapes: *The Well-Beloved'*, 142, 143, 165 n.10

Sacks, Peter, *The English Elegy*, 60, 160 n.30
sado-masochism, 10–12, 59, 82, 116, 121, 123, 157 n.17, 157–8 n.19
Sappho, Sapphic, 53, 59, 60, 161 n.2
'Self-Unseeing, The', 50
Shakespeare, William, 33, 100, 101, 110
Cymbeline, 113
King Lear, 107, 135–6, 164 n.8
Macbeth, 106
Measure for Measure, 113
Much Ado About Nothing, 70
Shelley, Percy Bysshe, ix, 35, 36, 44, 52, 61, 86, 97, 142, 154–5
Adonais, 111
Alastor, 53
'Defence of Poetry, A', 57
'Epipsychidion', 119, 166 n.19
'Ode to the West Wind', 51, 58
Prometheus Unbound, 150
Revolt of Islam, 134, 154
'Skylark, The', 51, 52–3
Triumph of Life, 58
'Shelley's Skylark', 52–3
Showalter, Elaine, 17, 133
Sexual Anarchy: Gender and Culture at the Fin de Siècle, 17, 158 n.24
'Unmanning of the Mayor of Casterbridge, The', 133, 165 n.6
Silverman, Kaja, 20–1, 158 n.28
'Singer Asleep, A', 58, 59
Smith, Barbara Herrnstein, *Poetic Closure*, 159 n.12

'Snow in the Suburbs', 38
Squires, Michael, *The Pastoral Novel*, 112, 161 n.3
'Strange House (Max Gate, A.D. 2000), The', 32
'Subalterns, The', 45–6
Swinburne, Algernon, 12, 28, 44, 53, 58–61, 65, 95, 161 n.2, 166 n.18
Atalanta in Calydon, 58
'Faustine', 59–60
'Hertha', 60
Love's Cross-Currents, 41
Poems and Ballads (1866), 58, 60

Tate, Allen, 36
Taylor, Dennis
'Hardy and Wordsworth', 160 n.23
Hardy's Metres and Victorian Prosody, 159 n.18
Hardy's Poetry, 1860–1928, 37, 159 n.18
Taylor, Richard, *see Personal Notebooks, The*
'Temporary the All, The', 53
Tennyson, Alfred, 34, 44, 69
Tess of the d'Urbervilles, viii, 3, 5, 7, 8, 11, 12–15, 18, 20–1, 22, 23, 24, 42, 43–4, 67, 68, 69–70, 77, 92, 96, 97, 106, 110, 116, 117, 119, 120, 126, 127, 141, 143, 157 n.9, n.14, 157–8 n.19, 158 n.20, 158 n.22
Thackeray, William M., 70, 161 n.7
Thomas, Dylan, 46
Time's Laughingstocks, 37
Tolstoi, Leo, 2, 156 n.3
Anna Karenina, 4
Tragedy, ix, 42, 67–9, 77, 80, 87, 90, 102–5, 107, 111, 112–13, 128, 140–1, 163 n.5, n.6, n.7
tragic hero and heroine, 108–11, 132–6
'Trampwoman's Tragedy, The', 42–3
'Transformations', 48–9, 50, 63
Turgenev, Ivan, 2, 156 n.3